SAFEGUARD

Stephanie Rose

Safeguard

STEPHANIE ROSE

HeartEyes Press

To my son, John,
Thank you for your awesome idea for the ending and for proving over the past year what a resilient and amazing kid you are. You're my hero and best friend, and we'll discuss your LEGO compensation for your input in the story, which you aren't allowed to read in full. Ever.

MATTEO

June

"Vermont has a *lot* of trees, Daddy," my five-year-old daughter, Lauren, said from her car seat. A laugh escaped me as I spied her wide eyes in my rear-view mirror.

"We had trees in New York, too. Maybe not this many but—"

"Does our yard have a lot of trees?"

When I rolled to a stop at the first traffic light I'd seen in hours, I craned my head and reached into the back seat to squeeze her legging-covered knee. The giggle she let out made my chest deflate in a little relief. I'd gone on for weeks about our new adventure in the country, and I must've done a good enough job for her to buy into it. It killed me to take her away from her grandparents, but as she jabbered with excitement from the back-seat, I prayed it was a sign that the crazy decision I'd made for us would work out.

"Here we are, Cookie," I told her as we pulled up in front of our new home. Other than the upstairs balcony, the small white house with the teal roof seemed plain to the naked eye, but the skylight windows on the roof plus the winding staircase made the

1

inside spectacular. We had a full basement, three bedrooms, and a dining room that was probably too big for the both of us, but I was excited about it all. There was nothing like this back in the Bronx, and when I came to Colebury a couple of months ago to scope out affordable housing options close to work, I knew we had to have it the minute I stepped over the threshold.

"That's our house, Daddy? *All* of it?"

When her mouth fell open, I didn't know whether to laugh or tear up. Whoever said real men didn't cry never knew what it was like to have a baby girl grab your heart right out of your chest the moment she was born. My family called us twins because Lauren and I had the same nose and mouth, but her eyes were all her mother. It was still confusing to love someone more than my own life who reminded me so much of someone I hated.

Maybe hate was a strong word since I could never hate Callie, but I resented the hell out of her for what she did, and as time passed it hadn't stopped eating away at me. I doubted it ever would.

I stepped out of the driver's seat and made my way to the back to open Lauren's door.

"It sure is our house." She squealed when I lifted her up and held her high over my head. "It has stairs and windows in the roof so we can see the sky, and a big yard with a ton of trees!"

When I brought her back to my chest, she looped her arms around my neck and cuddled into my shoulder. My life was the little lady in my arms, and I would do whatever I needed to in order to make this work.

While I had help from family back in New York, the job of both parents had always been mine. The only comfort I had was that this was all my daughter had ever known. I was all my daughter knew. Most would say a mother leaving her baby when she was an infant was tragic, but I'd found it a blessing. Lauren was too young to remember how indifferent her mother had been toward her, and she'd never worried when Callie left one day and didn't return.

All Lauren had was me. And although I felt as if I was screwing up daily, I was all she wanted.

It had always been my plan to move out of the city when I had a family. But I'd thought *when* would be years from now, and *family* would mean my little girl would have both a mother and a father, and I wouldn't be doing this alone at twenty-eight. My buddies back in the Bronx were mostly unattached and never really knew what to make of what my life had become.

There were times that I didn't either.

If I'd learned anything since I became a single parent, it was that life only laughed in your face at any plans you were foolish enough to make.

Lauren was used to the lower-level apartment my cousin rented to me out of his two family house. We shared the concrete backyard but it wasn't safe for her to play in. This yard had grass and trees, and I already had plans for a mini playground back there. The whole point of coming out here was to give her a different and—I hoped—better life.

I snatched my phone from the cup holder. After I scrolled through and replied to all the good luck messages, I shot my friend, Phoebe, a text. I worked with her at one of my first bar manager jobs in a restaurant in Manhattan and we stayed in touch. When she'd gotten a job as the executive chef at the new gastropub in Speakeasy, a trendy bar in Colebury, Vermont, she contacted me about an open bar manager position since she'd remembered that I'd always talked about moving my daughter out of the city and into the country. It didn't get more country than Vermont.

When I interviewed with the owners, the salary they offered was good, insurance was decent, and thanks to the savings I'd accumulated from free family childcare and cheap rent since Lauren was born, I could afford to give us the simpler and better life I'd always wanted for her.

At least that was my plan—a plan I prayed would work.

Matteo: *We're here. How are you holding up?*

Before she'd come to Colebury, Phoebe had endured a social media nightmare after an embarrassing breakup—photos and all —went viral on Twitter. She'd been looking to leave New York too, although her reasons had been more urgent than mine. I knew she'd be stubborn and insist she was fine, but it was a miserable way to start a new job in a new place.

Phoebe: *Welcome to Vermont! Is Lauren in shock from all the trees?*
Phoebe: *And fine. I'm acclimating very nicely. Small town living takes some getting used to. You guys may be in a little bit of culture shock at first.*
Matteo: *Trees are the first thing Lauren noticed. And I'm very glad to hear that. I'm around if you want to talk.*
Phoebe: *I'm glad you're around. I'm really okay. No one has called me meat girl once, and without losing hours scrolling through social media, I've had time to come up with some killer recipes. If anyone has recognized me, they haven't mentioned it. At least to my face.*
Matteo: *Let me know if I need to go Bronx on anyone.*
Phoebe: *Easy, tough guy. I appreciate the offer, though.*

"Matteo!" I recognized the shrill voice of Adeline, the rep from the home rental agency. After Phoebe convinced me to at least think about coming here, she connected me with both housing and school contacts, knowing I wouldn't make any kind of move unless I could guarantee an upgrade in both. From the time I'd made the first trip up here, Adeline had been all too accommodating.

"So nice to see you again. Aw, this must be Lisa." She shot Lauren a patronizing glance before meeting my gaze, a saccharine smile curling her red lips.

"Lauren," I corrected, my shoulders going rigid as I held my daughter closer to me. "Thanks for meeting us." The fact that I had a child in my arms didn't stop her from doing a shameless perusal up and down my body.

I'd casually dated here and there since Lauren's mother left, emphasis on casually. I would never bring another person into our lives who could hurt us both again and made it a point to never *ever* bring a woman I was seeing around Lauren. My daughter didn't remember her mother, but she'd been asking a ton of questions lately. The last thing I needed was for her to get attached to someone she'd only know temporarily. On the rare occasion I'd go on a date, it was a no strings attached and mostly one-time thing.

My friends used to tease me how my kid must be a chick magnet, but most of the women who thought single fathers were hot turned out to have no interest in children. Even if I had no intentions of introducing my daughter to anyone I'd dated, that was still a huge turn off.

"Here are all the keys. The kitchen appliances arrived, so all you need is some furniture to set onto those shiny wooden floors."

"That's all arriving tomorrow. We have an air mattress to sleep on tonight."

Adeline put the keys into my palm, sliding her finger over my wrist before I closed my fist around them.

"Sounds cozy. Well, you have my number if you need anything. The mailbox already says *Gallo*. Enjoy your new home."

She turned, an exaggerated sway to her hips as she made her way to her car.

I respected women who knew what they wanted and weren't afraid to ask for it, and Adeline was sexy as hell. In another time or place, maybe I would have asked to see her again. But barely giving my daughter an inkling of acknowledgment didn't make me want to take her up on anything she was offering. Not that I would anyway. Right now, we needed to make this place a home before I even remotely considered who I'd see in my spare time, which I didn't anticipate to be much.

Before I unpacked the car, I let Lauren down and led her by the hand inside the house, my heart swelling at all her gasps as we walked from room to room.

"Daddy, look!" She pointed her little finger to the ceiling and to the large skylight windows. "We don't have to go outside to see the stars."

"Nope." I lifted her up again. "And up here you'll see a ton of them without the city smog."

"How many?" she asked, eyes wide again.

"Thousands," I leaned in to whisper. She was still learning her numbers, but her hand flew to her mouth at the notion of all those stars right above us.

I could only hope that my attempt to reach for stars wouldn't make me fall flat on my face.

MELANIE

Three months later, September

"Don't be late," my mother warned in my ear. "Remember, Maria Rossi did you a favor."

I clenched my eyes shut, holding in a huff that would start another argument. "Yes, Mom," I said as evenly as I was able into the phone nestled into the crook of my shoulder as I rushed to get ready for my first night as a waitress at Speakeasy. "I very much appreciate Mrs. Rossi putting in a good word with her son, Alec, to get me this job because she's your friend. And on that note, I need to get out of here. I'll call you tomorrow."

Alec Rossi had done me a huge and undeserved favor by hiring me as I had no waitressing experience whatsoever—anywhere. As I zipped up my jeans and caught a glimpse of myself in my tiny bathroom mirror, I almost didn't recognize the frazzled and exhausted woman staring back at me.

I was only twenty-three, but this past year seemed to age me by a decade.

Six months ago, I was engaged and living with my fiancé. My

friends all told me I was nuts to move in with Chase so quickly, but what did they know? We were in love.

Or *I* was in love.

I hadn't realized when everything between us became one-sided, but looking back I could pinpoint clues that it probably always was. I'd put graduate school on hold to get a receptionist job until Chase's construction business got off the ground, because that's what you did when you were making a life with someone—or were naive enough to put what you wanted on the back burner without a second thought.

As I packed my purse for the night, the conversation that upended my life played on a reel in my head. I'd come home from work and asked Chase if he wanted to get takeout, and he told me he wanted to break up. He asked for his ring back and told me I could take as much time as I needed to pack. He admitted that he fell for his own receptionist, and it made him realize that what we had was nothing special—meaning that *I* was nothing special, at least not to him.

I flew out of there in a rush, not taking that much time to pack in my rage, and realizing with a bone-crushing shame that other than my boxes of books, there wasn't much in the apartment I could call mine anyway.

After crashing in my parents' spare room for a few months, I started applying to graduate schools like crazy. When I was accepted into Burlington University, or Moo U to the locals, with a partial scholarship, I accepted although it meant moving back to the town I'd grown up in. I thought if I ever came back to Cole-bury, I'd be a success at *something*. I'd be happily married with kids, or have that great teaching job I'd always wanted, maybe even both.

I wasn't bullied when I was a kid, but that was because I was invisible. I was one of the tallest girls in school with mousy brown hair and had managed to fly under the radar until I left. I wasn't even sure if most of my classmates realized I was missing during senior year after we'd moved. Granted, my loneliness was mostly my own doing since I'd hidden for most of my teenage years. I'd managed to cultivate a complex of crippling insecurity that had stayed with me for most of my life. Chase had been the first man I'd dated who'd made me feel wanted and loved or had fooled me into believing I was more than only a pastime.

I took in a sharp breath through my nostrils in an effort to straighten my spine. I was here to turn things around, and I'd be an awesome waitress if I put my mind to it. I'd set tables before, carried stuff from kitchens to dining rooms, how different could it be at a bar? The basics were the same. I'd manage. Somehow.

I groaned as I trudged out the tiny side door of my closet of an apartment. An old neighbor of ours was kind enough to rent me the space over her garage that was really too small to actually *be* considered an apartment, but it was in my minuscule price range. School was forty-five minutes away, but I'd only have a twenty-minute ride to work.

I may not have returned to Colebury as a teacher with a masters, but I'd leave as one—and that's when my real life would begin.

When I opened the door to Speakeasy, my eyes scanned over the bustling crowd. The din added to my frayed nerves as I searched for Ty, one of the managers Alec had put me in contact with after he'd hired me. My inexperience as a waitress would be obvious to anyone I came in contact with tonight, but I prayed it wouldn't make me a staff liability. I may have been given a chance because of my mother's friendship with Mrs. Rossi, but it would be a short-lived favor if I couldn't prove that I could handle it.

"Melanie!" My head whipped around toward a man's voice. I scanned the bar and noticed someone waving me over.

"I love it when new staff is early."

I cut through the crowd, forcing a smile as a large tray of beer glasses caught my eye. Visions of me dropping one in the middle of the busy crowd, shards of glass and craft beer splattered all over, made my heart leap into my throat.

"How did you know it was me?" I asked as I stepped up to the counter.

His head cocked from side to side. "Alec told me what you looked like, and you had that 'what the hell did I get myself into' look." I'm Ty. Nice to meet you."

My cheeks heated at how spot on he was as I took his extended hand.

"It looks like you can use another waitress tonight." A nervous laugh bubbled out as I took another glimpse around the busy floor. He needed another waitress who knew how to handle a night like this which although I'd try my very best to fake it, was not me.

"We sure could." Ty nodded, and I couldn't help returning his easy smile.

Ty was good looking in that scruffy, floppy haired way most of the guys around here had been when I was growing up, but it was easy to see how his friendly personality drew people in. Alec said Ty would be great to work for, fair but patient. I hoped that Alec meant that Ty was *very* patient.

"You can put your stuff into one of the lockers in the back. I'll tell Anne to come find you since you'll be shadowing her tonight. Don't get spooked by the crowd. It's five-dollar beer night so you won't have to worry about remembering any kooky cocktails on your first night. There are three beers on tap that ninety percent of the customers here will ask for, and they're all clearly labeled."

I squared my shoulders and nodded. I could handle that. This wasn't my first time around a tap. Well, it was a keg at a frat party, but I would force myself to believe it counted.

When I made my way to the locker room, it was empty. I found one vacant locker I assumed I could take, stuffing my jacket and purse inside before slamming the door a little harder than I'd wanted to.

I rested my hand on the cool metal as I clenched my eyes shut. This may not have been where I planned to be right now, but it was a means to a very important end. I wouldn't have made it through the past couple of months without a little resolve and persistence. A smile curled my lips as I mustered up the rest of my courage. I'd show Chase. I'd show everyone.

Mousy Melanie would make things happen.

"Hey," a female voice interrupted my internal pep talk. "I'm Anne, you must be Melanie."

I shook the tall brunette's extended hand. "Nice to meet you. I heard I'll be shadowing you, tonight."

She grinned while giving me a slow nod. "You'll be great. Here's an apron and pad and pencil. You can tuck that into the pocket. Nothing warms a Vermont heart like inexpensive craft beer. We have Goldenpour, Barclay Stout, and Read Rover. They actually have different colors if you can believe that. We have two Shipley ciders on tap, too, but I'd guess most our night will be running back and forth from the bar with Goldenpour. Give your orders to one of the bartenders, and they'll get whatever you need."

"Sounds good to me," I told her as I tied the apron around my waist and shoved the pad and pencil into the pocket, blowing out a breath of relief that I wouldn't have to work the tap tonight.

"I'll introduce you to as many of us as I can," Anne said over her shoulder as she made her way back inside. "You've met Ty, who's a pretty cool boss. There are a couple of other managers around if you need any help. This is Lily." Anne said when she arrived at the bar counter. "She's our awesome bartender slash artist who likes to force good energy on us." She nodded to the blackboard behind the petite woman with short blonde hair who looked oddly familiar. *You don't get what you wish for, you get what you work for* was written on a white dry erase board in perfect cursive with pink marker. Affirmations are always purposely generic, but this one hit me a little differently tonight.

I wished to be happy with my life and be proud of who I was and what I did, and I wasn't afraid of a little hard work to get there.

"That's what I get for being positive around here." She huffed with the hint of a smile pulling at her lips. "Nice to meet you, Melanie. This is Matteo, the bar manager. He loves it when you call him Matty."

"No, he doesn't."

My nerves were so shot, I hadn't noticed the man standing next to her with his back turned. When Matteo turned around, rolling his dark eyes at Lily, I had to hold in a gasp.

There was good looking, and there was *really* good looking. Matteo was two levels above that. He had gorgeous dark eyes, full lips, and a shadow of stubble covering his chiseled jaw. His black hair was thick and cropped short, falling a little below his ears, giving off a professional but boyish type of vibe.

As out of it as I was tonight, I'd have to be unconscious not to notice this man. Alec mentioned that I would be reporting to Ty and the bar manager, so although it was impossible to not notice how attractive Matteo was, I had to learn to ignore it. Besides, I had no time for anything but work and school.

"Hi Melanie, nice to meet you." Matteo extended his hand, the sleeves of his polo shirt shifting to reveal the bulge of his bicep and the tease of a black lined tattoo. I was almost five foot ten in height and wasn't used to a man towering over me. I wasn't used to the broad shoulders and megawatt smile, either.

Oh, holy Jesus, Melanie, get it together.

I took his hand and returned his strong grip. When our eyes met, I noticed his long lashes, another ridiculous addition to his overall masculine beauty. A jolt ran up my arm when my palm grazed his, and I pulled my clammy hand away as quickly as I could without being rude.

"You too," I squeaked out, forcing a smile before I turned to follow Anne.

By the third hour into my shift, it almost felt like I was getting the hang of it. I had some introductions in passing, but we were all too busy to chat. I loaded beer glasses onto a couple of trays and, while I hadn't attempted to balance anything onto my shoulder, I managed to carry them back and forth without incident.

Anne and Ty had been one hundred percent right. As long as we kept the beer flowing, the crowd was happy and blissfully satisfied.

Lily smiled as I approached the bar. "How's the first night going?"

"Not bad actually." I couldn't hide the surprise in my voice. "I need three Goldenpours, please."

"Of course you do." She winked as she started lining up the glasses. "So, what's your story? I guess you're new in town."

"Back in town," I corrected. "New to some, I guess." Or most, but I was too busy to dwell. "My parents and I moved to New Hampshire in my junior year. Manchester."

"Did you go to Colebury High School? Well, what else is around here, right?"

"Yes." I nodded slowly as it finally dawned on me where I knew Lily from. "I remember you—I was in the art club with you for a hot minute when I was a freshman."

"I loved that club! I helped start it in junior year. How long were you there? We were a couple of grades apart, but I knew everyone."

"I only went a couple of times. I realized I was out of my element among a bunch of talented artists." I coughed out a laugh, remembering how I tried to socialize by trying different clubs and never attended more than once or twice.

"I wish you'd have given it a chance." She frowned before shaking her head. "Art has always soothed me. So, what brings you back?"

"I'm taking graduate education classes at Burlington University."

Lily smiled. "So, you'll burn the night oil here and study the rest of the time?"

"Basically." I shrugged with a laugh, trying not to get anxious with every glass Lily handed me to line up on the tray. I could do this, I'd hold it with both hands and head over with a steady walk. I'd been helping load and unload trays all night and carrying them to tables, granted not this far of a distance. Piece of cake, I hoped.

"Melanie Thomas, is that you?"

My head whipped around at the sound of my name.

"Angie?"

I almost didn't recognize her without her waist-length long hair. Back in high school, she ran with most of the in crowd but always invited me along when she met up with other friends. I still remembered the ever-present hesitation that she'd spend hours trying to talk me out of.

On the rare occasions I'd agree to come along, she'd flutter through a crowd like the social butterfly she was while I was a gasping fish, alone and out of the water. It wasn't her fault I never felt like I fit in, but I always appreciated her trying.

College had been slightly different. I'd had a cluster of friends, and no one had to put a gun to my head to get me to join them at the bar. But coming back to Colebury, I still felt like that shy tall bookworm who'd never really belonged anywhere.

Before I knew it, I was tackled with a hug. "What are you doing here?" she asked when she pushed back, a big smile on her still beautiful face.

"Would you believe I live here now? I'm in graduate school at Burlington and working nights here at Speakeasy. First night here, in fact."

Since I'd returned to Colebury, even the familiar faces seemed strange after being gone for so long. Angie's presence reminded me of the good things about Colebury that I'd forgotten. While I was still talking myself down from the anxiety of carrying beer through a crowd, my shoulders relaxed from the unexpected comfort.

"Well, we need to catch up." She dug around her purse and pulled out her phone. "Give me your number. I don't want to hold you up on a busy night. Let's catch up one night this week!"

She handed me her phone, and I quickly plugged in my

number. "Let me get back to Milo before he thinks I got lost." She grinned before handing it back to me.

"Still with Milo?" Like I'd ever had any doubt. They'd been together since freshman year—one of those couples you knew would never break up even if their bickering gave you a headache.

"Yep. Married him, too. And had his babies."

"Babies?" I fell against the counter as my jaw dropped.

"Yup." She said with a slow nod. "Told you, lots to catch up on." Angie shifted but turned back to squeeze my shoulder. "Nice to see you back in town."

I smiled as she departed, still pleasantly surprised to have some good feelings about being back in town.

I held the tray with both hands as I crossed the bar floor to the table in the corner. Even with the loud buzz of the crowd, a heated argument grew louder behind me. I craned my head for a moment to see where it was coming from, but there were too many bodies clustered around me.

"I knew you'd be here!" an angry female voice yelled. "You're such a liar!"

The smell of warm beer crawled up my nose before a splatter landed on my arm. The glasses I was holding remained steady on the tray, and before I could figure out where the splash had come from, I was knocked over from behind, the tray flinging into the air in almost slow motion before I crashed onto the floor with the glasses.

It was almost a relief to watch my biggest worry for my first night at work play out. I cupped my forehead as I took internal stock of my injuries. Other than a raw scrape on my arm, I was okay. Humiliated enough for hot tears to burn my eyes, but I was able to pull myself to stand.

"You two, *out*!" someone with a deep timbre bellowed. "Ray, clean up the glass before anyone else gets hurt." Matteo rushed over to me and grabbed my shoulders. "Are you okay?"

I nodded, afraid if I spoke my voice would crack.

He looked me over with a furrowed brow. "You're bleeding. Let's get that elbow bandaged. Come with me."

Matteo pressed his hand to the small of my back and led me to the breakroom. The warmth of his palm through my shirt sparked tingles, despite my humiliation. When I slid into one of the chairs, he handed me a towel before rummaging through one of the cabinets.

"No other injuries?" he asked with his back still to me. When he turned around, he had a small case in his hand that I assumed was a first aid kit.

"Other than wounded pride." I coughed out a laugh as I wiped at the sticky beer on my forearms. "No, I'm fine."

He shook his head, and a warm smile stretched his perfect lips. "You were knocked over from behind. Don't be embarrassed for a second."

I winced when he swiped an alcohol pad across my bloody elbow.

"I've told Ty before that we should ban those two. This isn't their first fight here that ended with broken glass." My breath stilled when he quickly but carefully adhered the bandage onto my skin. The extra care wasn't necessary as he could have just pointed me in the direction of the first aid kit, but an odd warmth spread through my chest. It was nice to have someone take care of me, regardless of the reasons why.

"Did you work in triage before Speakeasy? You're good at taking care of injuries."

He laughed with a shrug. "I have a little girl who loves to play and run—and fall. I can set a Band-Aid in five seconds. I guess it's a skill that comes in handy sometimes."

A rush of shame washed over me. He had a daughter and probably a wife, and I could barely look at him without drool pooling at the corner of my mouth.

"She's lucky to have you," I whispered, a little breathless from this new information.

"I'm lucky to have *her*." He popped off the chair and stuffed the kit back into the cabinet. "Take a breather before going back out there." He handed me a clean Speakeasy T-shirt. "I'm sorry this happened on your first night."

"It's okay. Thank you for your help." My finger traced the bandage on my arm, and a rush of heat rose up my neck. I wasn't sure if it was still embarrassment or a spark between us as his eyes lingered on me. I sucked in a deep breath and let it out slowly.

"My pleasure." He smiled, stuffing his hands in his pockets before heading out of the breakroom.

I balled the shirt into my hands and leaned back on a long sigh. That's what I got for having good feelings about tonight. Between the embarrassment of taking a dive in front of everyone I was trying to impress and the budding inappropriate attachment to Matteo for coming to my rescue, I didn't know how to muster the energy to get back up and out on the tap room floor.

One of my bosses was a nice guy, a father, and most likely a husband. A nice gesture was just that—a nice gesture. And it would be wise to not twist it into something more.

Loneliness could do crazy things to someone's brain, and right now it was doing a number on mine.

MATTEO

"We need a bouncer here." Will, one of the other waiters, noted from his seat at the bar as I cleaned the counter for the night. "Or at least someone to keep watch for Ted Nealy. Whenever that dude comes in, trouble always follows." He snickered and shook his head.

"Trouble meaning Yvette, who tracks him here every time." I sighed as I straightened up the glasses behind the bar. I had no clue what their deal was, and I honestly couldn't care less. I wished they could just keep their angst out of Speakeasy.

"I had a girlfriend like that," Will mused with a wistful smile. "The fights were exhausting but the makeup sex…" A whistling sound shrilled through his teeth. "Made it worth it. For a little while, anyway."

Rolling my eyes, I filled tonight's purse and stuffed it into the safe. The nights I had to close always added about a half hour to my shift, but having a reliable babysitter had made it a non-issue. My stomach twisted every time I thought of that impending and dreaded change to my life.

"Speaking of sex." He lifted a brow. "I haven't seen Rochelle in here in a long time. Did you guys split up?"

"We weren't together to begin with. We just faded out, is all," I told Will without meeting his gaze.

I'd met Rochelle on one of my first nights at Speakeasy. She was beautiful and sweet, and I was ashamed to admit loneliness and stress had gotten the best of me when she'd slipped me her number one night. We hooked up a few times until she began to hint at making us more than a casual fling.

She was still young, a few years younger than me, and enjoying a life of bars and clubs and freedom. Getting saddled with a five-year-old wasn't in her plan, even if she'd never come out and said it. She'd never once asked to meet my daughter, and I'd had no plan to introduce them.

My mother told me that when I met the one, the first thing I'd want is for Lauren to meet her. It was the *last* thing I'd wanted with Rochelle, and I ended it as to not waste our time with each other any longer. Empty, no strings attached relationships did nothing but scratch a temporary itch. If anything, they reminded me just how lonely I was.

"You seemed to be a little friendly with the new girl." Will smirked as he stood from the bar stool.

"If by friendly you mean I picked her up off the floor after she was knocked over to make sure she wasn't injured—like any decent person in close proximity would, I guess. Why?"

The truth was, I'd tracked Melanie in my peripheral from the moment we were introduced. She was gorgeous, tall and curvy with crystal blue eyes and full lips, but that wasn't why I was aware of her the entire night. Well, not the only reason.

She had this vulnerability about her that compelled me to look after her. I'd never seen her before, and in a few months, I'd gotten to know most of the people in Colebury as they all dropped into Speakeasy at some point. Who I hadn't met yet, I'd heard about. I'd neither seen or heard anything about Melanie. When I saw Ted plow into her after Yvette pushed him, I rushed over to her before I knew what I was doing.

I could've just told her where to find the first aid kit in the breakroom, but something in me had to make sure she was okay. When she gazed at me with those big, grateful eyes after I set the bandage onto her arm, there was a spark between us that I spent the rest of the night forcing myself to pretend never happened.

"You crack me up, Gallo." Will shook his head as he shrugged on his jacket. "You have the whole dark, Italian brooding thing going on. With the crook of your finger, dating would be cake for you."

"Dark Italian brooding thing?" I had to laugh. "If you're asking me out, I'm flattered, but I'm sorry—you're not my type. Besides, I have a daughter. Dating will *never* be cake for me."

His smile faded. "I get it. I mean, I have no kids so I don't actually know how it is. But fathers can have a little fun, too. I would think, anyway." He slapped his hand on the counter. "And on that note, have a good night."

After Will made his way out the door, I headed to the breakroom to tell any stragglers I was closing up. I found Anne and Melanie chatting by the lockers. I forced my eyes away from the graceful slope of Melanie's neck. I was around attractive women all the time, why was this one distracting me so much on her first night?

"Hey, Matteo. Sorry for lingering. I was just telling Melanie she did a great job, tonight. Even if she ended up a casualty in another Ted and Yvette collision." Anne winced, nodding at the bandage on her arm.

"We all are at some point. It's become a Speakeasy rite of passage."

Melanie lifted her head, a shy smile pulling at her mouth.

"The arm is okay?" I asked, resisting the urge to move closer to inspect it.

"It's just a scrape. I've had worse, trust me." She smiled as she pulled on her coat and grabbed her bag.

"Follow me, ladies. I need to lock up."

"Seriously Matteo, can we ban them?" Anne asked from

behind me. I purposely walked in front of them in case I had the inappropriate urge to stare at Melanie from behind.

"I'm trying, Anne." I sighed as I locked the door.

"Goodnight, guys. And great job, Melanie." Anne said before she jogged over to her car.

"Goodnight, ladies," I told them before making my way to my truck.

"Hey, Matteo," Melanie called from behind me. I stopped and shifted back around.

"I just wanted to say thank you. If you hadn't come over, that fall would have ruined my night. Thank you for making me feel better and for patching me up." She laughed, her smile wide and easy and breathtaking.

I clenched my eyes shut as if to blink away a blinding ray of light.

"You're very welcome. I'm sort of new here, too, as I'm assuming you are."

She cocked her head from side to side. "Back, not new. Although, it's been a while since I've lived in Colebury. My family moved to New Hampshire years ago. We weren't very memorable." She barked out a laugh. "I think I hear a New York accent."

"I'm trying to say my r's the right way now that I'm a New Englander." We shared a chuckle. "It's hard when it's engrained into you."

"You shouldn't try to hide it. It suits you, and it's part of who you are."

Our eyes locked again—and I needed to put a stop to this.

"I better go relieve my babysitter."

"Oh," she said, more to herself than me. "Does your wife work nights, too?"

"I don't have a wife," I said, spying the slight widening of her eyes. "It's just Lauren and me."

"I'm so sorry, I didn't mean to pry." She draped her hand over her eyes.

"Don't be, trust me everyone makes that assumption. Not too

many single dads my age, I guess." I smiled and noticed her shoulders relax. "Even with the fall, pride yourself on a good first day."

"Thanks." She grinned, backing up a couple of steps before turning to make her way toward her car.

I raked my hand through my hair once I stepped inside my truck, blaming Will for jinxing me, tonight. I was technically Melanie's boss, and whatever misplaced attraction I might be feeling toward her couldn't continue past tonight.

Dating was cake. *Right*. Maybe seven years ago…but now, that felt like another lifetime.

I pulled my truck into the driveway and let my head fall back after I cut the engine. Before I committed to anything in Colebury, I made sure I had hired a babysitter I could trust. The last thing I wanted to do was have to figure out childcare and after next week that was exactly what I'd have to do.

Josephine was perfect. In fact, when I'd met her, she'd seemed a little *too* perfect. She reminded me of the Vermont version of my mother. She was in her mid-seventies but was strong and healthy with no issues driving or working at night. Her husband had passed away years ago and her own children had moved away. She'd told me babysitting for children in the area gave her a sense of purpose. After I interviewed her, I quickly hired her as Lauren's regular babysitter.

Childcare wasn't an issue during the day when Lauren was in school. I was able to get her off the bus, I only needed someone at night when my shifts started. Josephine would come over before I had to leave for work and watched her until after eleven when I came home. It was a sense of security I never expected to be ripped from me after only a few months.

Leaving my kid with someone I hardly knew, at night, brought on a roll of nausea every time I thought about it. Josephine was moving in with her daughter in Montpelier next weekend, which was too far for her to travel back and forth from each night. She was excited to be close to her family again, and I was happy for her—just worried as hell for *my* family and the delicate balance that was about to fly off kilter.

I slipped the key into the lock and opened the door. Josephine was wiping down the kitchen counter before she lifted her head.

"I was getting worried. Long night?"

First of many.

"Not too bad. I'm sorry I'm late. I forgot to mention I had to close up tonight, and it took longer than I'd thought."

I was still shocked that Speakeasy closed before midnight. In New York, the bar of the restaurant I'd worked at closed at three a.m. or later. Lauren would sleep over my parent's house, and I would pick her up after I'd gotten a couple of hours of sleep. I couldn't imagine doing that now, although she'd grown attached enough to Josephine to not look for me during the night. I'd bet she was the reason Lauren hadn't asked for her grandparents as much as I'd thought she might, another potential problem created from Josephine's departure.

"Don't be sorry. I was chatting with some friends of mine earlier today, and a few have daughters looking for a babysitting job. They go to school during the day, so they'd be free at night. I can give you their numbers if you'd like. Nice girls from nice families." Her smile was sad but hopeful.

I held in a groan. A young girl thinking she was going to get into my pants by taking care of my daughter was not what I needed. It was a dick assumption to make but after it had happened more than a few times back in the Bronx, I was hesitant to bring another student around my daughter.

But what choice did I have?

"Sure, I'll give them a call next week."

Her lips pursed as she shook her head. "I'm so sorry to leave the both of you. Lauren is such a wonderful little girl. And a lucky one, too."

I smiled, despite myself. The crushing guilt I'd always felt when it came to my daughter was because she *wasn't* lucky. She was abandoned by her mother when she was only six-months-old and left with a father who loved her more than his own life but struggled on a daily basis to fill the void.

"I know you always think you fall short," Josephine said as if she'd just read my mind, "but you love that little girl with your whole heart and soul. I haven't known many fathers as dedicated or harder on themselves than you." She shook her head. "She may miss me, and I'm sure she misses your family back in New York, but all she ever wants is you." She stepped closer and dropped a hand to my shoulder. "It's hard not to dwell on what she doesn't have, and I know you're afraid of failing her, but you won't. It's not possible."

Some days, no matter how hard I tried, failing Lauren seemed not only possible but inevitable. I loved her as hard as I could, and prayed that in the end, that would somehow be enough.

"Thanks, Josephine. I'm off this Thursday night. How about a thank you dinner? You pick the place. Our gift to you for putting up with us for the past few months."

"Thanks are unnecessary as Lauren is impossible not to love. Both of you are. But sure. We can go to the diner. I know Lauren loves it there."

"Lauren can probably *recite* the menu there." I snickered. We had dinner there every week when I had a night off, our date she liked to called it.

She gathered her coat and purse and wished me good night. I watched as she got into her car. Yes, Colebury was a safe small town, but the New Yorker in me always had his eyes peeled.

I fell onto the recliner, already exhausted from the energy that it would take to find my daughter a new babysitter that we both liked as much as Josephine. Rubbing my eyes, I smiled at the tiny hands squeezing my shoulders.

"You're supposed to be sleeping, Cookie." I turned to kiss Lauren's cheek then nodded toward the faded image of Belle from *Beauty and The Beast* across her chest. "I think if we wash that nightshirt one more time, it's going to fall apart."

"You look sleepy, Daddy," she said as she dug her palms into my back in an attempt to give me a massage. "You need a spa day."

I spied the spa "basket" by her feet with the hair clips, fake nail polish, and Highlights magazine. I'd been a client of hers at least three times a week and had memorized the magazine by now.

"It's a little late for a spa day, Laur." I cupped her cheek. "But I appreciate it."

I lifted her onto my lap and pulled her against my chest. Her contented sigh stalled when she jerked her head up.

"What's that yucky smell?"

I burst out laughing at her cute little crinkled nose.

"Someone spilled beer on me." I had been near Melanie when she'd been knocked over, and some of the spilled beer had ricocheted onto me when it splattered on the floor. It was another reminder of how I'd been *too* near Melanie tonight.

"On purpose?" Her mouth fell open. "That's mean."

I shrugged, holding in a laugh. "It happens, Cookie."

"I don't like beer." She folded her arms and twisted her lips into an angry pout.

"Good. Remember that." I picked her up and climbed the stairs to our bedrooms.

All I'd wanted was to make life good for my daughter but I'd never thought the good path we were on here would get derailed this easily.

As much as I tried, I always feared the gaping hole left by the mother she didn't even remember would swallow us both.

MELANIE

"Melanie! Over here!"

I scanned the crowded Colebury Diner, searching in the direction of Angie's voice.

I couldn't get over how much Colebury had changed. It still had that tiny New England town feel, but instead of sleepy and traditional it was vibrant and exciting. Even the diner I'd remembered from when I was a kid was somehow more upscale.

"Sorry if you were waiting long." I finally found Angie in a booth in the far corner. "I was trying to finish a paper for class."

She smiled, shaking her head. "I give you credit. I couldn't imagine going back to school now. I'm lucky I made it through four years of college." Angie laughed before handing me a menu.

"I'd always planned to go to graduate school. It probably would've been easier if I had just kept going instead of taking a hiatus." My mouth watered as I tried to decide what to order. With my tiny kitchen, I hadn't cooked much for myself since I moved in. A real cheeseburger sounded like heaven on Earth.

"I hope you did something good during your hiatus. Something fun at least." She crossed her arms and leaned back. I hated having to disappoint her.

"Well, I was engaged to someone who I'd thought was a

wonderful man and moved in with him in record time, then moved back home when he dumped me. I don't know if I'd call that fun."

Even the Cliffs Notes version of what happened with Chase and me was sad and pathetic.

"I'm sorry, Melanie." Angie's eyes were full of sympathy. I'd hoped that I escaped that look when I left New Hampshire.

"It's okay." I waved her off. "Everything happens for a reason, right? Now I can become the teacher I always wanted to be and start over. Did I think I'd start over here? No way, but life doesn't always turn out the way you think, I guess."

I tried to look at what happened with Chase as a lesson to not move too fast should I ever fall for someone else, but what it had really taught me was that I wasn't special enough for a man to want to keep. That unimportant and unnoticed feeling had manifested itself again, and no matter what I'd done lately, I couldn't shake it off.

"You'll be a great teacher. I credit you for my love of romance novels. Before I was friends with you, I'd never pick up a book that wasn't for school." I returned her warm smile. "Hopefully, when you get your masters you can teach in Colebury and make one of my kids a reader."

"I have two years before I'd be a teacher anywhere, but I'm not sure if I'd stay here or not."

"Right, you probably miss New Hampshire."

I nodded, even though I wasn't sure that I did. I missed my friends and my family, but I wasn't rooted there. If I was, I wouldn't have applied to every graduate school in the Northeast. My goal was to go back to school, but deep inside, I yearned to start over. Having to go back to Colebury to do that was both the sweetest and most bitter irony.

"Now that we're caught up on my sad life, tell me about you. I always knew you'd end up with Milo."

"I think I did too, even though I fought him for a while." She lifted her shoulder. "We got married right after college. I got pregnant with twins on our honeymoon. I never thought we'd have a baby before I was twenty-five never mind two, but what can you do? I have a boy and girl so unless I get unforeseen baby fever, I'm *done*."

I couldn't help but laugh at her pursed lips.

"I guess Milo has them tonight?"

She shook her head. "The grandparents fight over who gets to baby-sit when one or both of us go out. Milo is off tonight, but he's out with a couple of buddies while his mom takes care of the babies. We take advantage of their generosity whenever we can, and as parents of twins, we'd be stupid not to."

"I guess that's who had them when I ran into you at Speakeasy with Milo," I asked while seeking out the waitress.

"You got it. My college friends still ask me to come with them on weekends to Vegas or the Bahamas, but a night at Speakeasy and dinner with a friend are the extent of my good times. By the way, how is that going? It's a busy place, so I'm sure you must work your ass off."

"It is and I do. I thought working nights and going to school during the day was a good idea until I found out I had to choose between schoolwork and sleep. Lately, sleep is winning, and I'm already behind. I should load up on carbs here since it's going be a late night."

I rubbed my temple, my exhaustion creeping up on me no matter how much caffeine I ingested in a given day.

"I also don't sleep, so I hear you."

Her mouth lifted in a tired smile. When she dropped her head to peruse the menu, I glanced over the crowd and found Matteo sitting at a table with and older woman and a little girl who I assumed was his daughter. I could only see her side profile, but she was a beautiful girl. Her hair was cinched in a tight ponytail with a rainbow tie and her adorable laugh traveled all the way to our table.

Matteo had his back to me but it was clear how much he adored his daughter. He leaned in to whisper something that made her giggle even harder, and when she stood he pulled her into his lap.

"Isn't he the hottest single dad you've ever seen?"

I turned to Angie's sigh, embarrassed to be caught staring.

"Well I haven't seen many," I dodged her question although a *God, yes* was on the tip of my tongue. "Better not let Milo hear you say that." I smiled and leaned back on the soft vinyl in case I was tempted to steal another glance at their table.

"Milo is a great dad. Clueless at times, but I suppose we both are. I couldn't imagine doing this on my own, and for a father to be raising a little girl by himself in a new town? That has to be so hard on him. I forgot you guys probably work together at Speakeasy."

"He's one of the managers. He actually saved me on my first night." I still thought of how he swooped in like a superhero and bandaged the scrape on my arm along with my wounded pride. Since that night, almost a week ago, he always checked on me. *How was the night going? If I needed help just ask him.* I figured he was like that with most of the servers, and I tried not to fool myself into thinking I was special just because he'd stuck a Band-Aid on my arm.

The waitress came over to take our order, and I couldn't help sneaking another look at Matteo when she left our table.

"How long has he been in Colebury?" I asked before I could help myself. "He told me he was still sort of new here."

"He moved here in June, I believe. When he got here, the hospitality committee swarmed on him. A single father with a little girl and no wife or family anywhere? Plus, a single father who looks like…that? Every woman in this town offered her help in some way, even the married ones."

My head whipped to look at her. "You're kidding me? Married women hit on him when he first came here? God, doesn't anyone have shame anymore around here?"

She laughed, sputtering the sip of water she'd just taken. "I don't know if they all *hit* on him. I do think it's hard not to take an interest. I'm not only talking about wanting to date Matteo, but a little girl that age with no mother to take care of her in a new place?" She shook her head with a long sigh. "From what I heard, all his family is still back in New York. I don't know their back-story or anything, but it seems tragic to me, no matter what happened."

"It is." I cleared my throat and turned around, hating that I was gaping at Matteo and his daughter just like everyone in town still does. "I'm guessing that's his nanny."

Angie shook her head. "No. Well not anymore. That's Josephine Jenkins, remember her? She has that old Victorian house that everyone would hit for candy on Halloween, even the high school kids."

"Yes!" My hand fell to the table. "She made the best caramel apples. Why isn't she his nanny anymore?"

"She baby-sat Lauren while Matteo worked, but she's moving in with her daughter in Montpelier."

"Everyone still knows everything about everyone here, I see." I snickered and rolled my eyes.

"Well, yes." A smirk tipped her lips. "But she babysat for us a couple of times when I was in a jam. That was her thing in recent years, but when Matteo came to town she only watched *his* daughter and no other kids."

"Wow. It's probably going to be hard for Matteo to find someone to work at night," I wondered out loud, still entirely more invested than I should've been.

Angie burst out laughing. "I'm very sure there will be a line of very willing and able young babysitters to help him in his hour of need, day or night." I laughed when she brought her hands to her chest and heaved an exaggerated sigh.

"Where's the restroom? I obviously haven't been here in a while." I stifled a yawn. I needed some cold water on my neck to perk me up before my burger and fries got to the table.

"Right back there." Angie pointed to the far corner of the room —right behind Matteo's table.

"Excuse me for a minute." I slid out of the booth and felt a sudden wave of nerves. Watching Matteo with his daughter captivated me enough to have to force my eyes to tear away from him. I worried it would show if I spoke to him. But I was about to pass him and couldn't be rude.

"Oh hey, Melanie," Matteo said, noticing me as I approached.

"Hi Matteo. I guess this is still the town hot spot." I coughed out what I hoped didn't sound like a nervous laugh.

"It has been for us." He gazed down at the little girl in his lap. "Melanie, this is Lauren. Lauren, this is Melanie, she works with me."

"Hi, Melanie!" Lauren smiled at me as she cuddled into her father's chest. I rubbed at a sharp pang in my side, most likely from one of my ovaries exploding. She had the biggest brown eyes and longest real lashes I'd ever seen.

I'd worked at a daycare center near my parents' house after I moved out of Chase's apartment and it had been just what I'd needed. The kids helped me heal and reminded me of why I always wanted to become a teacher. Lauren reminded me of one of the little girls who'd always rushed toward me and hugged my knees the second she came in.

"Wow, you're pretty and tall like a princess!" Her dark eyes grew when they met mine, showing off the long lashes she inherited from her father. "You look like Belle. She's my favorite."

Matteo met my gaze with a tiny smile.

"Thank you, Lauren. Belle is my favorite princess, too."

"How do you know all princesses are tall?" Matteo asked Lauren while shifting Lauren on his lap.

She cocked her head to the side before blowing out an exasperated breath.

"They're all tall so they don't trip on the bottom of their dresses, Daddy."

"That makes sense." I couldn't help my smile at her resolute nod.

"Melanie Thomas. Didn't you grow up beautiful!" Mrs.

Jenkins stood from her chair and made her way over to me. "I haven't seen you since Halloween all those years ago!" She squeezed my wrists. "It's good to see you."

"Thank you. It's great to see you, too." I peered at Lauren over her shoulder. "Mrs. Jenkins always made the *best* caramel apples on Halloween."

"She made them for us too, even though she said it wasn't the right season. But Daddy only let me have half." Her bottom lip jutted into a pout.

"That's because I want you to keep your teeth at least until high school."

She burrowed back into his chest after he kissed her forehead.

"I'll let you guys enjoy dinner. Nice to see you all." I dipped my head." And it was very nice to meet *you*, Lauren."

"Thank you." Lauren's leg swung back and forth along the side of Matteo's chair.

"When someone says nice to meet you, you say 'Nice to meet you, too,'" he told her in a loud whisper.

"Oh. Nice to meet you, too!" She lifted her head to her father's, beaming at his nod of approval.

As I headed to the restrooms, I wondered how many potential babysitters would ignore Matteo's sweet little girl because they were too busy focusing on him?

It wasn't my business or my problem, so why did it bother me so much?

MELANIE

"Melanie, are you all right? You were due back inside fifteen minutes ago."

I nearly jumped out of my skin at the knock on my car window. My head fell into my hands, shame burning my cheeks that this happened *again*. The short breaks I had during the nights I worked at Speakeasy went one of two ways. Either I was so engrossed in what I was studying that I lost track of time, or I passed out and lost track of time. Both were becoming bad habits that weren't going unnoticed by my coworkers or my managers.

"Thank you, Anne. I'm so sorry." I threw my book onto the passenger seat and leaped out of my car. When it was too hard to focus in the noisy breakroom, I thought studying in my car was the perfect solution. It turned out that I was able to weed out the distractions from Speakeasy so well, I managed to forget I was even working while I was in the parking lot.

I ran inside and grabbed my apron off the wall in the break-room before rushing to the bar to see what orders I could fill.

"We were wondering where you were," Ty lifted a brow at me from where he stood with Matteo behind the bar. "Listen, I under-stand you need to use your breaks to study or catch up on sleep, but I need you to stay inside from now on. One of us can't keep running to the parking lot to bring you back when you're late."

"Sorry. Got it, Ty." I swallowed the lump of humiliation growing in the back of my throat. This was not me. I never slacked off in school or at any job that I'd had, and I never needed a job more than I needed this one. As much as I fought against it, something had to give. My course load was competing with my shifts at Speakeasy, and each day, it became clearer how much I needed to back off of one.

Cutting back on my hours wasn't an option since I needed silly things like a roof over my head and food. Although I'd managed to get a loan and partial scholarship to pay for most of my tuition, but it was still up to me to come up with the rest.

Dropping a couple of classes and extending my time in school —and in Colebury—was in the complete opposite direction of my goals but every night, that choice slipped more and more out of my hands. All I needed was for my extra-long breaks getting back to Alec, who would tell his mother, who would then mention it to my mother. I was too exhausted to have another, "What are you doing with your life?" conversation.

In trying to do it all, I was setting myself up for failure, but I wasn't ready to admit defeat, yet.

"Everything all right?" Matteo asked, concern creasing his forehead. "I was about to come look for you myself."

"Yes. I'm so sorry I've been late coming back from break. We're too busy for me to be so scattered. I'll look into adjusting my school schedule." I lined up the beer glasses on my tray. My balance had improved quite a bit in my weeks at Speakeasy, so at least I had that going for me.

"That's not why I asked. Are you still not sleeping at night? They shouldn't get on you for napping in your car if that's what you need." He frowned. "I know it's Colebury and not Manhattan, but being asleep in your car at night isn't the safest thing. They just put a couch in the breakroom, I'd rather you sleep there if you have to."

I guessed being a parent he had that innate sense to look after someone, but the more I got to know Matteo, the more it was obvious that it was just who he was.

"I was actually awake, this time. I was lost in early childhood development when Anne knocked on my window. I thought it would be easier to study without the noise." I shrugged. "Thinking I could do any kind of studying on my shifts was ridiculous. I don't want to be the scattered waitress not pulling her weight." I rubbed at my temple, the solutions to my problems even more nonexistent.

"You aren't, and you're not the only one scattered around here. I'm getting told about my breaks, too. It's hard to leave my daughter with new people at night and not call to check every hour." The tired smile stretching Matteo's full lips matched my own. I clenched my eyes shut to stop staring at his mouth and went back to checking my order.

"I didn't think it would take you this long to find someone new. I thought for sure you'd find someone regular by now."

"So did I." He raked his fingers through his thick, black hair. "It's been two weeks, and every time I think one may work out, something happens, and they can't come back. I suppose it's tough to find anyone willing to do this every night. I got lucky when I found Josephine." He leaned against the bar, the muscles in his forearm flexing when he rubbed at his eyes.

"It sucks when life interferes with work, doesn't it?"

I managed to pull a smirk out of Matteo. "It does." His chest deflated with a long sigh. "Things have to get better for us eventually, right?"

"They will for you, I'm sure. For me, we'll see." We shared a laugh before I grabbed my tray.

Since that first night when Matteo almost had to scoop me off the floor, we'd become friends. I was friendly with my co-workers at Speakeasy, but I never had the urge to open up about anything personal. Trading sad stories with Matteo was always the highlight of my night, and something I looked a little too forward to when I came in.

I worked without stopping for the rest of the night. It was the busiest night since I'd started working here, and I felt too guilty to take another break. By the time the customers cleared out, my feet hurt so much, they were numb.

After trudging back to the breakroom, I waited until the last two waitresses scattered before I slid down the wall onto the floor. Dropping my head into my hands, I took in a few long, slow breaths to try to recalibrate enough to stand.

When I'd come back to my hometown, I'd intended to stand on my own two feet and create the life I wanted. I tried to use the anger and shame over my wasted year as fuel to push myself forward, but I was too tired to push for anything. Hot and angry tears of frustration burned my eyes.

"Melanie, what's wrong?" I peeled my hands away from my eyes and found a panicked Matteo staring down at me. "Are you sick?"

"No," I said, letting my head fall back with a thud. "Just tired. Working half the night with no break isn't something I want to try again."

"Why would you do that?" He crouched down next to me, leaning back before stretching his legs out on the floor. "The last thing we need on a busy night is one of our waitresses to pass out."

"I guess…" I lifted a shoulder before trailing off. "Everyone was already annoyed at me for coming back late so often, I didn't want to piss anyone off more tonight and lose this job. I underestimated how hard this would be to balance it all."

"Sounds a lot like my life at the moment."

His head fell back with a quiet thud against the wall. I sat on my hands to quell the urge to squeeze one of his. That would be a little more than friendly.

"Do you have anyone else looking? Maybe ask her teacher if she can put you in contact with someone."

"My neighbor said she'd ask around. I'm hesitant to post anything because of what happened when we first came here."

"What happened?" I asked, noting his wince as he settled next to me.

"When we first moved here," he started, resting his elbows on his knees, "for the first month we had an endless stream of visitors. Most were nice, dropping off food, extra cookies and sweets for Lauren. She was so hopped up on sugar, I thought she was going to bounce off the walls."

"I bet she loved that." I laughed at Matteo's groan.

"Oh, she did. And I appreciated the gesture but…" he trailed off, cupping his forehead. "Half the women who…lingered, for lack of a better word, always hinted at the void we had," he lifted his fingers in air quotes at the word void, "because Lauren's mother wasn't around, and how they could help me fix it. The other half pretended to care about my daughter but were only interested in me."

"Ugh, that's awful." I shifted toward Matteo and sat on my hands. When he met my eyes, his gaze full of defeat—something I was all too familiar with—the urge to reach out to comfort him was again stronger than it should've been. "I was afraid of that happening to you."

"Afraid of what?" He reared back and squinted.

"Women lining up saying they'll take care of Lauren but only wanting to date her gorgeous father. I only met her once but she's such a sweet little girl and doesn't deserve that—" My heart dropped into my stomach when I realized what I said. I spied Matteo's lips twitch as I scrambled to figure out how to pull my foot out of my mouth. "I mean you know, hypothetically."

"Hypothetically, I'm gorgeous?" he teased, narrowing his eyes at me with a grin still playing on his lips.

"Look, I'm on four hours of sleep in two days. Don't pay attention to anything I say." I draped a hand over my eyes. "Anything."

Matteo peeled my fingers away from my heated face, flashing

me a smile that relaxed me yet drew me in. When the corners of his eyes crinkled, his long lashes stood out. That shouldn't have been sexy on a man, but Matteo didn't have an unattractive inch on his body. Not that I snuck any glances at it during my shifts. Well, glances that I hoped no one noticed.

I had a growing crush on my friend. My friend who also happened to be one of my bosses. My problems were piling up faster than my solutions and making my head ache.

"Hypothetically, thank you. It's frustrating when women try to talk to me and pretend Lauren isn't even there. She's getting old enough to notice things like that. I know people worry about us because they don't think a guy my age knows how to be a single parent—"

"No, you do. That's pretty obvious. Lauren is a lucky little girl to have such a dedicated father."

His eyes darted around the room before he popped off the floor, extending his hand to me.

"I'll walk you to your car. Are you okay to drive?"

I took his hand, my skin sliding against his and sending a shiver up my arm before I let him pull me up.

Being around Matteo reminded me of the awkward teenager I'd been before I left Colebury and seemed to become again once I returned.

"I'm fine." I shrugged on my jacket and shut the locker door. "Thank you for listening. I grew up here, but I'm more or less on my own now that I'm back."

"Well, I *didn't* grow up here, and no one gets my single father troubles, or at least wants to listen to them. So, thank *you*."

Our eyes locked, a long silence dangling between us before I followed Matteo out of Speakeasy, waving to the managers who were closing for the night before we headed out the door.

"I'd bet Lauren doesn't pay too much mind if anyone ignores her," I said as I unlocked my car. "She seems like she has a big personality and makes sure she's noticed one way or the other. And that's a good thing."

He groaned, scrubbing a hand down his face. "Her kinder-garten teacher told me she's trying to teach her how to quiet down her *big* personality when she needs to pay attention in class."

My hand flew to his bicep as if on its own accord. "See, nothing to worry about." The hard muscle under my fingertips made me pause. I slipped my hand away as quickly as I could without seeming obvious and opened the door to climb into the driver's seat. "Have a good night."

He nodded a goodbye, the crisp, early autumn air simmering between us before I shut the door.

I shook my head at myself as I drove away. Catching feelings for Matteo was a complication I hadn't needed, but I couldn't explain them or stuff them away.

Maybe being alone was a lot for two people to have in common.

MATTEO

"Matteo!"

Melanie's voice made me jump. I'd just sent my fifth text to my daughter's new babysitter and was staring down at my phone screen as if I could will it to respond.

"Are you okay?" Melanie's sympathetic gaze did nothing to calm me. She stuffed her pad and pencil inside her apron, her concerned eyes still fixed on me from the opposite side of the bar.

"I'd be better if Hayley would respond to my texts." I dropped my phone on the counter and groaned. I'd asked if Lauren had gone to bed on time at eight p.m. and hadn't gotten a text back. It was now after ten, and even though Speakeasy was crawling with people tonight, I was ready to grab my jacket out of my locker and run to my house to check on them.

"What happened to Amelia?"

After a parade of one night only babysitters, I'd met Amelia through one of our customers at Speakeasy. She was the niece of one of our regulars and a straight A college student. She seemed nice enough and was fine for a few days. At this point, as long as she took care of Lauren and didn't burn down the house, my standards were fairly low—as with most desperate people.

"She couldn't come back. Texted me this morning that her

friend was willing to take her place. On a Saturday night, at a moment's notice."

I'd known that leaving Lauren with this girl was a mistake.

Hayley seemed nice enough when we chatted over the phone about Lauren and what she'd need while I was gone, but when I opened the door and met her smoky-rimmed eyes, I considered calling out of work after telling her thanks but no thanks. She wore a short skirt with knee high boots, and gave me a breathy "nice to finally meet you," before she strolled past me into the house.

When she saw I wasn't up for flirting or whatever she was trying to do, she agreed to all Lauren's rules that I'd repeated so often for a new babysitter I recited them without thinking about it at this point. I tried to relax for a couple of hours when I'd gotten to work and prayed to just get through tonight. Until Hayley had stopped responding to my texts, that is.

I was about to stuff my phone in my back pocket and find Ty to tell him I had to leave when the phone vibrated in my hand, my stomach bottoming out when I recognized my landline number on the screen.

"Hello? Hayley?"

"Daddy?" My blood ran cold at the break in my daughter's voice.

"What's going on? Where's Hayley?" I lifted my gaze to where Melanie still stood in front of me, her expression reflecting the same panic squeezing my chest.

"I don't know. I can't find her anywhere. I had the bear dream again, and when I woke up, no one was here. I looked everywhere but I'm scared to go to the basement in the dark…" she trailed off, now crying in my ear.

"You can't find her?" I yelled, raking a hand through my hair trying like hell not to lose my shit and upset her more.

I turned around, inhaling a deep breath to sound calm enough to soothe my daughter until I ran out of here.

"I'll be right there. Go sit on the couch and stay there until I come home. Everything will be okay, I promise."

I had no idea what was going on there and had no right to promise anything, same as I had no right to leave my kid with someone I didn't trust.

When I turned back around, Melanie tossed my jacket at me. She must have gotten it from my locker.

"Go. I'll tell Ty why you left. Don't waste time."

"Thank you," I breathed before sprinting out of Speakeasy and into the parking lot.

When I signed the lease to rent our town house, the amenity that sold me before all the others was that I could be home from work in fifteen minutes if I needed to be. It was the one thing I was grateful as fuck for as I sped home, blowing through a few traffic lights on the way to get to my daughter.

No matter what Hayley's motivations had been for agreeing to babysit tonight, leaving a five-year-old child to fend for herself after she fell asleep was something I couldn't fathom anyone would be low enough to do, but, again, I really hadn't known who I'd been dealing with when I'd left tonight. I'd fought against my instincts, and now my little girl was suffering for it.

As horrible as it was, I prayed for Hayley's sake she'd hit her head and was unconscious somewhere my daughter couldn't find her. Because if this was deliberate, I had to figure out how to hold it together enough to not lose it in front of my kid and upset her even more.

I thanked God Josephine had taught Lauren how to dial my phone number when she babysat. It was a game to her when she'd call me before she went to sleep. She'd answer with, "See Daddy, I called you all by myself!"

The memory of those phone calls, contrasting with the one that had me tearing out of Speakeasy like a mad man, made me plunge my foot down on the gas petal that much harder. My hands shook on the steering wheel as I pulled into my driveway and leaped out of my truck.

I didn't even close the door behind me before I ran inside, scanning the room and holding my breath until I spotted Lauren curled up in her blanket at the edge of the couch.

"Come here, Cookie," I crooned, trying like hell to keep my voice even as I scooped her into my arms. She was tall for her age but still fit into the crook of my arm as she hiccupped sobs into my shoulder. "It's okay. I'm glad you called me." I dipped my head and met her teary gaze. I dug my nails into my palms to get a grip on the fear and rage coursing through me. "That was a really smart thing to do. You still can't find Hayley anywhere?"

She shook her head, her breathing still shaky. "There's a light on in the yard, but I was too scared to go outside."

"That's a good girl." My grip on Lauren grew tighter as I started to piece together where Hayley might have been. Lauren dropped her head against my chest and cinched her arms around my neck as I padded to the back patio door leading to the yard. Lauren was right, our porch light was on and while the yard was still mostly dark, my eyes landed on the glow of three cigarette butts around the bench in the far corner.

If something happened to Lauren tonight inside the house, Hayley wouldn't have had a clue. I sucked in a quick breath and shut my eyes, knowing losing my shit was inevitable but still trying to not frighten my daughter more than she already was.

"Listen. Since I'm home early, why don't we have a movie night?" I set her down gingerly in front of me and tried to give her an easy smile. Whenever Lauren had bad dreams during the night, it took her a bit to fall back to sleep. Waking up and being rattled by finding herself all alone would rile her up for the next couple of hours. "We can even have a sleepover in my room tonight, go pick something out and wait for me." I kissed her forehead and nodded my chin toward the stairs.

"I got Hayley in trouble, didn't I?" She frowned and dropped her chin to her chest.

"No," I whispered, cupping her cheek to make her look up. "She got herself into trouble. She broke a promise to watch you until I got home from work. So, she'll never watch you again. Did she give you dinner after I left?"

She nodded with a little sniffle, her tears finally subsiding.

"There were hard parts on the nuggets. I told her they were cooking too long, but she was looking at her phone and didn't hear me."

"Sorry about that, Cookie." I tapped her chin with my knuckle before crouching down in front of her. "Go upstairs, I'll only be a minute. I love you." I kissed her cheek and pulled her close. It would take me a while to calm down enough to fall asleep, too. Having her close by tonight wasn't only for her benefit.

"I love you too, Daddy." Lauren's red eyes lingered on me as she tiptoed away and up the stairs, regarding me like a ticking time bomb. She wasn't far off.

Three dark figures jumped at the loud slide of the screen door.

I stuffed my hands in my pockets and stalked over to where Hayley stood alongside a guy and girl I didn't recognize.

"I'm guessing you didn't expect me home so early. Would you mind explaining why you're out here in my yard, hanging out with people I don't know, when you're supposed to be in my house watching my daughter?"

Hayley peered at me, the whites of her eyes popping in the almost darkness.

"Lauren was sleeping. So, when my friends happened to be in the area and wanted to say hi…well…I…um, didn't want to wake her." The big smile she offered me was insulting, but it was hard to focus on anything as I could only see red.

Even though Lauren was okay, and I'd arrived back home before anything bad could happen, I struggled to dial back the urge to explode in a fit of rage. Laying into Hayley where neighbors could hear wouldn't do any of us any good. If word got around about what a loose cannon I was after berating one of my kid's babysitters, I wouldn't be able to find anyone willing to watch Lauren.

"Your friends shouldn't have stopped by at *all* since I told you no visitors under any circumstances." A sharp pain seared down my neck thanks to my clenched jaw. When I attempted another calming breath, my blood boiled at the unmistakable skunky scent from their "cigarette" smoke. I hadn't thought I could be more furious than I already was, but I somehow catapulted to that next level.

"Do you know what could have happened to a five-year-old at night—alone? She could have been hurt or sick. Do you understand what could have happened to her while you *weren't* watching her? My daughter called me at work scared to death because she'd thought you had left. So, thanks to you, I lost a night of work, almost had a heart attack, and came home to find you in my yard entertaining your friends when you were supposed to be taking care of my daughter."

"I should have asked you if they could come over," she said, still not getting the severity of how negligent she'd been. "I'm sorry—"

"You can leave now. Take your friends and go." I turned to her clueless friends, scrambling to grab whatever was on the table before rushing out of the yard.

She shrugged, having the audacity to huff before lifting her head. "I get it. I'll be gone as soon as you pay me."

"Pay you?" A laugh sputtered out before I could help it. "I hired you to babysit my daughter, and you were out here smoking pot with your friends for most of the night. If you can explain what exactly I'd be paying you *for*, I'd love to hear it."

She swiveled around like the petulant child that she was to run inside to grab her purse off the table and jet out the still open door. After I shut and locked it behind her, I turned off the lights inside and out. In the morning, I'd sweep up whatever mess Hayley and her friends had left.

I leaned against the doorjamb of my bedroom as my tired eyes lingered on Lauren. She was already burrowed into my comforter and clicking at the TV screen, ready to most likely play either *Beauty and the Beast* or *Frozen*. I doubted she'd fall asleep before two a.m., but after all the terrible possibilities that raced through my head on the way here, possibilities I had to entertain due to my own negligence, I wasn't going to refuse her anything, tonight.

She perked up when she noticed me standing there. "Come on, Daddy. Let's start the movie." She patted the bed next to her.

I kicked off my shoes and fell back onto the mattress as the movie started playing. When her head settled onto my chest, I dug my phone out to scroll through all the texts that had been blowing up my phone for the last half hour. Lily and Ty and some of the wait staff all wanted to know if Lauren was all right. Other than the young woman I threw out of my house tonight, the people we'd met in Colebury were mostly good and decent, and that was exactly how I'd wanted Lauren to grow up.

But if I couldn't make sure she was safe while I was at work, how could we stay?

I stopped when I got to a number that I didn't recognize.

Unknown: *Hey, it's Melanie. Is everything ok?*

All the wait staff had the managers' numbers, but I'd forgotten to key her number into my phone when she'd started. Or maybe that was accidentally on purpose so I wouldn't be tempted to talk to her outside of work. This town was full of beautiful women, but my urge to seek out Melanie was strong enough for me to attempt a little distance.

Matteo: *She's fine. Thank you for your help tonight. Her babysitter decided to have people over in my backyard and forgot she was here to take care of a child. So, Hayley isn't coming back.*
Melanie: *What? Who would do something like that? Is she okay?*
Matteo: *She is now, if a little shaken up. I offered a movie night sleepover, so we'll be up for a while.*
Melanie: *Are YOU okay? I was worried sick for you both.*

Matteo: *Tonight was my fault. I didn't vet this girl like I should have. I fucked up, and my daughter suffered.*
Melanie: *Stop. Go watch the movie and try to relax. You're doing the best you can.*

I gazed down at my daughter, wondering if my best would ever be good enough for her.

As Lauren focused on the TV screen, the adrenaline high I'd ridden for the last hour began to dissipate. I set my phone down and let my heavy eyelids shut, now exhausted but still too keyed up to sleep.

"Can we still go to the farm tomorrow, or do you have to work?" She lifted her brown eyes to mine, still wide awake and alert. I'd been scheduled to work tomorrow night, but I'd already planned to call out. I needed a one-night break before I could attempt to trust another stranger with my daughter. I hoped Ty and Alec would understand, but I couldn't make this a habit.

"I think I'm taking the night off, so we can maybe go to the diner afterward. Can't get any more Vermont than a hayride and pumpkin picking, right?" I kissed her temple and rested my aching head onto the pillow.

"I like Vermont." Lauren turned and settled on her side.

I liked Vermont, too. Maybe coming here was a little selfish on my part as the thought of starting over in a place where no one knew Callie and the sad story of how she'd deserted us both was a big selling point. Sure, people here thought it was a terrible tragedy when they found out that Lauren had no mother, but I never had to hear, "Oh, she looks just like Callie, what a shame."

I'd thought without the daily reminders, the reality of what had happened to us wouldn't force Lauren to grow up too fast. I wanted her to have hayrides and all the country stuff they have in movies. My daughter deserved a life full of simple goodness, even if it was only with her father.

I had a perfect plan—a plan that was about to unravel if I couldn't figure out a solution.

MELANIE

"It's like you never left, right?" Angie told me as she pushed her twins up a steep, grassy hill. She wrangled that double stroller like a champ as we headed up the path toward the Murphy Farm's pumpkin patch.

I nodded, marveling at how she wasn't out of breath by the time we arrived.

"That's some serious upper body strength you have to haul a sack of apples *and* two babies."

"You get used to it." She shrugged, letting out a long breath when she parked the stroller. "Anywhere in particular you'd like to see next?"

"I don't suppose that's a hard cider stand, is it?" I joked as Angie's infant son, Carter, let out a loud squeal as he reached his fingers toward the endless rows of pumpkins.

"I'd think you'd be sick of beer and cider by now." Angie laughed. "Although, Shipley cider is a delicacy."

"I usually serve it, not drink it, but yes, I agree about Shipley cider."

I'd sampled some cider at work last night, trying to feel a little looser with my coworkers. They'd offered me a sip of the special Audrey batch named after Griffin Shipley's wife, warning me that it's been known to kick off some hot nights in Colebury. I declined as I doubted any true hot nights were in my future.

"Are you excited for the pumpkins, little guy?" Carter replied to me with a gurgle and toothless grin while his sister Crissy slumbered next to him.

"He's *always* excited." Angie smiled at Carter, still bouncing in his seat. "Thank God his sister learned to tune him out so she could sleep." As if on cue, Crissy stirred and fussed, her bow mouth twisting with an angry wail as she started to wake.

"Come here, my girl." Angie bent to unbuckle Crissy from the stroller. The twins were eight months old, and from the few times I'd seen them, their polar opposite personalities were obvious. Carter was always ready to party while Crissy preferred to chill.

"She needs a new diaper and a bottle. Would you mind picking up Carter so I can push the seat back?" Angie asked, as she rocked her daughter back and forth. Crissy's cries had decreased to a low whine as Angie rummaged through the diaper bag with her other hand.

"Sure. I can carry him over to the patch if you want." Carter lifted his arms as soon as I released the safety restraints around his tiny waist, giggling as I crinkled my nose at him. He had that adorable sweetness that I'd loved soaking up from the children at the daycare. My plan was to teach the younger grades once I had my masters. They needed the most care and patience, but the pure and innocent love they gave back made it worth it.

"You're a natural. If you ever want to babysit, you're hired," Angie mused as she pulled down Crissy's tights.

"I worked at a daycare center all through college and the last four months before I came back. Hopefully, the experience helps when I finally graduate and teach somewhere."

"I'm sure it will. Thank you for coming with us today. Milo works weekends, so I'd planned to go alone, but two against two is always better odds." She smiled at us over her shoulder. "I'll take care of Crissy and meet you over there."

"Sounds good." I propped Carter on my hip and headed over,

tiptoeing over the bumpy patches of dirt and skirting the family photo ops around the largest pumpkins. This was the Colebury that I remembered. My parents used to take me to this patch when I was little, and I still remembered running back and forth, refusing to pick a pumpkin until I'd made sure I'd seen them all.

Too bad I hadn't had that same resolve when I'd said yes to Chase's proposal.

I headed down to the patch, trying my best to shake it off. That was my old life, and I had to learn to push away the sour intrusive thoughts that sometimes distracted me from my new one.

My gaze fell on a little girl up ahead, wrapping her arms around a pumpkin that almost came up to her waist before attempting to lift it. A laugh slipped out of me when she tripped backward, but it hadn't fazed her one bit as she reached for it again.

"Easy, Cookie." My head swiveled toward a deep and familiar chuckle. "Let me help you."

Matteo jogged over to his daughter and lifted the pumpkin as if it were nothing but a small rock, hoisting it onto his shoulder. A little air drained out of my lungs as I watched them. At work, Matteo had a perpetual furrow in his brow. He was never stand-offish, but always seemed as if something was weighing on his mind. Here, laughing with his daughter and peering down at her with nothing but adoration, like he had when I'd met them in the diner, he looked unburdened and completely happy.

They'd been on my mind ever since last night. I was worried about Lauren but terrified for her father. When he mentioned Lauren to me, which was often, it was obvious that little girl was everything to him. When I asked if he was okay, I knew he wasn't, and even sadder than that, he sounded like he felt he didn't deserve to be.

"Oh, hey." Matteo's greeting startled me as he approached. A wave of heat washed over the back of my neck, embarrassed that he'd probably caught me staring. No matter how much watching Matteo and Lauren enthralled me, I needed to learn not to gape.

"Hey, guys." A smile stretched my lips as I looked between them. "That is the perfect pumpkin. Good choice, Lauren."

Lauren nestled into her father's side, shooting me a wide grin.

"Daddy said we can carve it when we get home. I saw it when we were on the hay ride, and I was afraid someone would take it first." She rested her chin on Matteo's hip and lifted her head to meet his gaze.

"I'm glad to see you guys here and having a little fun."

Matteo shut his eyes and nodded. "It was a long night, for sure." He smiled, motioning to the baby I'd forgotten was in my arms. "This is Milo's little guy, right?" Carter reminded me of his presence with a grunt.

"Yes, I'm here with Angie. I told her I'd entertain Carter while she took care of his sister." I dipped my head to meet Carter's eyes. He was too busy staring at all the action in front of him to notice my gaze.

"I don't know how they do it with two. When Lauren was that age, one was plenty." He laughed to himself as he swiped the loose hairs off of Lauren's forehead. He still held the pumpkin on his shoulder, bringing out the bulge in his bicep. Although I'd seen Matteo's arms almost daily, once my eyes landed on them, I had to force myself to look away.

I wondered if Matteo had taken care of Lauren alone when she was a baby or if she'd still had her mother around back then. He never spoke about Lauren's mother other than noting how it was just the two of them, and since that first awkward night after I'd asked about her, we'd never spoken about her again. The pain in his eyes when he mentioned it made me hesitant to ever bring her up.

"I used to come here when I was your age. Did you have an apple cider donut?" I chuckled when her eyes lit up.

"She had two." He peered down on her with a frown. "So, now I get to carve the pumpkin while she bounces off the walls tonight." He exhaled an exaggerated sigh and shook his head. "But I may have some good news. I ran into one of Josephine's friends after we got off the hay ride. She offered to babysit a couple of nights a week."

"That's awesome! I knew you'd find someone soon."

"Well it's good—not awesome quite yet." He set the pumpkin down in front of him, offering me a glimpse of his flexed shoulders.

"I called out tonight, but I still have to go in Sunday. Carol can't watch Lauren until next week, so I need to figure out who can take care of her tomorrow.

"I can," I blurted out before thinking about it. "I mean, if you can't find anyone else, I'm off tomorrow. I used to work in daycare and have plenty of experience taking care of children."

Matteo's brow pinched at my offer.

"I trust you, I just don't want to take away your day off. I know you could use the rest."

"It's totally fine. I had a hot date with a good book, but I could reschedule." I was happy to see a relaxed smile from Matteo.

Maybe getting out of the tiny space I could barely afford and not going to work or school would do me some good. Plus, I'd be helping a friend. A very hot friend, but I could ignore it, or try to—like I had during almost every single conversation we'd had.

"I like her, Daddy. She talks to me." Lauren peered up at him with an innocent smile. It sounded like this last babysitter and quite a few other women ignored Lauren while in Matteo's presence. If it broke my heart that she noticed, I couldn't imagine the effect it had on her father.

"Could you come at four? I need to be at Speakeasy at six and could take you through everything before I have to leave. What she has for dinner, bedtime, all of that. I'll make sure her homework is done before you come over since I'm sure she's going to be distracted." He flashed a relieved grin. "Thank you, this is a huge help."

"My pleasure. I'm looking forward to it," I told Lauren as she beamed at me. "If Belle is your favorite princess, would you mind if we watched *Beauty and the Beast* when I come to your house? It's my favorite movie."

Lauren's jaw dropped as she bounced next to her father. "We have the first one and the new one. We can watch both of them!"

"No, you can watch *one*." Matteo told her. "You have school the next morning."

"Now, I have to think about it." She folded her arms with her bottom lip jutted in a pout.

"I'm a mean dad, what can I say?" Matteo shrugged before he squatted down to lift the pumpkin.

"Sorry that took longer than it should have," an exasperated Angie said behind me. "Oh, hey Matteo. Wow, that pumpkin is huge!"

Lauren straightened, squaring her shoulders with pride after forgetting she was mad at her father. "I picked it out myself."

"Hi Angie," Matteo's smile faded as his gaze slid to Crissy. She burrowed into the crook of her mother's neck while her chubby fingers wrapped around a lock of Angie's hair. "We better get going, this is a lot of pumpkin to carve. We'll see you tomorrow, Melanie." He led Lauren away by the hand. She swiveled her head over her shoulder to wave back at me.

"*We'll* see you tomorrow?" Angie quirked a brow at me. "Are you hanging out with Matteo outside of work?"

"No," I said, shaking my head. "Nothing like that. He needs a babysitter for tomorrow, and I volunteered. The last one was awful, so until he finds someone regular, I'm happy to help." I walked Carter closer to the pumpkins without looking back at Angie.

"Poor guy. I figured it was something like that since he really doesn't date."

"Really?" My head whipped toward Angie's snide grin at my surprised and oddly hopeful reaction. I cleared my throat as I tried to find a way to recover. "Well, he has a little girl to take care of, so I can see why he can't."

"Very true. He did sort of date someone when he first got here, or so I'd heard, but not since. In all the months he's been here, women have been trying, and he refuses. He's hung out with Milo and the guys a couple of times, and he even said he wished Matteo would let himself have more fun. I guess he'd rather just be with his kid. It's sweet. Rare as hell, but sweet."

"Or maybe he's been so hurt that he won't let anyone get too close to either of them," I mused as I buckled Carter back into his stroller. The sadness in his eyes when he took in Angie holding her daughter broke my heart.

Matteo *was* rare and sweet. And my urge to both be close to him and protect him was dangerous.

MATTEO

"Lauren…" I groaned from the doorway of her bedroom. After I'd spent the morning helping her put away her toys, she now had every *Beauty and the Beast* doll lined up on her little play table. Helping usually meant cleaning up myself while she plucked out a new toy for each one I packed up.

"Melanie hasn't seen any of my toys. She needs to see them *all* to pick which one she wants." My head jerked up at her huff. Yes, my daughter huffed at five-years-old. I was in for it in about ten years, but I thanked God for her resolve. She'd been a tough cookie as a baby, grunting and taking what she wanted before she could speak. When she started fisting cookies when we weren't looking, the nickname "Cookie" stuck. Either way, it was perfect for her. She wasn't shy about how she was feeling and always wanted to take care of herself.

Maybe that's what motherless little girls figured they had to do.

I blinked away the repetitive thought that always triggered a pang in my chest. In the end, it was truly Callie's loss. She had no idea how amazing Lauren was and what she was missing by not being in her life. I guessed that's why I'd made it my mission to make sure that Lauren had the very best I could give her.

While I was relieved to find someone reliable for a couple of nights a week, I still needed a solution for the other three. Cutting back on hours wasn't an option and neither was adjusting my shifts. Although I took the occasional day shift, I was hired to manage Speakeasy at night.

Daycare centers weren't open at night, so that was never an option unless I completely changed jobs, and right now, I didn't have time to work, find childcare for Lauren, *and* job hunt. It was doubtful that with my lack of degree and experience, I'd find the same pay and benefits anywhere else.

The multiplying issues ran through my brain on a daily loop and robbed me of any chance of a good night's sleep.

Lauren raced down the stairs at the sound of the doorbell ready for a play date, not another babysitter. I hoped Melanie wouldn't have a hard time getting her to sleep, because I had the feeling my daughter wasn't going down without a fight.

Another twinge of guilt poked at me as I followed Lauren to the front door. Josephine had taken her to play dates with kids around the area that she knew. Because I'd been so engrossed in finding her another babysitter, I hadn't reached out to the few parents I'd connected with at her school. My poor daughter just had me and whatever temp sitter she had to tolerate.

"It's Melanie, Daddy." Lauren pressed her face to the side window. "Can I open the door?"

"Go ahead." I came up behind her as she reached to open the top lock and pull the door open.

"Hey, Lauren!" Melanie dipped her head and met Lauren's gaze with a wide smile. She wore a fitted yellow shirt under a light jacket and jeans, her hair down in loose waves. My gaze was tempted to sweep along the lean curves of her body and unlike the diner and the farm, I had nowhere else to look. I'd kept the boulder-sized pumpkin on my shoulder to distract me until I'd almost dropped it.

"Hi Melanie! I took out all of my *Beauty and the Beast* toys and I decided I wanted to watch the new movie. I like the prince better at the end."

Melanie covered her mouth as her gaze slid to mine. I rolled my eyes and shook my head.

"I would agree with that, Lauren. Hi, Matteo." Her lips stretched into a warm smile. She seemed relaxed, not exhausted and frazzled like I sometimes noticed she was at Speakeasy. Her eyes were somehow even bluer.

I rubbed my neck as I tried to get a grip on myself.

"Hi, Melanie. Come in, Lauren is a little excited to have you here in case you couldn't tell." Before I could push the door fully open, Lauren grabbed her hand and pulled her inside, dragging her upstairs.

"I'm excited to be here." Melanie craned her head toward me and smiled. Warm, genuine, beautiful.

Since Callie, my feelings for a woman never went beyond the superficial. A date here and there before we moved to Vermont would satisfy me for weeks. My cousin, Dom, liked to tease that I was a sexual camel. Without my heart in it, it was easy for me to walk away. Staying with anyone long term was never something I'd allow myself to consider.

I liked Melanie, and if things were different, I could grow to like her even more. It was why the usual distance I put between me and other women was even more important when it came to her. But for the past few weeks at work, I couldn't seem to do it. And now, she was in my house, giggling with my daughter as she handed Melanie toy after toy.

"Before you guys settle in for the night, I have to go over a few things with Melanie. Then she's all yours. Okay?"

"Okay," Lauren said before plopping onto the little seat at her play table.

I shot Melanie a grin before I motioned her toward the hallway.

"For dinner, she usually eats grilled cheese or chicken nuggets and fries. The nuggets and fries go into the toaster oven. I usually encouraged the sitters we've had to do that since I wasn't sure who would or wouldn't start a kitchen fire, but with you, she can pick."

"Well, thank you. I appreciate the confidence." Melanie laughed as she followed me down the stairs and into the kitchen. "If she asks for snacks—"

"There's a tub of chocolate chip cookies." I opened the cabinet and pointed to the top shelf. "She can have a cup of milk and two cookies if she finishes dinner. I keep it up there because she's been known to sneak more than only two."

"A girl after my own heart. Is that why you call her Cookie?"

"Yes," I answered, somehow taken aback by the question. Melanie paid attention, unlike the sitters who'd come and gone over the last few weeks and did just enough to get paid and leave.

"Bedtime is at eight. She loves to read at night, but try to keep it to two books, because she'll always try to talk you into one more."

"She loves cookies *and* books?" Melanie clutched her chest. "I think I've found my new best friend."

I laughed, not dreading heading to work like I usually did when I left Lauren with someone new. It was a luxury I wished I could get used to.

"Thank you, Melanie. Really. This is a huge help—"

She waved a hand at me. "This is absolutely no trouble. I miss taking care of kids. Go to work, and don't worry about us for a minute."

"Well, I'll always worry, but I think tonight I may actually be able to relax. Usually, Sundays aren't busy, but there's live music tonight, so we'll see. I'll be home as soon as I can."

"Take your time. I brought my laptop so I can study after she goes to sleep." When she made her way over to the kitchen table and slung the strap of her laptop bag onto one of the chairs, my eyes followed her. A stray lock of hair fell in front of her face as she shrugged off her jacket.

She was my friend and babysitter for the night, I shouldn't have been noticing her hair, or soft rosy lips, or the tease of her collarbone when the neckline of her shirt stretched as she leaned across the table.

"Text me if you need anything. I'll go tell Lauren goodnight, not that she'll notice I'm gone." I coughed out a laugh and headed back to her bedroom upstairs.

"Okay, Cookie. I'm headed to work." I squatted by the doorway and held my arms open. Lauren rushed over to me and tackled me with a hug. I squeezed her tight before kissing her cheek.

"Be good, and don't give Melanie a hard time when you have to go to bed. I love you, and I'll see you in the morning."

"I love you too, Daddy." She planted a wet kiss on my cheek. I always savored the hellos and goodbyes. They were quiet moments of pure love that reminded me what I was fighting for.

Her. *Always* her.

"I like Melanie. She's pretty and nice."

I bit back a smile and kissed her forehead. "I do too, and yes she is."

I shifted to leave when Lauren went back to stacking her dolls.

"Have fun at work." Melanie smirked, leaning against the wall by the kitchen when I came back downstairs. "I'll go ask Lauren what she wants and get dinner started. We have two games to play, so I'd better get an early start."

"She's a little bossy. I already told her not to give you a hard time." The familiarity of all of this unnerved me. How long had it been since I'd left Lauren with someone I trusted? That had to be it. I was too exhausted to ponder any weird feelings or try to talk myself out of them.

Work was nonstop from the moment I'd walked in. The restaurant crowd lingered at the bar before and after dinner thanks to the band.

"Hey Matteo, you got a second?" Ty asked when I was behind the bar, motioning to the back where the office was.

"Sure," I said, wondering what was so bad that we had to leave the floor to talk in private.

"What's up?" I asked before settling onto the couch.

"Alec is looking to hire more staff in the coming weeks now that the restaurant is getting busier." Ty leaned against the desk. "Usually, in November, the bar crowds are light until ski season kicks off, but with everything going on with the restaurant and the live music nights, we need more help, which is a good thing."

"Then why do I hear a *but* coming."

"I know you're friendly with Melanie, and I like her, too. But there've been complaints."

My shoulders stiffened as I reared back on the couch.

"Complaints?" I squinted at Ty. "From customers?"

"No, from one of the waiters annoyed that she's coming back from breaks late. I know she's struggling, but we're too busy to police the hours of the staff every night."

"I think that's a little unfair. It's not every break. I bet I know who complained and why."

Ty shut his eyes and shrugged. "Troy's been asking for more hours and brought her up when I said we weren't extending shifts at the moment. I agree, but maybe you can talk to her without making her panic. Alec told me there's a long list of applicants if anyone isn't working out, and I don't want one of them to be her if this makes it up to him."

"Neither do I," I said, rubbing my forehead. She'd said Alec gave her a chance because their mothers were friends, but I knew that he cared too much about his business to let her stay if he thought she couldn't handle it.

Ty was right, it was getting too busy to watch who was coming back from break and when. Melanie already knew people noticed her disappearing and falling asleep during the night. Telling her this would only make her panic even more. Anger bubbled in my gut at that tool throwing her under the bus for his fucked up selfish reasons.

"I just wanted to let you know. We'd better get back out there." Ty let out a long breath before opening the office door.

My head fell into my hands. My concern for her, however

inappropriate, gnawed at me. She needed this job to keep going to school, and I'd hate for this to derail her plans. She was doing the best she could, and I wished I could find a way to help her. After trudging out of the office, my phone buzzed in my pocket.

Melanie: *Just wanted to let you know that Lauren has been sleeping since 8. She ate all her dinner, and while I kept the cookie limit, she talked me into a third story. I was weak.*

It had been so busy, and I'd been so unburdened knowing Lauren was with Melanie, I hadn't texted once. It shocked me a little when I realized the time.

Matteo: *She's pretty persistent, so I'm not surprised. Glad to hear all is okay.*
Melanie: *All is great. She's a joy.*
Matteo: *It's a little nuts tonight, so I may be later than I thought.*
Melanie: *No worries at all. Nowhere for me to be and relaxing outside of my shoebox apartment has been nice. You get home when you get home.*

She'd stepped in to help me without a second thought, and I had no idea how to return the favor. Melanie was spreading herself too thin, and telling her she was being watched would only push her to the brink even more. Her only option would be to cut back her hours somewhere, either at school or at Speakeasy which I knew she hadn't wanted to do.

Unless she had a different job at night.

I couldn't make Melanie Lauren's regular babysitter, could I? It would solve both our problems. I wouldn't have to worry about finding someone I could trust, and after Lauren went to bed, she'd have all the time in the world to study until I came home.

I went through the rest of the night running the option in my head. Melanie had experience taking care of children, and I trusted her, so I wouldn't have to step out a million times a night to check on them both. And Lauren seemed to like Melanie. It really was the perfect solution, except for one thing.

I liked Melanie, too. I wasn't sure if asking her to work for me would end up the best idea I ever had, or my biggest regret.

9

MELANIE

As I flipped through channels on Matteo's TV, I tried to remember the last time I was able to truly relax. After Lauren went to sleep, I managed to finish the first draft of a paper due next week and catch up on chapters for another class. I regretted leaving my e-reader at home, but it had been so long since I was able to use it, it was dead. Matteo kept thanking me for doing him a favor, but I needed to thank *him* for this rare opportunity to breathe.

I stood from the couch and scanned all the pictures on the hallway wall, stopping at one with Matteo holding a chunky Lauren as a baby, the both of them beaming at each other. There were shots of an older couple, the man resembling an older Matteo with salt and pepper hair, and a few others with family and maybe friends.

None of Lauren's mother.

I hadn't wanted to be nosy, but I couldn't help being curious. All Lauren talked about was how she and her daddy did this or that, how he loves the bagels at the Busy Bean Café, but she gets the pretzels, how their house here is so much bigger than their old one at home, but not one mention of her mother.

He'd said it was the two of them but never alluded to where Lauren's mother was. I almost wanted to believe that she had passed away because I hated the thought of her leaving them, especially leaving Lauren. In all my time in daycare, I'd known one single father. Usually, it's the mother taking care of her child alone because it's simply easier for a father to leave.

Again, Matteo was rare.

I wasn't lying when I'd said Lauren was a joy. She was a happy little girl, full of energy and giggles. I hadn't even noticed when we played three rounds of a princess game, ending with a spa session "just like the ones she gives Daddy when he's tired from work" with her little kit of clips and fake polish. Thinking of her trying to take care of Matteo made me smile. Someone had to.

I scrubbed a hand down my face and groaned. Why was I so invested in Matteo and Lauren? It went beyond friendly concern, and I had my own issues to focus on. I had to figure out this week which course to drop so I could at least make the cutoff for a partial refund on tuition. The problem was that every time I looked over my schedule, the sour taste of defeat rose in the back of my throat, and I'd move on to something else.

Pulling back on my schedule wouldn't delay my degree that long, but I loathed having to delay it at all.

My head jerked to the click of the front door lock. Matteo gave me a tired smile before he peeled off his jacket.

"I guess she stayed sleeping?" Matteo came over to the couch and sat next to me. "Thank you again, it was nice to work without a brick on my chest for once." I smiled at his crooked grin.

"I was happy to help. You have her in a solid routine, so this was an easy night for me. How was Speakeasy tonight?"

Matteo's smile faded before his gaze fell to the floor.

"Fine. Busy like I expected, especially for a Sunday. I actually wanted to talk to you about that."

The drop in Matteo's tone made my stomach flip. My back went rigid against the couch cushions.

"Did something happen?" I squinted at Matteo, trying to decipher what the crinkle in his forehead meant.

"No, nothing like that. How would you feel about cutting back on your hours at Speakeasy to work somewhere else?"

"Somewhere else?" I reared back. "I don't understand. Where?"

"Here," he said, the corners of his mouth lifting. "How would you like to watch Lauren four nights per week? I have someone for Thursdays and Saturdays, and I'm off on Fridays. It would really help me out if Lauren had a babysitter that I could trust, and maybe this would work out for you, too. You can study or do whatever you need to here without worrying about a time limit. And you'd still be at Speakeasy on the busiest nights to make the best tips."

"Can I just change my schedule like that? Alec gave me this job, and I'd hate to look like I was slacking or throwing it back in his face."

He held up his hand. "I'll talk to Alec and Ty. I'll play the desperate single father card and say you're doing this to help me, which you are. I can pay you twenty an hour, more than what you'd make at Speakeasy even with tips during the week. I know you didn't want to have to drop any classes, and maybe now you wouldn't have to. Of course, you'd have to deal with me more. Sorry about that."

I huffed out a laugh at his exaggerated grimace. I wouldn't mind dealing with Matteo more at all, and that was the exact reason I wasn't jumping up to say yes.

"You can totally think about it. It's just," he trailed off, raking his hand through his hair with his eyes clenched shut. "It's been so hard to find someone that I can trust, and even though I haven't spoken to Lauren about how tonight was yet, when I left she was having a blast with you. She needs more people like you in her life. Her father is too tired to be fun."

Any chance of me refusing his offer vanished at Matteo's hopeful and bottomless dark eyes.

"All Lauren talked about is the fun you guys have together, so I don't think that's entirely true." I pushed off the couch and stood. "And if Alec and Ty are okay with it then, yes. I'd love to be Lauren's babysitter."

I spied Matteo's shoulders drop in relief before he popped off the couch. "Thank you so much. Come by Speakeasy tomorrow afternoon after you get out of class, and we can work it out." I stiffened in his arms when he pulled me in for a hug. "I can't begin to tell you what a huge relief this is."

I let my hands fall on his back and returned his grateful embrace, hating that his hard body against mine would be another thing I'd have to push out of my mind if I took this job.

He pulled back, panicked. "I'm sorry, I didn't mean to…"

I stifled a laugh at the blush creeping up his cheeks. "It's okay. Thank you. This is a good solution for both of us. That being said, I better get going. Early morning classes tomorrow." I made my way into the kitchen to snatch my laptop and jacket off of the table. "I was just thinking how weird it was to feel ahead for once. I didn't anticipate getting used to it."

"Same." He grinned, stuffing his hands into his pockets. "Goodnight. Get home safe."

"Goodnight," I said, reaching for the door before Matteo caught my hand and leaned in, almost as if he was about to kiss me goodnight. Which would be a little odd even after the relieved hug he'd given me a few moments before. Still, my breath caught as my feet rooted to his floor, all too willing to accept it if he did.

What did I just agree to?

"I guess you're Lauren's new spa customer." He pulled a hair clip from behind my ear. Tiny hairs on the back of my neck stood up when his finger grazed the shell of my ear, my pulse thrumming from that simple touch.

"I didn't even realize it was still there." I patted the side of my head, now feeling the absence of the oversized pink clip.

"This is usually in my hair a couple of times per week." He moved it back and forth between his fingers, a weak smile pulling at the corner of his lips. There was something about the way his eyes seared into mine, a weird current between us that both drew me to him and made me want to leap back.

"I heard. See you tomorrow, Matteo."

I pushed the door open and headed to my car, plopping my head onto the steering wheel after I started the engine.

I'd watch Matteo's adorable little girl, keep up with both my rent and my schoolwork, and maybe even stop falling asleep every time I sat down for more than ten minutes without a book or bar tray in my hand.

I only had to stop watching Matteo.

MELANIE

"You're not working at Speakeasy anymore?" my mother asked, her tone grating on my nerves.

"I am, but only three nights a week. Babysitting is better for my schedule when I have school the next day. The hours every night combined with my early morning classes was getting to be too much."

"Which is what I told you." I felt more than heard her loud sigh. "I wish you would have just gone to school in New Hampshire. You could have stayed here and not had to worry about working nights at all."

"Burlington University was the only school that gave me a partial scholarship, and I can't ask you and Dad to pay any more tuition than you already have. This is all a good thing. And I know what you're thinking, so I promise you Alec and his mother aren't upset or insulted at all."

In fact, when Matteo and I proposed pulling back on my hours and adjusting my schedule at Speakeasy, Ty seemed relieved and all too accommodating. I was unsure how to take that. Maybe I wasn't the best waitress, but I worked hard not to be the worst. And now that I was able to do my schoolwork at Matteo's house after Lauren went to sleep, I wouldn't have to worry about passing out on my breaks or not having enough study time.

I tried to ignore my conflicting feelings and go with being relieved rather than insulted.

"I know you probably missed kids, too. I ran into Jackie from the daycare center the other day, and she told me how much they all wish you still worked there." If I wasn't mistaken, there was a little pride in my mother's voice. "I think you're going to be a great teacher."

"Thanks, Mom." I smiled at the rare compliment.

While my parents supported me, they'd always pushed me to do things their way. I'd spent most of my life complying until I met Chase. They'd lost it at how quickly we'd moved in together and become engaged, but they at least spared their errant only child an "I told you so" when it all blew up in my face.

"Lauren is so adorable. She's a little spitfire but impossible not to love. Matteo has done an awesome job with her."

This was my second week watching Lauren, and it still hadn't seemed like work. I missed her during my shifts at Speakeasy and always looked forward to seeing her again.

I was starting to miss her father, too, and until I figured out what to do about that I simply ignored it.

"It's a shame he has to raise a child on his own. Especially raising a daughter. There's a lot of men who don't know how to handle little girls."

"He knows how to handle Lauren. Trust me." Irritation poked at me from my mother's judgment. I was sure others shared her opinion before they got to know Matteo and Lauren, and it made me angry. As rambunctious as Lauren could get, he never raised his voice or lost his patience. Lauren loved to talk about all the fun they had on Daddy's days off, filling me in on all the places he'd taken her to around Colebury or cool things they did at home.

Lauren wasn't a burden to him, and he wasn't simply going through the motions of being a parent. When someone insinuated he was, it irked me more than it probably should have.

"I better go. I have to be there at four. We'll talk soon."

When I can muster the energy to defend my life choices and deny my inappropriate affection for my boss.

After I hung up, I packed my computer and books, plus a surprise for Lauren, and headed for Matteo's. Her love of books excited me, and instead of reading a few tiny books each night, I decided to be ambitious and brought my favorite book from when I was a kid. I thought she could easily handle a couple of chapters each night, and it filled me with an odd joy to share this with her. I wasn't lying when I'd said Lauren was lovable, but what my mother said echoed in my head the entire drive there.

Matteo was doing a spectacular job raising a little girl on his own, but I worried for both of them as she got older. Then I felt guilty for worrying because one, I was already too invested and spending time with them only made it worse, and two, it felt like I was shortchanging Matteo as a parent. I was sure that whatever he needed to do for Lauren, he would figure it out.

I parked in front of their house and fumbled with the keys on my chain. He'd given me a key in case I ever had to take Lauren somewhere in an emergency and told me to feel free to use it when I came to the house, but it still felt intimate to just walk into Matteo's house. The little crush I had led to silly fantasies in my head.

When I opened the door, my stomach growled as the smell of roasted tomatoes and garlic wafted in from the kitchen.

"Hey, you're here!" Matteo greeted me with a wide grin. "I thought it was time Lauren expanded her horizons from nuggets and fries every night, so I decided to start cooking actual dinners. I'd love for you to eat with us if you haven't eaten yet. I hope you like macaroni and meatballs."

"Absolutely," I said, happily forgetting about the protein bar in my bag that I'd brought to eat for dinner. I left my bag near the coat rack and followed Matteo into the kitchen.

"Can I help?" I asked as he stirred a huge, bubbling pot of sauce.

"Nope. Table is already set, I just have to put this together." The corner of his mouth turned up. "Unfortunately, I'm not smart enough to know how to make it for only three people since I was always taught to cook for an army of family, so we have leftovers for the week. Makes things easier."

"Leftovers are good." I leaned against the wall, a little breathless at how sexy Matteo was as he effortlessly maneuvered around the kitchen. Of course, there wasn't much Matteo did that I hadn't found to be sexy. Cooking dinner pushed it over the top.

"Will Lauren eat this? I never asked to make her anything other than what you told me, so I assumed that she was picky."

He shrugged with his attention on the sizzle of the meatballs in the pan.

"Josephine used to make her better meals. When we lived in the Bronx, her grandmother used to make this every Sunday for us and buy wagon-wheel shaped pasta because my daughter found it funny that the meatballs had wheels." He smirked at me before adjusting the heat on the stove. "I made this meal so many times for me and Ca—before Lauren was born. Anyway, I got lazy and used my night schedule as an excuse. It's time I made a little more effort. I actually enjoy cooking. My mother gave me no choice but to learn." He grinned as he drained the pasta into the sink. "I was her only child, so she had to pass along what she knew to someone."

"What else can you make?" I asked, wondering if he was referring to Lauren's mother earlier. He'd never mentioned her before, and I'd never asked, but I couldn't help growing more and more curious.

"Steak, Chicken Marsala. I'm a pretty decent cook if I do say so myself. I just lost my motivation when Lauren was a baby." He gulped a bottle of water, and I was unable to take my eyes away from the sinful roll of his throat.

They must've lost Lauren's mother when Lauren was just a baby, however she left. While, again, it was none of my business, I paid attention to all the tiny clues. Thinking of Matteo alone with an infant to take care of broke my heart.

"We're having wheels and meatballs!" Lauren announced after she rushed to the dinner table, patting the seat next to her. "Come sit."

"I only had to visit three stores before I found them. Go sit, I have this covered," Matteo said and nudged his chin toward the table.

"I finished my homework, so maybe we can watch two movies and read three books." She grabbed her cup and sipped through the purple straw.

"My daughter—always the negotiator." Matteo shook his head as he set the large bowl of pasta onto the table.

"We can see how it goes for two movies, but I actually brought over a new book that we can read. It's a chapter book, so instead of reading different small books, we can read a few chapters every night in *this* book." I piled a scoop of sauce-covered wheels onto her plate. "How does that sound?"

"Cool," she said, grabbing her little fork and digging in.

"What do you say, Lauren?" Matteo prompted as he put two meatballs onto her plate.

"Oh, sorry. Thank you, Melanie. Thank you, Daddy."

"You don't have to wait for me." Matteo reached for the big spoon and filled my plate with a generous helping of pasta before taking a seat next to me.

"Thank you. This is nice." I darted my eyes away for a moment, trying to ignore the warmth spreading across my chest at Matteo going out of his way for me once again.

When he cracked another smile before he filled his plate, butterflies filled my stomach. We had a close friendship, at least closer than I'd had with others I'd connected with in Colebury, with the exception of Angie. But when his eyes would linger on mine, it sometimes seemed like there was more to it. It almost felt as if it was seeking me out rather than simply looking out for me.

I shook off the ridiculous notion and scooped some pasta onto my fork. This dinner seemed intimate, comfortable yet not at all weird—which was weird in and of itself.

"Do you have a lot of homework, Melanie?" Lauren asked as she chomped on a meatball.

"Nope, I can start after you go to sleep. I'm all yours until bedtime."

"Yes!"

Matteo and I shared a chuckle at her fist pump.

I couldn't recall anyone I'd known in my lifetime who was so happy to be in my presence, and the feeling was already mutual. Spending time with Lauren made me forget my daily struggle for balance and the uncertainty of coming here in the first place. In the past couple of weeks, the books, the princess games, and the Disney movies with an amazing little girl were just what I'd needed to forget my adult issues.

"You guys have all the fun while I'm stuck at work," Matteo teased before taking a sip from his water glass.

The time I'd spent chatting with her father when he came home from work was a nice distraction too, but that was part of those adult issues.

After we ate, I cleaned off the table and helped Matteo load the dishwasher.

"What book did you bring?" Matteo asked after we finished.

"*The Velveteen Rabbit*. It was my favorite book as a kid, and since she's always begging to read more, I thought she might enjoy it."

He nodded, linking his arms over his broad chest as he leaned back against the sink. "Her mother was a huge reader. I think that's where she gets it from. Our apartment was filled with all kinds of books. Mystery, romance. She never liked to watch TV because she thought books were always better." A sad smile ghosted his lips for a moment.

"I hope you don't mind me asking, and you don't have to answer," I gulped, praying I wasn't stepping over the line. "What happened to Lauren's mother? Did she pass—"

"No." Matteo cut me off. "She's alive and well, or was the last I'd heard." He shrugged. "She left when Lauren was six months old." He exhaled a long breath, as if he'd been holding all of that in for a long time.

"I'm sorry, I didn't mean to pry. I'll go upstairs and get Lauren set up for the night."

He grabbed my wrist before I shifted to leave. "You didn't. I haven't said it out loud since we came here because…I didn't want it to define us like it did back home. In the Bronx, everyone knew Callie and how she left. Whenever they'd see me pushing Lauren's carriage in the neighborhood, all we'd get were looks of pity. Not that we don't get them here, but it's different. I can't explain it. I didn't want it here, too." He dropped my wrist and let out a deep sigh.

"I can understand that." I reached out and squeezed his shoulder, unable to help myself. "Thank you for trusting me enough to tell me."

His head jerked up, his dark eyes glossy. "You're the first person here who I've actually wanted to tell."

"How long should we wait for cookies?" Lauren asked. I hadn't even noticed her footsteps behind me because I was too lost in Matteo's sad gaze.

"Give it a half hour, Cookie. You ate a lot of meatballs, and I don't want you to get sick."

Lauren's shoulders scrunched in a reluctant shrug.

"We should start the movie anyway if we have a whole real book to read later. Let's go upstairs." Lauren pulled at my hand, but I couldn't move. Something anchored me to his kitchen floor as our eyes stayed locked.

"Go, I have to get ready for work anyway." A tiny smile lifted his lips. I guessed it was his way of reassuring me that he was okay.

I let Lauren drag me up the stairs as she rambled about what to watch tonight. She plopped on one of the oversized beanbag chairs in her room while I searched for her movie of choice on screen.

"Sit down!" she demanded for a second time. "I mean, sit down, *please*." She squinted at me before I gave my nod of approval and settled next to her.

Lauren rested her head on my shoulder as the opening credits rolled. Warmth filled my chest as I leaned my head against hers. She was becoming so much more than just a little girl I babysat for, same as her father was becoming more than just my friend and boss.

How could anyone lucky enough to have them both leave and never come back?

MELANIE

I sifted through my notes, trying to eke out one last paragraph for this damn paper. Ending any kind of schoolwork after ten-thirty was probably in my best interest since my brain stopped working right about this time each night.

I rested my head onto my folded hands and closed my eyes, as if the words I needed would magically appear behind my eye-lids. Cutting back on my hours at Speakeasy had at least helped me not be a total zombie, but there was still enough schoolwork to knock me on my ass from exhaustion occasionally.

"Hey,"

I jerked awake, my moment of rest longer than I'd wanted it to be.

"Sorry for startling you."

I blinked a few times, my tired eyes landing on Matteo's smile and tingles radiating from where his hand rested on my back. His warmth and concern relaxed me for a moment before I straightened, finally alert enough to be unnerved by my visceral reaction over a friendly touch.

"It's okay. I shouldn't have dozed off to begin with. I really thought I could do this. What was I thinking?"

I scrubbed a hand down my face, finally voicing what had been echoing in my head for weeks.

"Thinking when? Deciding to go back to school?" He slid into the seat next to me. "I admire you for going back and how hard you work. When we first moved here, I thought of taking online classes at Burlington."

"Really?" My head craned to look at him. After a full shift managing Speakeasy, he looked just as gorgeous as when he'd left. I was sure I looked as disheveled as I felt. "For what?"

"Restaurant management. I always wanted to run my own place. When Phoebe first got the job as executive chef and called me about working at Speakeasy, even she suggested it for when I got settled, telling me how Colebury had huge potential and how I could make a life and a future here." He shrugged. "Trouble is, I never felt *settled* enough to look into it. At least, not yet." The corner of his mouth curved up. "You're helping with that."

"How?" When Matteo's eyes met mine, he cleared his throat and looked away for a moment.

"I mean, you and Carol. It helps to have reliable childcare. Until I did, I was afraid this whole damn thing wouldn't work out. When you make a big, life-altering decision, even if it's the right one, it's hard to fight against that first urge to pack it all in and go back when it gets tough. At least for me."

His easy smile combined with the glimpse of the tattoo on his arm when he slid a hand through his hair brought on a whole other urge. I exhaled slowly, blaming tonight's fixation on Matteo on lack of sleep.

Yes, Matteo was attractive. *Very* attractive. But my pull toward him went beyond the allure of his sexy dark eyes and chiseled jaw. He was kind and considerate, a good friend who looked out for me without making me feel I was some kind of damsel in distress in need of rescuing.

"I'm glad I'm helping with that. And that you don't have to deal with the parade of bad babysitters every day."

I laughed at his widened eyes.

"Yes, that's something I don't *ever* want to go back to. But honestly, you help more than that, though. It's nice to have a friend to unload my problems on. I always seem to tell you more than I tell most."

"Same." I returned his easy smile. "You're pretty easy to talk to. Or just the one who's around often enough to get a front seat to all my issues."

He shook his head. "I don't see issues. I see a woman who sells herself short entirely too much. Test?" He nodded to my laptop and the array of papers across the keyboard.

"Paper due this week. I have one last paragraph before I'm done, and I'm blocked and stuck." I sighed, resting my head on my hand. "I think I need a break."

"You think?"

I scowled at Matteo's snide grin.

"Put the books away. I'll make some coffee to perk you up a little before you have to drive home." He tapped my wrist and stood, pulling two mugs out of the cabinets before setting up the coffee machine.

"That actually sounds perfect." I closed my laptop and stuffed it back into my bag. "As bosses go, you're pretty thoughtful. Making me dinner, coffee."

I spied his cheeks lift with a smile.

"That's all so you stay." His lopsided grin drained the air out of my lungs.

He never had to convince me to stay. Limiting our time together would have been the smart thing to do, considering my inappropriate growing feelings for Matteo, but I always ended up extending it.

"Thank you," I whispered when he set the steaming mug down in front of me. My gaze caught the black ink of his tattoo peeking out of his sleeve again as I took my first sip.

"What?" he asked when he caught me staring.

"I'd never seen your full tattoo, and I guess I'm nosy."

"Oh, I'll show you. I'd love to tell you it has some kind of meaning, but it was what I picked off a wall after a night of drinking." He rolled up his sleeve, revealing a swirling black design that surrounded his corded bicep.

When I leaned over to look, I grasped the handle of my mug tightly to ward off the temptation to trace the lines on his skin with my fingertips.

"It's nice," I choked out. My crush would be easier to ignore if he didn't get exponentially more attractive to me with each passing day.

He stood, shrugging before he lifted his shirt halfway up his torso.

"This is Lauren's birthday." He motioned to the thin cursive numbers along his ribs, right above his sculpted abs. "That at least had thought and meaning to it, and I remember getting it."

It was sweet how open and honest he always was with me, but if he showed me any more lines of ink over lean muscle, my brain would short circuit.

"That's sweet. I bet it hurt getting it there."

Also, please put your shirt down, and have mercy on me.

"Not terrible." He lifted a shoulder and sat back down. "Ever consider getting one?"

"I don't know… I've thought about it. There is this quote I wanted to get, but I'm not sure if I can handle all the letters. I'm not tough like you and have never been really big on pain."

He laughed at my crinkled nose as I stood from the table to carry the already empty mug to the sink.

"I don't know if I'm as tough as you think." He linked his arms over his chest and leaned back against the counter. "If I hadn't been blitzed, the one on my arm would've probably made me cry. What's the quote?"

I broke my gaze from his, the heat of embarrassment rushing up my neck.

"*Once you are Real, you can't become unreal again. It lasts for always.* It's from *The Velveteen Rabbit*. You can go ahead and laugh at me now."

"I'd never laugh at you." His smile faded as he leaned in closer. "I haven't read the book, so I don't know what it means."

"The short version of the book, or the lesson I suppose, is that when someone loves you, you become real, and it lasts forever. Growing up, I always felt so unseen, almost like I hardly existed. Maybe that's why I'm killing myself trying to accomplish something. I want to be real and stop feeling like that."

His eyes held mine, dark and focused and making me feel even more raw and exposed. I'd never said that to anyone before, but it was my life in a nutshell. Why I was here burning myself out and risking it all, and why I couldn't let myself be drawn into whatever I was feeling for Matteo—any more than I already was.

He stepped in front of me on my way back to the table.

"You're more real than you know, Melanie. In fact, I've never met anyone more real than you." His tone dipped to a husky rasp as he dropped his hand on my shoulder, squeezing until I lifted my head. "I don't want to see you slumped over books anymore. I hoped watching Lauren would give you a little bit of a break. Promise me you'll at least try to stop burning yourself out like this. You're amazing and have absolutely nothing to prove." His gaze softened before he swallowed. "Anyone who takes the time to really know you can see that."

A jolt ran down my arm from where his thumb drifted back and forth on my shoulder. What was probably meant as a soothing touch was having the complete opposite effect on me.

I wasn't tired anymore, the urge to close the space between us and taste his lips so intoxicating my head spun. I felt myself inch toward him and sobered, clearing my throat before shooting him a tight smile.

"I promise. And I better get going. Early classes tomorrow." I made my way around him and started piling and packing up my books, my neck hot from the weight of his gaze.

I couldn't let my yearning to be real screw up my real life.

MATTEO

"Everything is like a forest, except where Daddy works and where we get pretzels." Lauren said as she shifted back and forth on my lap. I caught my cousin, Dominic, shoot his wife, Thea, a smirk on the screen as Lauren went on about our life in Vermont. Even after months of living here, whenever we had a video call with family, she always mentioned the trees first. As a city kid myself, I was still getting used to the lack of sidewalks whenever we went anywhere. She was right, a lot of Colebury was like a forest to us.

"Even where you go to school?" Thea asked. Dominic and Thea lived in a small town by the Jersey shore. This was the longest we'd gone without seeing them. I usually tried to visit at least once per month during the summer, but we hadn't made it out there before we moved in late June.

Dominic co-owned and managed a restaurant in a hotel, and when we'd come down to see them, we'd stay the weekend in a discounted room and soak up all the sun and sand. Lauren missed their twins and all the fried food we'd get along the boardwalk, and I missed my cousin's sarcastic way of making life not seem as bad as I thought. I'd leaned on Dominic a lot since Lauren was born—especially after Callie left.

"School is just a big building, but there's a greenhouse there!"

Lauren slammed the desk on either side of the computer, her eyes saucer-wide in the reflection screen of us in the corner. "I forgot to say that. It's really a big hole in the ground with walls around it to keep it warm. It *has* to be warm so plants could grow, in case you didn't know that."

"A country greenhouse at school? Wow, you guys really are one with nature." Dominic quirked a brow before leaning back with his arms crossed.

"Yep! Where are Lyndee and Luca?" Lauren asked, probably already bored talking with adults.

"They fell asleep. Both of them woke up too early today, so they're taking a power nap." Thea laughed. "Next time I promise to make sure they're up, okay?"

"Okay." Lauren's shoulders fell in disappointment.

"Well, what else can you tell us that's new? Although, I don't think that you can top the greenhouse. Thanks for explaining what it is." Dominic said, his lips twitching as he shot me a glance.

"Not much, except that Melanie and me are reading a *chapter* book. *The Velveteen Rabbit*." My daughter lifted her chin, never much of a humble bragger.

"Oh, is that your new babysitter?" Thea asked.

"One of them. Carol is the other one. Melanie is awesome. She's pretty and tall like a princess, and she's Daddy's friend."

Dom narrowed his eyes when she said "Daddy's friend."

"She's my friend from work. She goes to school during the day and babysitting three nights a week is better for her schedule than late nights at Speakeasy," I tried to explain, but Dom still scrutinized me.

She was my friend from work who I had to talk myself out of kissing so many times I'd lost count. Dom's ability to see through me from behind a screen several states away was fucking annoying.

"I didn't realize she was so young," Thea said, squinting at us the same way that her husband was.

"She's twenty-three, not that young. Well, younger than me. She goes to graduate school—"

"We *really* like her. Daddy cooks dinner when she comes over, and she eats with us, too."

"Daddy cooks, huh?" Dominic stroked his jaw. "I think she's the first sitter to eat dinner with you, right ?" He leaned in toward the screen, his gaze sliding to mine as he spoke to Lauren.

"No, they all did." Lauren's lips pursed as if Dominic had just asked a ridiculous question. "Just Daddy didn't cook it and eat with us."

I groaned to myself when I spied four brows shoot up.

"Why don't you go play in your room for a bit so I can talk to Dom and Thea, too?"

"Okay. Bye!" She waved at the screen before jumping off of my lap.

"Something you want to tell us?" Dominic tapped the desk with his finger.

"No, there's not much else than what Lauren told you. No need for both of you to hurt yourselves jumping to conclusions."

"Well, from what Lauren said, Melanie sounds like she's more than a babysitter if you're cooking for her." Thea said.

"It's not a big deal," I denied, not wanting to admit Melanie was something special to both of us. I looked forward to the nights when Melanie babysat, too, but I argued with myself enough about that. My cousin's help wasn't needed.

"Do you cook for the other babysitter, too?" Dominic wasn't going to let this go.

"I cook for my daughter. Carol arrives just a little before I have to leave. Melanie usually comes straight from school in the afternoons."

Carol was great. With older kids and grandkids of her own, she knew exactly what to do without me having to hover when I was at work. I'd always come home to a clean house and sleeping daughter, but it felt empty. Like I was missing something. Or someone.

Nothing felt odd or out of place when Melanie had dinner with us on the nights she babysat. But judging by Dominic and Thea's reaction, maybe it was a milestone I'd ignored up until this point.

"It's not the worst thing in the world to let someone in, Matt." Thea's sad smile made me all the more uneasy now that they were both making me think about it.

"But letting the *babysitter* in, especially since it was so hard to find someone you could trust, may not be the best thing either." Dom leaned forward again. "Don't get me wrong, we'd love to see you with someone that the both of you *really* like so much, but this can get complicated pretty fast if you're not careful. And she still works for you at the bar, right?"

"Yes, she works at the bar with me two nights per week. We have different nights off." I cupped my temple and dragged a hand down my face. I knew all too well how complicated things could get. I saw Melanie five days a week, and she was always someone I had to manage, or was supposed to. We had a constant boss/employee relationship, so for that reason alone, she was off limits.

The other reason was that liking another woman as much as I liked Melanie freaked me out. I never saw myself with anyone, really *with* anyone, after what had happened to us. To trust anyone after the one person we were supposed to count on, the one person who was supposed to love us both, up and left with hardly a word, I couldn't fathom it.

Until now.

I couldn't go through that again, and I couldn't risk Lauren going through it at all.

"Talk to us, Matty," Dominic whispered, using the childhood nickname I hated but only allowed him to still use. "What's going on?"

"I can't do it again. Maybe someday, if I can get a handle on my schedule, I could go out with a woman for a good time, but letting someone get close to both of us like that… I can't do it."

"It sounds like you *are* doing it, Matt. That's why you look so scared." Thea frowned, scooting her chair closer to the desk. "I agree with Dominic, this can get complicated. But, maybe it's worth the complications if you both really like her. Callie leaving the way she did was awful, and I understand every bit of your hesitation. Truly. But, don't deprive yourself of something that could make you happy. You *both* deserve that."

Protecting us was the one thing I'd never had to think about. It was always my first priority and factored in every single decision I made. Even considering not being careful made panic rise in the back of my throat.

"Thank you," was all I could say. "You should figure out a way to come up here. Aren't you in the off-season, anyway?"

"Yes, but it's busier than you'd think. Tell you what, how about we try to make it up for Thanksgiving? A holiday in Vermont has to be like one of those paintings, right? Maybe you can get a turkey from the farm you probably have next door?"

I laughed, relief easing the knots of tension always in my neck.

"I've never done a whole Thanksgiving dinner myself before, but if you guys come here, I'll figure it out."

"Then, it's settled." Dominic looped his arm around his wife's shoulders. "And I agree with Thea. Be careful, but don't let the fear and the anger cheat you out of love, little cousin. The both of you deserve more than that."

"Thanks. I better go, I didn't realize what time it was. Give the two troublemakers a kiss from us, okay?"

"Absolutely." Dominic smiled. "Take care, Matty."

I shut the laptop, realizing that was the first time I'd sort of admitted out loud to having feelings for Melanie. My wimpy acknowledgment made it too real, especially when Melanie was due here any minute.

As if on cue, the lock to the front door opened with a loud click. My daughter somehow heard from all the way upstairs and raced down the steps after the door creaked open. My heart cracked a little when Lauren squealed before tackling Melanie with a hug. At least one of us wasn't losing sleep over their growing affection for Melanie.

"Hey, girlie!" Melanie laughed as Lauren looped her arms around her thighs. She hugged her back with one hand while balancing large bags on the wrist of her other arm.

"So, I hope this doesn't get me into trouble," she said as she approached me with a sheepish grin. Her cheeks were red from the chilly autumn air, and the urge to pull her into my arms and warm her up made me take a half a step back.

"You said that Lauren's school is closed tomorrow for a teacher's conference. Would it be okay, if we promise not to make a huge mess, if we could stay up slightly later to bake cookies tonight?"

Lauren gasped loudly before bringing her hands to her mouth.

"I won't make a mess, Daddy. I promise, really, *really* promise." Lauren bounced as she pulled at the bottom of my shirt.

A laugh escaped me before I could help it.

"I think you both made it pretty impossible to say no." I glanced at Melanie while Lauren bounced between us. "I trust you both to not destroy the kitchen, so have at it."

"Yes!" Lauren lifted both hands in the air before she scurried away.

"Sorry if I put you on the spot. I was in the grocery store this afternoon when the idea came to me. Baking anything isn't really possible in my kitchen, if you can even call it a kitchen, and I guess I got the baking itch." She lifted her shoulder. "I was about her age when my mom let me bake with her, so I think she can handle it." She turned to hang her coat on the rack and froze. "Oh God, I'm so sorry."

"For what? I'm a cook, not a baker. I depend on the Busy Bean for most baked goods but I think baking with you would be good for her."

"No. I mean," She draped her hand over her eyes. "To mention my mom cooking with me, I didn't mean to upset you or make you think Lauren was missing out on—"

"Stop," I said, grabbing her wrist and pulled her hand away from her face. "It is what it is. You can tell us about what you did with your mom at her age and not upset us. Lauren doesn't remember her mother, so a mom is more of an idea to her than anything else."

She exhaled and nodded.

Lauren never got upset when someone mentioned the word mother in her presence, at least, not that I could tell. She'd ask a question or two from time to time, asking things like who her mother's favorite princess was or did her mom like chocolate chip cookies as much as she did. I'd answer, and she'd say "Oh," and go back to whatever she was doing without missing a beat.

I wanted to believe that was a good thing. Having no memories of Callie, Lauren couldn't miss her or be angry with her, or get confused on the days she did both.

That was only my burden.

"What smells so good?" Her adorable nose crinkled. I found a lot of what Melanie did adorable. That was my burden, too.

"Beef stew in the crock pot. Little potatoes and all. Dinner will be ready in fifteen minutes, so you're right on time."

"I'm still getting used to having actual meals three days a week. You guys are spoiling me. Let me get this all into the kitchen."

"I'll help you," I reached for one of the bags, but she snatched it away before I could grab it.

"You made dinner. Relax, I'll take care of this."

With a warm smile that robbed me of a reply, Melanie headed for the kitchen.

Being careful was a moot point because I was already getting too attached—a brand new and scary as hell feeling for me. Melanie was poking cracks in the walls I'd built to protect my daughter and me, and I wasn't sure what would happen when they came tumbling down.

MELANIE

"Free appetizer night is my *favorite*," Angie gushed, mumbling with her mouth full. "What are these again?"

I couldn't help the laugh that escaped me when Angie shut her eyes and leaned back. "They're goat cheese puffs. We try new appetizers out on customers, and the chef adds them to the menu if they're a hit."

"Oh, please pass along my praises so I can have more next time." She studied me as she licked one of her fingers. "You look different."

"I think you mean *awake*." I leaned my elbows on the table. "Or, at least more awake than usual. Now that I babysit on school nights, I have time to study. So, when I'm here, I'm not spreading myself thin trying to do both."

I'd been trying to take Matteo's advice and gave myself a schoolwork cut off point of ten p.m. for the past couple of weeks. It was enough time to study and rest, and it freed me up to chat with Matteo for an hour or two when he came home. Angie didn't need to know about my other motivations for backing off the books at night.

She usually came to Speakeasy on her date nights with Milo, which they hadn't been able to pull off for a couple of weeks. As much as all the grandparents loved to babysit, Angie said that once both babies started teething, they were a handful. Instead of spending my break in the back, I slid into the booth across from her while Milo picked up their drinks at the bar.

"I'm glad it worked out for you. Lauren is a cutie, I can't imagine her being much trouble. Unlike the two screaming kids we ran away from tonight." She groaned and ran a hand through her hair.

"They'll get better soon." I reached across the table to pat her hand. "And no, Lauren isn't much trouble at all. She's a great kid." A smile snuck across my lips whenever I thought of Lauren. I tended to fall in love with some of the kids when I'd worked at the daycare. At times it was impossible not to, but there was something extra special about her. I loved her adorably blunt attitude and how her eyes lit up when she ran to me at the door.

"You and Matteo spend a lot of time together, now." She motioned to where Matteo laughed with Milo at the bar. "That's… been okay?"

My eyes narrowed at her question. "It's been fine. We were already friends, and he's great to work for."

Angie's scrutinizing gaze hadn't budged. "You know you can talk to me, right? If anything is wrong or you're worried about anything."

I glanced at my watch, making sure I wouldn't end my coming back from break on time streak. I had ten minutes before I had to get on the floor, but my inkling was this conversation would have to continue later. Too many ears listening at Speakeasy, even over the din of the crowd. Bad enough a couple of waiters nicknamed us "M&M" whenever we were in the same space. I was sure some speculated that Matteo and I were closer than simply boss and employee.

It was easier to remain in denial if I kept it inside. Saying it out loud was admitting it to myself as true. My stomach turned at the thought.

"I know, but there is nothing to tell." My shoulders went rigid as my back straightened against the cushion.

"I've been watching you guys tonight. I'll be honest, I'd bet most are. You know how this small town is. No one can help themselves."

A laugh escaped me when she rolled her eyes.

"You…gravitate toward each other a lot. Whenever you pick up drinks at the bar, he's always right there, or when you need a hand carrying trays, he's usually the one to help."

"That's his job, Angie. And he's a nice guy, he'd do that for anyone."

"But he doesn't," her voice dropped as she glanced over my shoulder. "Any time I've come here, he only does it for you. And when you aren't at the bar, he looks for you. And you look everywhere else but his direction as if you're afraid to."

"I don't know if he looks for me in the way you think. Remember, I fell on my first night here, he probably wants to make sure I don't ruin anymore glasses."

I broke my gaze from hers and shrugged, my denial hollow to even my own ears.

"Honey, I know you like him and that makes both of your jobs complicated, so you deny it, but he likes you right back. You'd see if you let yourself pay more attention."

"I have two minutes left," I sighed, rubbing my temples. "He's lonely. I am, too. What you see is two friends commiserating over common struggles, that's all."

Angie exhaled a long breath before she crossed her arms and leaned back. "What I see is two friends who yes, may be a little lonely in their own right, but two friends who want to be *more* than friends." The side of her mouth lifted. "You guys would look good together."

"Stop." I pushed off the seat and stood. My eyes darted from hers before I had the guts to lift my head. "It's too…complicated like you said. We both finally have a routine that works, I can't bring that into it."

"Sometimes, *that* gives you no choice." I turned away from her raised brow.

"How long before we need to get home to the rugrats?" Milo asked behind me. "Oh hey, Melanie. I was trying to convince your boss over here to come out with us on Thursday." He set a tall glass of beer in front of his wife and slid into the seat I'd just vacated.

"And I was trying to tell Milo I don't have a babysitter lined up. Carol needed this Thursday off."

My head swiveled toward Matteo's voice. My eyes fell on the quirk in his lip as his gaze slid to mine. Although his close presence was something I'd become used to, the conversation I'd just had with Angie about him made me antsy enough to take a half step back.

"Thursday is my night off. If you want to go, I can watch Lauren for you."

He cocked his head to the side. "Exactly, it's your night off. I wouldn't ask you to do that."

"You're not asking, I'm offering." I dropped my hand to his forearm and craned my head toward Milo. "He'll go. Give him a couple of drinks so he loosens up."

He dipped his head, shooting me a wry grin.

"I better get back to work. Find me before you guys leave."

I busied myself for the rest of the night, making it a point to get my orders from the opposite end of wherever Matteo was standing behind the bar. Coming back to Colebury was more and more like high school in so many ways. Angie asking me why I wouldn't go out with whoever she said liked me, blowing her off because I never could believe it and choosing to wallow in my self-imposed isolation.

But now I was an adult. An adult with goals and responsibilities who couldn't make a man the center of it all—again.

"Is it just me, or did this night seem long and short at the same time?" Matteo asked as I slid my arms through my coat in the breakroom. After an evening of avoiding him, I had to suck in a breath before I turned to face him. Entertaining any possibility that he had feelings for me was both ridiculous and terrifying.

"Busy nights do that I guess." I pulled my purse strap onto my shoulder and stuffed my hands into my pockets. Maybe people thought something was going on between us because of all the friendly touches. My hands seemed to always find his arm or his shoulder in a conversation, and sometimes he'd do the same. Angie's words made me mentally scrutinize our every interaction.

"Thank you for Thursday night. I can always cancel if you change your mind."

I shook my head as we stepped into the parking lot. A shiver ran up my spine. I'd forgotten how cold it was in Vermont on fall nights.

"You need some fun. You deserve it."

My hands shook as I pushed the unlock button on my car key.

"Cold?" Matteo nodded to the jiggling keys, his throaty chuckle giving me a whole different kind of chill.

"A little. I should use gloves even though it's only a short walk out here."

"Yeah, I underestimated how cold the fall could get here." He rolled his shoulders under his jacket. "Can I ask you something?"

"Sure," I said, trying to sound light, even though my heart dropped into my stomach at the serious tone in his voice.

"Why don't you go out on your nights off? I know you hang out with Angie sometimes, but you're young and pretty. I hate the idea of you being alone all the time."

"Pretty?" I teased, trying to ignore the skipped beat of my heart.

"Yes. Beautiful, in fact. And don't dodge the question."

I shifted and leaned against my car, wrapping my arms around my torso.

"Before I came back, I was engaged and broke it off. Well *he* broke it off. It's a long embarrassing story, and although I never thought I'd come back to Colebury again, it's nice to get away from that. Where it's not in my face all the time."

"You know, I hear that." He sighed, resting a hand on the roof of my car.

"It was a while ago. And I jumped into it and got burned, so I thought it was better to just lay low. Take it easy. And I could probably be better at connecting with people to get actual invitations to go out. Angie is used to forcing me from when we were in high school."

I had to look away from Matteo's sad smile.

"So, that being said, I can usually help you out on my nights off, and it's no big deal. I'll see you guys tomorrow."

I opened my car door when Matteo grabbed my arm. Something about the way his hand slid around my bicep made me freeze. It was purposeful and intimate. Not a friendly jab or pat on the shoulder.

"I don't know the whole story, and I don't have to. But only an idiot would let you go. I'm probably not one to talk, but don't let him stop you from enjoying life, okay?"

When I lifted my head, I saw more than a friendly gaze. His eyes fell to my mouth before they clenched shut for a second, as if he was thinking about kissing me. Did he feel it too? It always seemed impossible but at that moment, his eyes bored into mine as if he wanted to get closer but something was holding him back.

"See you tomorrow," he rasped, a husky edge to his whisper.

Or maybe it wasn't holding him back.

"Not sure what's for dinner yet, but it can be a surprise to both of us."

I laughed at his shrug.

"I look forward to it." I took one last glance at him before I stepped into my car and blasted the heat the minute I started the engine.

I held my hands in front of the vents and flexed my fingers, trying to shake off whatever that was with Matteo.

I was paying attention now, but didn't know what to do with what I saw.

MATTEO

"How do you do it?" Milo asked me through a yawn, rubbing his eyes before he lifted his head.

"How do I do what?" I squinted at him before taking a long pull from the only beer I could have tonight since I was driving. When he'd suggested the Gin Mill, I'd been relieved. I never liked hanging out at Speakeasy on the rare occasions I went out, because I was still too in tune with what was happening around me to feel like a customer. He offered to pick me up so I could have a couple of drinks and relax, but I never liked to depend on anyone to get me anywhere in case I had to get home quickly.

Not that I ever really worried when Lauren was with Melanie. Parent teacher conferences were scheduled for tomorrow at Colebury Elementary, giving the kids an unexpected Friday off. When I'd left, Lauren had pulled out every princess game she had so I expected them both to be up well past Lauren's usual bedtime. I smiled at the thought of them. Melanie was in my head a lot lately, even when she wasn't at my house wearing a matching tiara with my daughter.

"Be a father all by yourself. I love my kids, but God, it's exhausting." He dragged a hand down his face. "If I'm lucky, I get to have two nights out a month where Angie and I spend most of our dates trying not to nod off in our beer. It does get better eventually, right?"

I had to laugh at the desperate plea in his eyes.

"Yes, it does get better. Once they have all of their teeth they'll at least sleep at night for the most part. But then they also get more mobile and curious, which can be a dangerous thing. I guess when one thing gets easier, something else gets harder. That's life, right?" I shrugged, the memories of Lauren as an infant flashing in my brain, feisty even back then. When I'd had to take care of her by myself, it hadn't been the huge adjustment everyone assumed it was. I'd been a single parent from the beginning, long before Callie physically left.

"I give you both credit. The idea of having kids now?" Milo's brother, Dan, twisted his lips in disgust. "The thought of marriage makes me break out in a cold sweat." He shook his head and motioned to the waitress for another round.

"Things happen. You can't always plan. And not everyone gets lucky enough to be a dad. My time came a little early, but I wouldn't change a thing."

Dan studied me as if I'd just lapsed into another language, but I'd meant it. Even after everything I'd gone through, I'd never see Lauren as a burden. Staying out all night or taking a weekend trip on a whim was fun while it lasted, but I never missed it. I was ready to grow up, and it took me a long time to accept that Callie never was.

"So, this is your big night out?" I smirked before I took a last gulp of my beer glass. "Where are the other guys?"

Milo still had his head in his hands and pinched the bridge of his nose before he met my gaze. "All had different excuses. Out with girlfriends, tired from work. Once I have something scheduled, I have to go out, or I don't go. A couple of times, I even sat at the bar alone." He motioned to the bar with his glass. "But don't tell Angie."

I laughed at his wince. "I won't, promise. And I get that. When you have kids, you have to make arrangements before you can go anywhere."

"That's right, good thing you found Melanie, or Lauren would have had to learn how to tend bar."

I cracked up, not wanting to think how close it came to something like that.

"I went to school with Melanie," Dan said, swirling the last drop of beer in his glass. "I sat behind her in, I forget what class, oh yeah, English. It was the first time I'd heard her speak. I used to tease Angie that Melanie was her mute friend until then." Dan's snicker made me bristle.

"She wasn't mute." Milo rolled his heavy eyes. "She probably knew, like everyone else, that you were a dick back then." He turned his head to me. "And he hasn't gotten much better."

"I wasn't a dick. Well, not all the time. And I didn't say anything bad about Melanie. I actually liked sitting behind her, especially when I'd watch her get up." My hand balled into a fist when he wiggled his eyebrows. "I guess being a single dad has its perks, like hot babysitters."

I took in a deep breath and let it out slowly, wanting to take my fist and ram it through his face. But he really wasn't saying anything wrong. Yes, he was a dick as his brother had noted, but Melanie was just a friend who happened to be Lauren's babysitter. If she wanted to date someone like this douche for any reason, I had no right to stop it.

But I wanted to. Because I wanted Melanie for myself. Even though I swore I'd never let anyone else in, she was already there, and I had no clue how to handle it.

When I couldn't deny it, I tried ignoring it. Neither worked. On the nights she was with Lauren, I always tried to leave work as quickly as possible so I'd get to talk to her longer. When we worked together, I'd make an excuse to stay close to her. I wasn't stupid enough to not think people noticed, but I was stupid enough to keep doing it.

"Seriously, dude?" Milo washed a hand over his face and shook his head. "Ignore him. Most of us do." He rolled his tired eyes.

"Shit, I didn't mean to…" Dan stammered, his eyes wide with panic. "I didn't realize you had something going on with her."

"I don't," I said through gritted teeth. "What makes you think that?"

The corner of Dan's mouth quirked up. "When I said Melanie was hot, you looked ready to leap out of your chair and slug me."

"You did," Milo whispered. "Your jaw clenched so tight just now, I could almost hear your teeth grinding. Even I sat up a little straighter." He snickered and shook his head.

Great, even a guy who hardly knew me and had spoken to me for less than an hour had figured out how I felt about Melanie. I was doing a shit job of hiding it. I'd told her to get out more because I hated thinking of her alone so much but never gave a lot of thought to how I'd feel if she actually dated someone. As the notion drifted into my brain, my fist clenched again.

I was fucked no matter how I looked at it.

"Listen, I'm going to head out." I stood and dropped two twenties on the table. "Next round is on me. Enjoy it." I clasped Milo's shoulder and nodded at his brother with a tight smile before I made my way to the parking lot.

I glanced at my watch after I stepped into my truck and laughed. It wasn't even nine yet. I shouldn't have wasted a rare night out, but out wasn't where I wanted to be. And Milo and his brother weren't who I wanted to be with.

Matteo: *I'm heading home, want anything on my way?*
Melanie: *Now? I thought you'd be out at least until 11.*
Matteo: *I guess drinking in a bar isn't a novelty for me anymore.*

Or, I just wanted to be with you, and I'm sick of pretending I don't.
My thumb stilled over the screen, wishing I could punch that

out on text but I couldn't. When I had the guts to tell her, it would be face to face. We both deserved that.

> **Melanie:** *No thanks. We made cookies already tonight, and everywhere is closed anyway. See you when you get home.*

I loved seeing her when I got home. Why would I waste time anywhere else?

When I opened my front door, Melanie lay on my couch with her eyes closed and clasped two carrots in her hand.

"I think this is the Sleeping Beauty reenactment Lauren always does, but why are you holding carrots?" I whispered as I hovered over her.

Her shoulders shook with a silent laugh. "Because I'm supposed to have flowers, but we couldn't find any, so Lauren said since the carrots had green on the ends we could pretend."

"Her improv is always good."

Melanie laughed harder as she sat up on her elbows. She wore T-shirts and jeans whenever I saw her, but she was always gorgeous. In a dress that showed off her long legs, she'd be stunning. I spent too much time picturing that, and what she'd look like out of her T-shirts and jeans. I'd bet she'd be fucking breathtaking.

"You're home early. How come?"

"Wasn't feeling it tonight. I went for Milo's sake. It was only him and his brother."

Her nose crinkled. "Dan isn't like Milo. He was in a couple of my classes in junior year. He's kind of a dick."

A laugh escaped me. "I kind of noticed. Sorry you wasted a night off, tonight."

She grinned and shook her head. "Not a waste at all. We played that princess game where the winner gets to tell a story after she collects all the objects. Lauren loved my story so much that she wanted to act it out. She told me to stay here while she went to get a second crown."

"Dolls and crowns are plentiful in this house." I settled on the edge of the couch, lost for a moment in Melanie's blue eyes and the way her dark hair fanned over the cushion. "I usually let her win so I can hear the stories she tells. Most have a princess in charge of everything and everyone does what she says."

Melanie gave me a slow nod. "Art does imitate life."

"Daddy, you're home! Perfect!" Lauren ran over, balancing two crowns on her wrist. She plunked one on top of my head and handed me the other one.

"You wear that one," she said, pointing to my head. "Then you kiss Melanie, and when she wakes up, you put the small crown on her head. *Melanie*, you have to keep your eyes closed."

Melanie nodded and complied, but not before I noticed her eyes bulge at my daughter's request. I bit back a smile as she squirmed back into position.

I'd imagined kissing Melanie more times than I could count, but this wasn't quite how I'd pictured it. I'd run my thumb along her jaw, trace those lips to see if they felt as pillow-soft as they looked, then I'd let my hand slide to the back of her neck and drag her to me until my mouth was on hers. I'd take it as slow as I could stand it before I...

"Daddy, what's taking you so long?"

My head whipped toward Lauren's exasperated sigh and tapping foot. In my all too often recurring fantasy Melanie and I were alone. My daughter's presence pulled me back to the present, reiterating all the reasons why a real kiss couldn't happen.

I steadied the cheap plastic crown on my head before I pressed my hands into the couch on either side of her. I spied Melanie suck in a breath and hold it as if she were bracing herself. Going in slowly, I pressed my lips to her cheek, close enough to the corner of her mouth for me to feel her shallow breathing.

I lingered for a long minute, watching her chest fall on a soft, almost inaudible sigh. I knew she felt it too and probably fought it just as hard. Maybe she spent her days talking herself out of it and was just as exhausted as I was.

This tiny kiss seemed big, and made my heart pound and my palms sweat more than all the meaningless sex I'd had in the past years. This meant more than all of that, more than I was ready for.

I grazed my stubbled cheek against her soft one and took in her sweet scent one more time.

"Wake up, Princess," I whispered. She squeezed my elbow for a second as if she were attempting to break a fall. Goosebumps broke out along the patch of her collarbone showing under her V-neck T-shirt.

My gaze locked on hers when she opened her eyes. Wide again, but not with panic this time. They were dark, her crystal irises almost invisible behind her dilated pupils.

"And now, Melanie sits up, and you put the crown on her head."

We both jerked away from each other, as if Lauren had caught us doing something we shouldn't have. Melanie shot up, folding her legs under her as I set the tiny crown on her head.

"Was that okay?" I asked Lauren, scooting away from Melanie and off the couch.

She shrugged, looking between us. "Yes, but you took too long to kiss Melanie. It's supposed to be quick. But yeah, I guess it was okay," she relented before gathering our crowns and heading upstairs.

"I'm sorry if I," I trailed off as I studied her for a reaction. "I'm sorry if I made you uncomfortable."

Her shoulders relaxed as she shook her head. "You didn't. I've learned during play time, you have to do what the boss lady says." She motioned up the stairs.

The laugh we shared relaxed me. "That's for sure."

"And as far as kisses to bring a princess back to life, that was my first, but it was…nice." A blush filled her cheeks. My eyes fell on her collarbone again, wondering how much of her skin flushed. My cock poked at my zipper from the urge to find out.

"Thank you. Not *my* first time kissing a princess back to life, but yeah it was nice." My gaze stumbled back to hers, and my hand itched to thread my fingers through her hair, feel her move against me as I ran my hands and mouth all over her.

Melanie sifted her hands through her hair and cleared her throat.

"I'll help Lauren clean up. I know she doesn't have school tomorrow, but she should get into bed. Both of us can have an early night." She smiled, dropping the carrots on the coffee table before she pushed off the couch.

"I could make us some coffee. You could stay for a bit since you don't have early classes tomorrow. If you want to."

She stilled and craned her head toward me. This wasn't the first time she'd stayed after Lauren went to sleep, but something had shifted between us tonight, and she looked just as confused as I was. I only knew that I didn't want her to leave yet.

"Sure. I can put her to bed, but since you're here, want to read a chapter with us?"

"I'd like that, but I don't want to intrude or anything." I held up my hands. "I already hear how no one reads a story like you do."

"You can be in the audience." Melanie tilted her chin upstairs.

I followed her into Lauren's room, settling on the floor and leaning against the wall as Melanie started reading. Lauren and I regarded Melanie with the same rapt attention. I stifled a laugh when I noticed my daughter fight the drooping of her eyelids until she conked out. Melanie smiled and gingerly stood from the bed, sliding the book back onto Lauren's shelf before turning to pull the covers over her.

The affection in Melanie's eyes for Lauren before she turned off her lamp caught me right in the chest. I'd never thought this was just a job for Melanie, and Melanie was never just another babysitter—to either of us. The realization of that fact didn't give me any idea about what the hell to do about that or what my next move should be.

"I'm sorry your night wasn't what you planned," Melanie said with a sad smile as we both crept down the stairs. "I wanted you to have some fun for once."

I did have fun—when my lips grazed her cheek and I finally found out how soft her skin was. But I couldn't say that, could I? There were lines we couldn't cross, or *shouldn't* cross. The problem was that one little kiss made it hard to remember the important reasons that those boundaries were there in the first place.

"I actually have coffee left in the pot. I could just heat it up. I'm used to cold or reheated coffee, but if you're not I can make more."

"Reheated is fine." I grabbed the pot and filled two mugs before shoving them into the microwave. I couldn't have cared less about coffee at that moment, as long as Melanie stayed.

"Lauren rolled out most of the cookies herself. That's why they're all different sizes." She folded her arms, letting out a nervous chuckle when her eyes met mine. She seemed just as unnerved as I was. We stood there, gazes locked, until the beeping of the microwave gave us somewhere else to look.

"She loves baking with you. Between that and the chapter book, she thinks she's a big deal."

Melanie's lips curved into a bashful smile before she slid into a seat at the table.

"She's a *very* big deal." A wistful smile crossed her lips before she took a sip from the mug I set down in front of her.

So are you, I wanted to say. More than I expected. And more than I could force myself to ignore. At least, not anymore.

"You can ask me to watch her if you ever want to go out again. Maybe tell Milo to leave Dan home next time."

I shook my head, peeling back the foil on the plate of cookies in the middle of the table and stealing one.

"Sometimes, out is overrated. Dan mentioned he had a couple of classes with you in high school."

She sighed, nodding and grabbing a cookie for herself.

"I was pretty quiet in school. I did speak with friends, but sometimes in class I'd clam up. I always enjoyed talking about books, so English was the one class I'd participate in." She rolled her eyes before she took a bite. "I remember in junior year, every time I'd answer a question, Dan would make a big deal that I could talk."

"Maybe he wished you were talking to him."

I cracked up at her disgusted wince.

"I guess part of why I wanted to become a teacher was to help kids like me. Lauren has this booming personality that always has to be heard, and I love that, but some children need a push. I want to be that push." She shrugged as she took another sip of coffee. "Sounds a little cheesy, I know."

"No."

When her gaze whipped to mine, I realized it had came out more forcefully than I'd meant it to.

"You draw people in more than you may think. You make them open up and see things that maybe they hadn't noticed, or didn't want to. I think you'll be an amazing teacher."

Her crystal eyes, wide and glassy, held mine as she sank her teeth into her bottom lip. I wondered if she realized I was talking about us, about how she made me feel, how I was considering all sorts of things that I never thought I would ever again.

"Thank you. I hope so. Or this detour back to my old hometown would be pointless, right?" She shot me a smile before she stood, draining her mug before setting it into the sink. "I better go. Late classes tomorrow and then a long night at Speakeasy."

I nodded, following her to the door and hating myself for gawking at her the same way Dan said he did when they were at school.

"I hope you and Lauren have a nice diner date tomorrow night. I'll hold down the fort at work until Saturday."

"Yes, ma'am." I brought two fingers to my temple and gave her a mock salute. "Don't work too hard tomorrow."

She shot me one last beautiful smile before stepping out the door.

A princess had just brought *me* back to life, and she had no clue.

MELANIE

Matteo: *Go to sleep.*

I shook my head at my phone, unable to stop the smile across my lips.

Melanie: *How did you know I was up?*
Matteo: *...Really?*
Melanie: *Twenty more minutes, and I'll be good. I promise.*
Matteo: *Which means an hour.*
Melanie: *Haha. Well you'll be happy to know after this test tomorrow afternoon, I have plans to go out on my night off for once.*

My grin faded when he didn't respond for a few minutes. I picked up my textbook and started reading through my high-lighted lines when my phone buzzed against my knee.

Matteo: *That's good. I told you to get out more.*
Melanie: *Look who's talking?*
Matteo: *I'm sure college kids are a lot more fun than the friends I have.*

Melanie: *We're not kids, or at least I'm too old to feel like one. They actually want to come to Speakeasy.*
Matteo: *Out doesn't mean where you work.*
Melanie: *Ah, but I'll be a nameless customer. One of the rowdy ones screaming for more Goldenpour.*
Matteo: *Granted, I haven't seen you drink yet, but I can't see you as rowdy.*
Matteo: *So, it's a lot of you?*

I couldn't see him, but he seemed strange. He'd told me to go out, so I wouldn't think he'd have an issue with it. Unless he thought I had a date or something. Was he jealous? Any other time I would have laughed it off, but ever since that princess kiss on the couch, things had been odd between us. Long silences with lingering stares and jumpy touches were how we interacted lately. On text, we were still us. Meaning we were still friends, or so I thought.

Melanie: *Two, maybe three of us.*
Matteo: *Another reason to go to sleep early. So, you're not pathetic like me and can stay out past nine.*
Melanie: *Maybe since I'm younger than you, I can handle it better.*
Matteo: *Says the girl who likes to sleep on my kitchen table.*
Melanie: *Goodnight, Matteo.*
Matteo: *Go to sleep, princess.*

I smiled, my heart hammering into my rib cage with both elation and fear.

As much as I wanted it to be true, if Matteo was jealous, I didn't know what to do with that. I wanted him to want me.

I piled up my books and stuffed them back into my bag, as Matteo, once again, took over my headspace for the rest of the night.

The next day, I made it through my grueling exam and

pretended to be excited about going out that night, all the while wondering how to react to Matteo when I saw him. We were in each other's space too often for it to be this tense, and it was starting to wear on me.

"This place is amazing," Sheila, one of the friends I'd made in language development class, mused as she scanned the busy crowd at Speakeasy. "How do you work here *and* go to school full time? I'm exhausted just watching the waiters and waitresses zip back and forth." Her crimson lips pulled into a smile. "I forgot to say when we picked you up, it's nice to see you out of hoodies." She elbowed my side as she reached for her beer glass.

Sheila never had a wavy hair out of place, always showing up to class perfectly put together. We'd started chatting after I complimented her patent leather knee-high boots one day and found her to be sweet and down to earth, even if she came to school looking like she was headed to a club.

Speakeasy was a totally different experience as a customer. Watching the crowd knowing I wouldn't have to weave in and out of it all night and enjoying the appetizers that always made my mouth water whenever I brought them to tables made this sometimes-grueling place fun.

"Two Goldenpours and one cider," Tim said from behind me, balancing three glasses as he gingerly set them onto the table in front of us. "I have to say, I have new respect for Melanie after that trip to the bar. It's a Thursday night, and I could barely get through."

I laughed as I reached for my glass. "Thanks. I guess I've gotten used to it. The first night I worked here I was scared to death of dropping beer glasses. I kept it cool until I was knocked over from behind." I shrugged, smiling at their widened eyes.

"Did you fall?" Sheila asked.

"On my face." I shut my eyes and nodded. "But it wasn't terrible. I guess after my biggest fear came true so early, I was able to move on and focus."

I left out the part about Matteo swooping in like a knight in a polo shirt and taking care of my injuries. That seemed like a life-time ago now, but the memory always made me smile.

"I guess that's where you got those shoulders from." Sheila motioned to where my top hung over one shoulder. I'd worn leather leggings and open-toed booties tonight, even curled my hair and put on makeup. I managed to sit with Tim and Sheila for an hour without being noticed, so I'd bet no one recognized me without a T-shirt and ponytail.

"That's a big muscle," Tim agreed. "Maybe I should get a job here." We laughed when he flexed his bicep. "I guess if you do that all night," he pointed over his shoulder to Anne, balancing beer glasses on a tray as she crossed the floor, "it would beat weight lifting at a gym any day."

I zoned out when I spotted Matteo over his shoulder. He spoke to one of the new waitresses with his arms crossed, treating her to a nice view of his corded forearms. I always wondered when he had the time to work out until I found his dumbbell tower next to Lauren's Barbie Dream House in their basement.

"So, do any hotties come here on the regular?" Sheila sipped her cider as she studied the room. "Do you work with that one?" She pointed a blue painted fingernail in Matteo's direction.

"I do. He's one of my bosses here, and he's Lauren's dad."

She jerked back with saucer-wide eyes. "*That's* Matteo? No wonder why you don't mind working six nights a week."

"Five, usually. But he's my boss, and we're friends."

Sheila pursed her lips and rested her head on her hand. I couldn't blame her, as my denial sounded hollow even to my own ears. Every time I closed my eyes at night, I heard his low whisper in my ear and felt his warm lips on my cheek. It was supposed to be a silly game, but when my knees melted into his couch after Matteo kissed me, the moment played over and over again while it lived rent-free in my head.

Wake up, princess.

Chills ran through me when I thought of how close I came to turning my head to capture his lips—with Lauren only a few feet away. The reasons why I couldn't let anything happen between us were burned into my brain, yet I'd been forgetting them all too much, lately.

I tore my eyes away from where he stood, too tempted to moon over him like the waitress was.

"I could use some water. I'll get us some glasses from the bar and you both can see me in action." I winked before standing, hoping for a change in subject when I returned.

"Melanie, is that you?" Lily gawked at me when I approached the bar. "You look great! You should wear your hair down more often."

"Thank you. It's a good way to stay incognito around here. No one's noticed me until you for the past hour. Three waters, please."

"That top is hot, too. Matteo!" I craned my head to find Matteo standing right behind me.

"Doesn't our girl look good?" Lily prodded.

A sheepish grin curved my lips as I met Matteo's gaze, but he didn't smile back right away.

"I wasn't sure if you still planned to come tonight." A slow smile spread his lips. "You look amazing." His voice was low and gruff as his gaze swept up and down my body. I shuddered, my skin heating along its path.

I'd gotten used to my feelings for Matteo, but I didn't know how to react to the possibility that he may feel something for me.

"Thank you. I clean up okay, I guess," I joked, letting out a nervous laugh. "I actually don't mind. It's nice being a nameless customer who fades into the background." I gathered up the waters, nodding a thanks at Lily. "Nice crowd, tonight. Hits different when you don't have to take any of their orders."

"I'm sure it does." He smiled before stepping closer. "Tomorrow's your late night at school, right?"

"No, actually. My two classes were cancelled tomorrow, and since I covered for Anne last week, I'm off tomorrow night, too."

"Oh," he replied, more to himself than me. "A real Friday off. I hope you have good plans for the day."

"Oh yeah," I nodded slowly. "Laundry followed by outlining my final paper."

Matteo laughed at my exaggerated wink.

"I promised Lauren a cheeseburger at the diner and that cupcake place she's been begging to go to."

"Oh, For Heaven's Cake, yes! She told me all about that place, too. She must be so excited."

"Why don't you come with us? I'm sure she'd want you to come." I spied his chest rise and fall before he took a small step toward me. "I'd like you to come, too."

Even though I tried to avoid it, I always wound up in Matteo's orbit and never made a real attempt to find a way out. Hard to do that when it was the only place you wanted to be.

This went beyond babysitting. This was almost like a date—with both of them. Dinner and cupcakes with Matteo and Lauren was an invitation I couldn't refuse, even though I should. It both thrilled and frightened me the way things were shifting between us, but I had no desire to stop it.

"It would be nice to do something fun with my time off. The whole reason I'm here, tonight." I shrugged, not wanting to acknowledge the hope in Matteo's chocolate eyes and what it meant. "I'd love to. Thank you for asking."

Matteo's lips split into a slow grin, and although I was balancing three water glasses in my hand, my feet were stuck. Words, again unspoken, dangled between us, making the air thick and tense.

"Go hang out with your friends and enjoy the rest of the night."

When he wrapped his hand around my elbow, it reminded me of when I clutched his arm during our Sleeping Beauty kiss. I still had no idea why my instinct was to grab onto him like that. I was lying on the couch, and yet I'd reached for him as if I was falling.

Maybe because I already had.

"For the record," he whispered, leaning in close. "You never fade into the background. Not tonight. Not ever."

MATTEO

"But, Daddy…" My daughter whined at the counter of Oh, For Heaven's Cake. "Ice cream comes with the cupcakes. Like when we get a cheeseburger and French fries."

"No, it doesn't." I cocked my head to the side while I stifled a laugh. "Not for you, and especially not after a big dinner. One or the other, Cookie. You pick."

I snuck a smile at Melanie over my shoulder. Lauren was a master negotiator and manipulator, and sometimes, she was so cute about it that I was tempted to give in.

"Okay," she relented, shooting me a look that was half still pleading and half scathing as she leaned against Melanie's hip. "The rainbow one, please."

"How about, I'll get the ice cream, and you get the cupcake. And then we can swap one bite." Melanie crouched in front of her. "That way, you can taste a little of the ice cream but won't get sick from filling your belly too much." Melanie tapped on Lauren's stomach. "If that's okay with your dad."

Her gaze slid to mine, her crystal blue eyes zeroed in on me, and I almost forgot what she'd asked me. My only instinct was to give her whatever she wanted, because I wanted *her*.

And I was starting to make reckless decisions because I just couldn't help myself.

I was falling for my kid's babysitter and playing a dangerous game. When I'd seen her at Speakeasy last night, gorgeous and dressed up and laughing with a guy I didn't know, a rage I had no right to feel swelled inside my chest even when I found out later he was only a friend. Either way, it was none of my business, but it ate at my insides because I wanted to be that guy. The one who could be with her without a slew of complications.

The invitation to come with us today had left my mouth last night before I even knew what I was doing.

"Daddy, is it?" Lauren pressed, dragging me back into the present and away from the memory of Melanie in leather pants.

"I think that's okay. Just a couple of bites, though."

Lauren bounced as she lifted her head, beaming at Melanie in adoration. I wondered if I had the same goofy expression when I looked in her direction lately. After Gigi, the owner, took our order, I tried not to let my gaze linger on Melanie. Her hair was down today, and she wore a tight black sweater over her jeans. Still casual, but more dressed up than usual. I stuffed my hands into my pockets to fight what seemed like the overpowering urge to pull her into my arms.

I was losing my mind, and this wouldn't end well if I couldn't somehow get myself together.

"This was a great idea!" Lauren marveled before taking a scoop of chocolate ice cream out of Melanie's bowl.

"I have my moments." Melanie's snuck me a grin as she sucked frosting off her finger, shutting her eyes when she inched it out of her mouth. "That's delicious. Great choice, Laur."

I never thought I'd find myself jealous of a cupcake, but since I'd met Melanie, I'd done a lot of things that surprised me.

"I can't wait to tell Molly at school that I finally came here!" Lauren took a big chomp out of the cupcake, leaving a trail of icing on the tip of her nose.

I was just about to reach for a napkin when Melanie swiped

the frosting away. This felt cozy and familiar, and weird. It was as if Melanie belonged with us. She was close enough to Lauren to know how to handle her little demands and actually wanted to spend time with her, not only because I was paying her to do it.

Melanie also knew my moods, recognized when I was more tired than usual and cooked dinner with me when she came over. We'd text about Lauren but would end up having conversations about everything and nothing until one of us had to go to sleep.

It had always been my daughter and me against the world because I never planned on bringing in a third person.

I scanned the space, waving to a few customers I'd recognized from Speakeasy who were sitting with their families. Seeing the three of us out together wouldn't help the rumors already circulating. I'd overheard a couple of waiters talking about how hot Melanie looked last night, but they'd shut up as soon as they'd noticed me approaching. Even though we weren't together, people assumed it anyway. As the old saying went, we were doing the time without enjoying the crime.

And I'd enjoy Melanie if I had the chance, of that I was certain.

When I gazed across the table, all those complications I kept reminding myself of seemed unimportant. Lauren adored her, and I liked her a lot more than I should have. She made us happy. What was so wrong about that?

"Hey, Matteo! Lauren," our neighbor, Riley, greeted us as she came to the table. "This place is great, isn't it?" She held up a big bag of what appeared to be trays of cupcakes as she looked between all of us. She was nice, but on the nosy side. She'd been trying to set me up from the moment she'd brought over a welcome apple pie back when we first moved here. It was why I'd declined when she offered to find me a babysitter.

"I don't think we've met." She set down the bag and extended her hand to Melanie. "I'm Riley, I live next door to Matteo."

"I thought you looked familiar." Melanie took her hand. "Your yard is opposite of theirs. I remember from when it was warmer and we could play outside." She nudged Lauren, too into her cupcake to participate in any kind of conversation.

Riley gave Melanie a slow nod. "I think I recognize you now, too. You're one of the babysitters, right?"

"She's my favorite one," my daughter said after she swallowed. "But I don't say it to Carol, because it will hurt her feelings."

"It's nice to have a favorite." Riley picked up the shopping bag and adjusted it on her wrist, quirking her brow at me. "You all enjoy." When she stalked out the door, I laughed to myself. Now, our neighborhood, along with most of the staff and some of the customers at Speakeasy thought Melanie was *my* favorite babysitter, too.

Melanie folded her arms and leaned on the table. "So how many people on your street will think you're dating your babysitter by the time you get home?"

"She isn't exactly subtle." I held her gaze, but she seemed amused, not panicked. "Does that bother you?"

"No, because I'm used to it." She shrugged. "Most assume at work. You've never heard them call us M and M?"

"Yes," I grumbled, crossing my arms as I leaned back in the chair. "Does anyone hassle you about it?" I never factored in some of the staff bothering Melanie because they thought I gave her special treatment.

"No, it's more of an unspoken thing. Like a given that everyone knows, or thinks they know, but won't say." We shared a smile while Lauren slurped the rest of her juice. "This is the most interesting I've been since I'd lived in Colebury." Her shoulders shook with a laugh. "We know the truth. The gossip current in a small town is mighty and pointless to fight against."

I nodded as we cleared off the table and headed to the parking lot. Melanie had met us at our house so we'd all piled into my truck. I stole a glance at her as I drove us home, her hair swaying on her shoulders as she rubbed her hands together. Usually, my passenger seat was empty, and I'd gotten so used to it, seeing her there should have been strange.

But it wasn't. I knew the truth, too. But I didn't know if our truths matched up. Although it would make things worse, I needed to find out.

"Come inside," Lauren pulled Melanie's hand when we stepped out of my truck. "We can watch a movie on the big TV downstairs. Right, Daddy?"

"You're more than welcome to stay." I shrugged, trying my hardest to pull off aloof but was most likely doing a shit job of it.

"You guys aren't sick of me, yet?"

"Never!" My daughter yelled as she yanked Melanie toward the front door, answering for both of us.

I scooped Lauren up, drawing out a giggle when I tickled her side. "How about putting on your pajamas, since I'm sure you're going to fall asleep down here?"

"Can I leave my penny on?"

"Pendant," I corrected, thumbing the resin image of Belle from *Beauty and the Beast*. In the days when I was struggling for childcare and had to bring her to work for a little while if a babysitter showed up late, Lauren was a big hit with all the staff. Until Melanie, Lily had been her favorite co-worker of mine, and she'd made her a two-sided mood pendant. She turned it to Belle when she was happy and showed the Beast when she was upset, which wasn't very often or didn't last too long. I never allowed her to wear it to school since I was sure she'd be more concerned with switching her moods than paying attention in class.

"I can tell what mood you're in without Belle or the Beast telling me." I dropped a kiss to her forehead before I set her down on her feet. "Go." I tapped her hip and nodded toward the stairs.

I watched her scurry up to her room before I felt Melanie's gaze on me.

"What?" I asked when I caught her wistful smile.

"I love watching you guys. You are the best father I know.

That's why she adores you so much." Her eyes were glossy when they met mine.

"I don't know about best." I walked over to where she stood. "I'm sure I come up short in a lot of ways, but I try. I can't give my daughter less than all I have, you know? Even if it's not enough, sometimes."

Melanie shook her head. "You're a wonderful man with a huge heart. Lauren is the luckiest little girl in the world." Her voice cracked before she wrapped her arms around her torso and headed for my couch.

I grabbed her arm, gently pulling her toward me. I'd been grabbing her arm and wrist a lot lately, in a constant battle with myself to not let her get too far but at the same time not pull her too close. My lack of resolve made me brazen as I cupped her cheek and turned her gaze toward mine.

"Thank you. That means a lot, coming from you." My lips grazed her cheek, not lingering on her skin too long like when she was playing a princess on my couch, but I stayed close enough to smell her fruity shampoo and the sweetness of her perfume. My hand feathered down her cheek, tracing the delicate curve of her jaw quickly before I let it drop.

Melanie huffed out a laugh.

"Who am I? Just the babysitter." She peered at me, her eyes both asking me to come closer and step back. I knew which option I preferred, and had a good idea what she wanted, too.

"Do you really believe that's all you are to us? To me?" I asked, sliding my palm against hers. Her hand stiffened before it relaxed, our fingers lacing together.

She met my eyes with a pained gaze, slowly shaking her head.

"Good," I whispered and gripped her hand tighter. "Because you're so much more. More than I could ever tell you. But I'd like you to let me try."

She sucked in a quick gasp when I cupped her cheek with my other hand, running my finger along her cheekbone to try to soothe her quivering jaw. This was it. Tonight, there would be no going back because I was fucking exhausted from this pointless game of pretend.

"Okay, I took the penny off and put my pajamas on." Lauren said as she stomped down the stairs and walked past Melanie and me, not noticing our hands were still joined. When Lauren plopped onto the couch, Melanie tried to slip her hand out of mine, but I wouldn't let go right away. I squeezed it one more time before I dropped it, my silent assurance that this conversation wasn't over.

"You aren't sick of *Beauty and the Beast*, yet?" I asked when I noticed what she'd queued up on screen.

"This is the cartoon one that matches my penny—pend*ant*. I usually watch the real people one, so this is different, Daddy."

"Of course."

I smirked at Melanie before we settled on the couch on either side of Lauren. She started yawning through the opening credits and passed out right before "Be Our Guest".

"Stubborn, but constant like gravity." I kissed Lauren's cheek before gingerly sliding my hands under her and resting her head on my shoulder. She whimpered a "goodnight, Melanie," when I was halfway up the stairs.

"Sleep tight, Cookie," I pressed my lips to her forehead before pulling the sheet over her. "Wish Daddy luck," I whispered before rushing down the stairs in case Melanie got spooked and was heading for the door.

Sure enough, she was shrugging on her coat.

"This was great. Thank you for dinner and for ice cream." Melanie's mouth stretched into a tight smile as she reached for her bag.

"You don't have to go. Stay. I'll switch the movie to something we both haven't seen a hundred times."

"Yes, I do." Her arms dropped to her sides. "If I stay—" she trailed off when I framed her face.

"If you stay, what are you afraid of?" I ran my thumbs back

and forth over her cheekbones. Her full bottom lip quivered as she took in a shaky breath.

"Everything." She clenched her eyes shut and grabbed my wrists.

"This is probably a bad idea," I confessed, so close to her lips I could almost taste her.

"The worst," she agreed with a breathless whisper.

I wasn't sure who went in first, but before I knew it, my mouth was slanted over hers. I ran my tongue along the seam of her lips, pushing inside her mouth when it opened on a whimper. She looped her arms around my neck, my body shaking against hers as I forced myself to go slow. She felt too good, tasted too good. With Melanie in my arms, all of my control and reason evaporated.

She broke the kiss, both of us panting as I kept my hands on her waist. I studied her face for a reaction. I wanted her so much that my vision was hazy, but I was letting her take the lead.

Melanie pressed her hands against my chest, drifting them down my torso until she hooked her fingers into the belt loops at my waist.

"What do you want, Melanie? Tell me."

She straightened, flicking her eyes to mine before grabbing the back of my head and pulling me in for a sloppy, mindless kiss. I kept my lips on hers as I backed her against the wall, dragging my lips down her neck and running my tongue along her throat.

I sifted my fingers into her hair, weaving them around a fistful to tilt her head back.

"Look at me," I whispered.

She met my gaze with hooded eyes and swollen lips, and she never looked more beautiful.

"What I want is you, and I'm sick of denying it."

"Matteo," she said on a throaty groan that made me dive in harder, my teeth scraping the creamy skin along her collarbone as she clutched both sides of my head.

"What is it, baby?" I murmured against her lips.

She pressed her hands against my chest to push me back.

"The blinds are open," she turned her head, nodding her chin at my side window.

"Let them see." I ran my hand up her thigh, lifting her leg higher and bringing her closer. "Let them know the beautiful woman in my arms is mine," I growled, crashing my lips against hers and not giving a single fuck who was watching.

"Daddy, can I have my water bottle?"

Melanie's head jerked up as Lauren's voice drifted down the stairs. Thankfully, she was still in her room and hadn't seen her father grope her favorite babysitter.

"I'll be right there," I answered, steadying my hand against the wall to bring down both my heart rate and hard-on before I had to face my daughter.

"I'm going to go," Melanie whispered, cupping the back of my neck. "I don't want to, but one of us needs to put this on pause for tonight." She kissed my cheek, her soft lips lingering against my skin before she leaned into me. "Go take care of Lauren. I'll see you tomorrow night."

She jetted out the door before I could say a word to stop her.

As I trudged up the stairs, I knew she was right. We needed to put this on pause before either of us made a huge mistake we not only couldn't take back but that would ruin everything.

The problem was that I only wanted full speed ahead, and anything less wouldn't be fast enough.

MELANIE

"Are you sure you're okay?" Angie asked, her confusion and concern evident as I held my phone to my ear.

"Yeah, fine. I haven't spoken to you since the twins were sick, and I just wanted to say hi." I rubbed my hands together as I sat in my unheated car, waiting until the last possible second to go inside Speakeasy and start my shift for the night.

"You sound jumpy. Did something happen? Don't you start work in a few minutes?"

"Yes, about seven minutes actually. I...um..." I clenched my eyes shut and sucked in a long breath. "I kissed Matteo last night."

I braced myself for Angie's reaction. I expected a loud "What?" Or "What were you thinking?" Instead, she replied, "You only kissed him last night?"

"You thought I was kissing him all this time?" My head fell back on my seat. "Of course you did."

"Don't get upset." Her attempt to calm me down did nothing to help my frayed nerves. "There's something strong between you two. I told you that a while ago. This was only a matter of time. I expected it and am impressed you've held out this long. So, now I see the purpose of this phone call. You kissed Matteo, and now you have to spend an entire shift around him and you're not sure how to handle yourself. Am I right?"

"Mostly," I mumbled. I put the call on speaker and pulled up Matteo's text from last night to read it for the millionth time.

Matteo: *I'm sorry if I pushed you, but I'm not sorry I kissed you.*

"You're adults, as long as you don't grope each other in the breakroom, you should be fine tonight. But you need to figure out what to do about what's going on. He's in your life a lot unless you change both jobs. So, you're going to have to pull up your big girl pants and deal with it."

"You aren't telling me anything I don't know. It's just—"

My head fell onto my ice-cold steering wheel. I had three minutes to run inside and clock in for the night.

"He's an awesome kisser, isn't he?"

"Angie, don't make me get into that now."

"Ah, I knew it. The strong silent types always are. Come on, indulge me. I spent my week checking both babies' diapers for a solid poop a million times a day. Give me a little something."

"He is awesome." I sighed. "Thorough, hot, bossy." The entire kiss replayed in my head over and over since last night, but the part that gave me the biggest chill was when he fisted my hair and pulled my head back with a feral look in his eyes. His lips were gentle yet demanding, and if we hadn't been interrupted he could have done whatever he wanted to me.

It took all I had to leave his house last night, but if a single kiss freaked me out this much, I couldn't imagine what a night in his bed would do. Or what his mouth and hands could to my naked body if we had the time and space.

Let them know that the beautiful woman in my arms is mine.

Between his words, his mouth, and his hands, I'd almost burned up right next to his coat rack.

"Bossy? Yeah, I need more details on that."

I jumped out of my car, hoping the cold would douse some of the heat from the memory of Matteo's body grinding against mine as he pinned me to his wall.

"You'll get them. Up for a late breakfast tomorrow?"

"For this kind of tea? Absolutely."

My unexpected laugh relaxed me. "I'm glad I entertain you."

"Go to work, and we'll talk tomorrow. This could be a great thing. Don't worry all the good out of it. Or try not to. Okay?"

"I'm about to punch in, but I'll try," I lied, knowing that was impossible.

When I made my way into the breakroom to get ready for my shift, I felt dozens of eyes on me. Ridiculous, since I doubted the entire crowd was peeping at us through Matteo's window. It felt as if I was wearing a red sign saying, "I just made out with my boss." I shook my head, dragging my hand down my face as I scolded myself to get a damn grip. Angie was right, we were adults, I'd get through tonight and we'd both shake this off.

Somehow.

Maybe.

I was so screwed.

I gathered a couple of orders from the tables and made my way to the bar, both looking for and avoiding said boss. I did a double take when I found him, sitting with a pretty brunette I'd never seen before at the opposite end of the bar. They were huddled in conversation, and when she playfully reached out to squeeze his shoulder, my face heated as a sting of envy pierced my gut.

Maybe he was just being friendly. Matteo was a nice guy, and being social at Speakeasy was part of his job. I turned my head, focusing on the glasses under the taps instead of whoever Matteo was speaking to.

"I haven't seen Rochelle here in a long time," I heard one of the waitresses whisper. "Think she and Matteo are hooking up again?"

"Don't tell the other M," a male voice snickered. I was too focused on keeping my breathing even to turn around to see who it was.

Matteo never dated, at least that's what I'd heard and what

he'd told me. He said he'd go out casually back when he had the time, but it was hard to be serious with anyone after what happened with Lauren's mother. He'd never gone into it beyond that, and I'd never pushed. Because then and now his love life was none of my business. A kiss didn't mean that I was part of any of that or that he was reconsidering anything.

But it had meant something to me, and although I exhausted myself to downplay whatever it was between us, I felt every bit of the want I saw reflected in his gaze. I knew enough of Matteo to know that he wasn't dating anyone right now, but seeing him speak to someone that he had some kind of history with awakened all the lousy and familiar insecurities. It was like being trapped under an itchy blanket. The more you tried to escape it, the more it scratched you and wouldn't let you out.

I hooked my finger into my collar and pulled, needing some relief from the sudden sheen of sweat.

This was going to be the longest night ever.

Even though it was ice cold outside, I walked into the parking lot when it was time for my first break. I leaned against my car, not wanting to get inside. I took in a deep breath of air, hoping the chill would soothe the burn of jealousy and irritation of being jealous in the first place.

"You are going to speak to me again eventually, right?"

I lifted my head to Matteo's tentative gaze.

"I thought you didn't take breaks outside anymore." His boots crunched against the light coating of snow on the ground as he made his approach.

"I needed some air. I thought if I didn't get comfortable in my car, I wouldn't lose track of time." I kicked my foot against a rock, still trying to get my bearings. "It's been a little busy, in case you hadn't noticed. When I had a minute, I saw you talking to someone at the bar, and I didn't want to be rude and interrupt."

"Is that what this is about?" His brow furrowed as his head jerked back. "Watching me talk to a woman bothered you? Or was it that someone inside told you I dated her for five minutes when I first moved here?"

"No," I replied too fast. "It was hot and I needed some air. That's all. I'd better get back."

He stepped in front of me, blocking the path back inside Speakeasy.

The corners of his lips twitched, reminding me of the contrast of his soft mouth and the delicious scrape of his stubble.

"I was jealous of that guy you were with the other night."

"Tim?" I squinted at Matteo. "He's a friend from school. More Sheila's friend, actually. Why would you be jealous?"

His smile grew as he moved closer. "Because he was sitting too close to you. Or at least he was in my stupid mind," he laughed to himself, shaking his head. "I don't want you with anyone else because I want you with *me*. Even though it's been a long time since I've *wanted* to be with anyone, and our daily lives are so entangled that just imagining us together is complicated. Sound familiar?"

I pinched my index finger and thumb together. "A little."

We shared a chuckle before he stepped closer. "So, it looks like the both of us were worried over nothing, right?"

"Right." The hairs on my neck stood up, a new chill that had nothing to do with the temperature rushing up my spine from the heat in Matteo's eyes. I took a half step back. Whatever this was between us, we couldn't show it here. Even if everyone thought we were together already, *being* together at work wasn't an option. We weren't the first Speakeasy co-workers to date, but since he was my boss, I wasn't sure if there were rules around that.

"You don't have to move away from me. I'm not going to kiss you here. Because once I start," he rasped, his gaze raking over me. "I won't stop, and we'll both come back late."

"Please don't bring up kissing here." I groaned and dropped my head into my hands. "It's hard enough to concentrate, tonight."

Matteo was like a magnet. The force between us was so strong, it wouldn't matter if I tried to run in the opposite direction.

He put a knuckle under my chin and raised my head to his beaming smile. His eyes bored into mine, dark with lust and none of the fear we'd just admitted to.

"See you inside, Princess."

MELANIE

"I wish I could find a way to just set up an IV and put this into my veins," Sheila lamented as she tilted her head back and drained her cup. "I guess I shouldn't complain since you have two jobs plus school."

I shrugged, leaning my elbows on the table. All my Monday classes ended at noon, but instead of going back to my apartment to study or catch up on assignments before I had to be at Matteo's, I'd started meeting Sheila at the coffee shop on campus and did whatever I needed to do here. I was glad to have somewhere to go today, even though my mind was too scattered and distracted to focus on school no matter where I was.

"It's really not bad. On the nights I babysit, I get a lot of schoolwork done after Lauren goes to sleep. Working late on school nights at the bar and getting up early for class every day almost broke me, but this is a good balance."

"Plus, both jobs give you the best kind of eye candy. Seriously, how do you not drool over Matteo?" I would have laughed at Sheila's exaggerated shiver if she hadn't nailed my exact problem.

"What?" Sheila's brown eyes narrowed as she leaned her elbows onto the table.

"What do you mean *what?*" I tightened my ponytail and

scooted closer to the table, mindlessly flipping through my note-book without reading any of the handwritten words.

"Something happened, didn't it?" Sheila raised a brow. "I mentioned Matteo, and your back went rigid on the chair. I've never seen you do that. Come on, we're friends. And thanks to my overloaded schedule this semester, I need to live vicariously through *someone*." Her smile faded before she leaned closer. "I won't push you, but if you need to talk it out, I'm right across the table."

I smiled, nodding but not confirming or denying how spot on she was.

Angie had picked me up for breakfast bright and early Sunday morning and wouldn't let me leave until she pulled every single detail out of me. She was so excited we "finally got together," I had to shush her when she squealed.

But, Angie knew the dynamic between Matteo and me, and wouldn't think I was some cliché for having the hots for the father of the little girl I was paid to take care of. Sheila was nice, but our friendship was new, so I didn't feel comfortable telling her about the interesting turn my life had taken in the past couple of days.

I didn't think she'd judge me for it, but I couldn't be sure since *I* already judged me.

"Sorry, I'm not the best company today." I wrapped my hands around my coffee cup, running my finger along the plastic top. "I guess I have a lot on my mind lately."

"No worries, honey." She patted my hand and stood. "I think we both need one of those big cookies." She pointed to the counter of baked goods by the register. "I'll be right back."

Matteo wasn't the only thing on my mind, although he was front and center. My parents were going to visit my aunt in Cali-fornia for Thanksgiving in a couple of weeks, and I couldn't afford to go with them. They'd offered to pay, but it made me feel like a little kid to have my parents still paying my way. I wasn't as lonely as when I'd first arrived in Colebury, but having a turkey sandwich on my bed as I binge watched crime documentaries was a special kind of pathetic on a holiday.

Of course, I didn't have to be alone. Matteo said he wanted me, wanted to be with me, and in a heated moment he'd called me his. As much as I obsessed over it, I had no idea what to do about it.

Giving in meant trouble for both of us, and I swore that I wouldn't let my sappy heart rush into something reckless again and make me lose myself. What was brewing with Matteo and me had been simmering since we'd first met, but that didn't make it any less dangerous. In fact, it made it worse.

Chase and I had been a whirlwind. The rush of the new passion high made me believe what we had was real and forever and clouded my judgment. Yes, I'd been attracted to Matteo from day one, but I knew him in a way I'd never really known Chase. Matteo was my friend first, even if I ached for him to be more than that. And that made the pull to him all the more palpable.

"Melanie, are you sure you're okay? You look like you fell asleep with your eyes open." Sheila studied me with concern when she came back to the table.

"Sorry," I said, covering my eyes. "Like I said there's a lot on my mind, sometimes it drifts."

I needed it to stop drifting to Matteo's lips and the inevitable way our delicate balance was about to fall off-kilter.

I was so zoned out, I almost jumped when my phone buzzed across the table. Matteo was calling, not texting, and my stomach lurched with a bad feeling. I wasn't due at his house until four, and while we texted back and forth often, he never called me.

"Give me one minute," I said before I scooped my phone off of the table and rushed outside to answer the call.

"Hey, what's up."

"Hey." Matteo answered, the gravelly but tense tone of his voice unnerving me. "I'm so sorry to bother you, but I need a favor. Lauren's been sick since last night, and I can't leave her with anyone because she's still throwing up. Would you mind picking up some Pedialyte? I thought your classes were over for the day, but I wasn't sure." My chest pinched at Lauren's whimpers in the background.

"They are, I can absolutely go pick it up. Is there anything else you need?"

"We're low on children's Motrin. She's running fevers on and off. I'm so sorry to put you out like this. Everyone I know is working right now or not home."

"Don't apologize, I'm always here for you guys."

"I know you are." The exhaustion in his voice was laced with defeat. "And I appreciate it more than you know."

They both meant a lot to me, and I was too concerned for them to worry about whatever was going on between Matteo and me.

"I'll be there as soon as I can." I ended the call and darted back inside the coffee shop.

"I am so sorry, but I can't stay." I explained as I quickly shoved all my books back into my bag and scooped up my half cup of coffee and threw it into the trash. "Lauren is sick, and Matteo needs me to pick up some medicine. She's throwing up, and he can't leave her." I sucked in a breath after all the words came out in a rush.

"Hey, breathe." Sheila stood to touch my arm.

I stilled, exhaling a long gust of air.

"They…" I stammered before meeting Sheila's gaze. "They both mean a lot to me. Too much actually."

Her warm smile helped me relax, if only for a moment.

"I know. Go. We'll talk tomorrow. Take this for the road, you probably have a long day ahead of you." She wrapped the cookie in a napkin and handed it to me.

"Thanks," I smiled, stuffing the cookie into my bag before I headed to my car.

Forcing myself to only go ten miles above the speed limit no matter how much my foot wanted to plunge on the gas, I arrived at the pharmacy and picked up Pedialyte, some children's Motrin, and grabbed some orange Gatorade from the fridge by the register. She loved orange drinks, so I hoped she'd keep this down once she stopped throwing up.

I looped the bags on my wrist as I fumbled with my key when I arrived at their house. I'd worked with kids enough to know that stomach bugs were not only common, but expected. I guessed it all hit differently when it was a child—and parent— you really cared about.

Matteo's lips lifted in a weak smile when his gaze stumbled to mine from the couch. His hair was wet as he held a limp Lauren in his arms, her damp locks of hair sticking to the back of her shirt.

"We just finished shower number three." He stood, keeping Lauren in his arms, before tiptoeing over to me. "I shampooed my hair while she was in there since it had puke in it."

"Sounds like you guys have had a rough day." I rubbed Lauren's back and shot Matteo a smile. He shut his eyes and nodded, my heart sinking a bit when he didn't smile back. He was obviously stressed and tired from taking care of a sick kid, but there was something more to it. I sensed more than exhaustion and worry.

"She just took the last of the Motrin we had, and hasn't thrown up since right before I called you. I think she's wiped enough to sleep for a little bit." His weary eyes met mine as he dropped his chin toward Lauren, her head buried into his chest as she pinched the cotton of his T-Shirt between her fingers. She held on to her daddy like a lifeline, and it both made my heart swell and break.

"Come on, Cookie." His voice was sandpaper as he trudged toward their winding staircase. "We'll take your temperature one more time before you go to sleep, okay?"

"I want Melanie to do it," she whispered as she reached for me over his shoulder.

"Sure," I gave her a little nod as I followed them, tempted to place my hand in between Matteo's shoulder-blades to keep him upright. The poor man looked like he was about to pass out alongside his daughter.

"Thank you," he mouthed before he stepped into Lauren's room.

After a lifetime of always feeling like an outsider, I'd never felt as wanted or needed as I did in this house, which made me need them all the more.

MELANIE

The thermometer bobbed in between Lauren's parched lips, the poor thing too zapped of any energy to hold it under her tongue herself. I held the other end with the tip of my finger until it beeped.

Matteo shot me a desperate glance and exhaled when I gave him a little smile.

"One hundred."

"Is that good?" Lauren rasped with her eyes closed.

"Better than one hundred and two," Matteo grumbled, rubbing at his eyes from the doorway.

"That means the medicine is working," I tried to reassure them both before I pressed a kiss to her forehead. Clammy but not too warm. By the time I straightened, Lauren was already asleep.

"Hopefully, she passed the worst of it," I chirped, attempting to be upbeat for Matteo's sake, but he only nodded, exhaustion evident in his heavy eyes before he shifted to leave her room. He seemed drained in every way possible, more than just physically tired.

"I'll take this downstairs." He grabbed what looked like a small TV from Lauren's dresser. "I hooked up her old baby monitor so I'd hear her downstairs. Not that she doesn't have a big enough mouth." He gave his sleeping daughter a sad smile before huffing out a laugh. "I'm extra paranoid when she's sick. I never got rid of it for reasons like this."

"That's not paranoid. That's smart."

He nodded without muttering a peep in reply and headed down the stairs. Even his shoulders had a sad slump I'd never seen before.

"When was the last time you ate something?" I asked when he fell onto the couch. "We don't need you sick, too."

He scrubbed a hand down his face and shrugged. "Last night. She woke up at midnight and this has been us ever since." He turned his hazy gaze to mine. "Thanks again for coming over."

"Don't thank me. I wish you would have called me sooner. I could get you some coffee maybe? Beer?" I smiled, but he didn't lift his head. He covered his face with his hands and pinched the bridge of his nose.

"If you make coffee, I wouldn't mind some."

"Stay here, I'll get it." I went into the kitchen, setting up the coffee pot before heading back into the living room.

I leaned against his living room wall and smiled. Matteo was out cold, his head laying on the arm of the couch while his feet were still on the floor.

Careful not to disturb him, I lifted his legs off of the floor and set them on the couch and covered him with the blanket off the back of his recliner.

I grabbed the monitor off of the end table to listen for Lauren and headed back into the kitchen. After I spread my books on the table, I fell into a seat and waited for the coffee to be ready. My eyes drifted to Matteo's refrigerator, draped with all of Lauren's drawings for school.

I stood, attracted more to Lauren's art than the paper I had to finish when I noticed something odd in one of the pictures. There was a square red building with *Speaky* written across the roof, a large boxy figure next to the door, and two girls behind it. When I took a closer look, I noticed the names she'd written in pencil over each figure. Daddy, me, Melanie.

My hand flew to my throat as my vision clouded. Lauren saw us as a family and instead of being put off or panicked about it, an unexpected yearning burned in my chest.

I loved being here and being with them. In this house, eating meatballs and wheels with a beautiful little girl and her equally beautiful father. It felt like home. Maybe it shouldn't have, but the heart wanted what it wanted, and it was telling me it wanted both of them.

I glanced at a still sleeping Lauren on the screen and checked on a softly snoring Matteo. After pouring myself a cup of coffee, I dug into my schoolwork for the next hour until I noticed Lauren stirring on screen.

She was sitting up in bed when I got to her room.

"I'm thirsty, Melanie," she rasped in her little voice.

"How are you feeling?" I draped my hand over her damp and thankfully cool forehead. "Besides thirsty?"

"Hungry. Can I have a waffle?" She rested her head on my shoulder when I sat on the edge of the bed.

"That's good that you're hungry, but how about some Pedialyte first? Then if you hold that down, we can see about making you something to eat. I'll fill your cup and be right back." I kissed her cheek and turned to go. She wrapped her arms around my torso and squeezed.

"I'm glad you came."

"Me too, Laur," I pressed a quick kiss to the top of her head and headed back downstairs to pour some Pedialyte into her cup and run it back upstairs. She was half asleep again by the time I came back to her room.

"Hey," I whispered, smoothing her matted hair off of her head. "Take a couple of sips for me. Then you can sleep for a little bit, okay?"

She nodded, taking exactly two tiny sips and settling her head back on the pillow.

"Can you stay in here when Daddy goes to work?"

"Sure," I said, pulling her covers higher. "I'll do my homework on the bean bag chair if you need me."

She lifted her head in a half nod, already fast asleep again.

Matteo was awake when I came back into the living room, sitting up with his head against the back of the couch.

"How long was I asleep?" He rubbed his eyes with the heels of his hands and squinted up at me, extra stubble covering his cheeks and his hair sticking up in all directions, I wanted to crawl into his lap and loop my arms around his neck. He still looked exhausted and drained with worry, but so damn sexy I had to look away.

I settled next to him on the couch, rubbing his shoulder before I could help myself.

"A little over an hour. I just brought up some Pedialyte to Lauren. Still no fever, but she went back to sleep. She did say she was hungry, so that's a good sign."

"I heard you guys on the monitor. She feels better that you're here." A small smile drifted over his lips as his eyes focused on the floor.

"Talk to me. What's wrong?"

He finally picked up his head, his red eyes meeting mine.

"She told me she started feeling sick yesterday but didn't want to say anything because they had some kind of show at school today. I should've noticed."

"How could you notice if she didn't tell you? *I* didn't notice last night when I was here either, although her saying no to a second cookie should have tipped me off."

"Because I *have* to notice these things." An angry glare narrowed his eyes. "Her temperature was one hundred and three this morning and it scared the shit out of me. Even when she was a baby, it was never that high. I should've noticed and stopped it."

"Come on, Matteo. You know that you can't stop her from getting sick. Kids share germs. It's how it goes."

He lifted a shoulder without looking up.

"Can you call out? You've been up all night and won't be much good at work. I'll stay and watch Lauren while you rest. I can heat up some coffee for you if you want—" He grabbed my hand and held it in both of his. My breathing halted along with my heart when his palm slid back and forth against mine like a caress.

"I used to call my mother when Lauren got sick. She'd come over and knew what to do and I'd just do whatever she said." He blew out a frustrated breath. "Sometimes, I wonder what the hell I was thinking bringing her all the way out here, away from all of our family. Thank God we have you."

"Matteo," I inched closer, forgetting the distance I was trying to put between us. "You knew all the right things to do. Anyone could get overwhelmed taking care of a sick child on their own. You had it handled. And other than the stop at the pharmacy, you didn't need me, or anyone." I leaned in and squeezed the nape of Matteo's neck, the tight muscles melting under the pressure of my fingertips. He rested his elbows on his knees with a throaty sigh, bringing our joined hands to his forehead.

My heartbeat echoed in my ears at being this close, holding onto each other like this. Even though I'd tried to convince myself the past couple of days that being too close to Matteo was wrong, I couldn't pull away. I slid my hand across his back and kissed his cheek, smiling when I caught the scent of Lauren's candy apple shampoo. That must've been the first thing he could grab when he gave her a shower. He leaned into me, gripping my hand tighter.

Matteo's breaths were just as shallow as mine were as I watched him worry his bottom lip between his teeth.

I was terrified of what would happen if we really gave in, but desire was blinding any inkling of self-preservation.

My fingers sifted through his hair, my nails dragging shallow scrapes along the nape of his neck.

"I do need you." He dropped my hand, shifting toward me to frame my face. "I need you so much."

He pressed his lips to mine, and I was lost. Nothing else

mattered in that moment. All I wanted was more—more of his lips, more of his hands, more of his hungry gaze. I'd starved for this man for so long. And now that I had a taste of what I shouldn't want, I couldn't let go.

He slid his tongue along my bottom lip before pushing it into my mouth. An embarrassing moan escaped me, the satisfaction bringing on a full body sigh. He broke the kiss to drag his lips down my jaw, weaving a fistful of my hair around his fingers before he gave it a gentle pull to lift my chin. Just like the first time he did it, I drew in a gasp when I met his eyes.

His breath was hot against the shell of my ear, "You taste so good." He cupped my chin and brought my mouth back to his, sliding his arm under my legs to pull me on top of him.

I backed away from the kiss, my quivering hand feathering down his stubbled cheek before I traced his swollen lips.

"Do you want to stop?" His eyes were dark and full of the same lust that consumed me. I shook my head before I grabbed his face and crashed my lips into his.

If I was going to regret this, I'd make it the best regret of my life.

His hands roamed my body and slid up the back of my shirt as I straddled him on the couch, my drenched core grinding against his hard length.

"Don't stop," I murmured against his lips, afraid if I stopped kissing him this crazy spell would be broken and we'd have to deal with the reality of how any of this would work. Right now, my body wanted his so much, it blinded me to anything resembling reason and logic.

"Now that I have you, I never want to stop, baby."

My head fell back as he trailed open-mouthed kisses down my throat, my racing heart speeding up even more when he said baby.

He had me, all right. They both did.

This was still so wrong, but it was too damn good.

He pulled back, his eyes wild before he slipped the tie out of my hair, my locks falling around my head like a wavy, disheveled mess.

"So beautiful," he growled before sifting his hand through my hair and yanking my mouth back to his.

"So are you," I panted, gliding my hands down his arms to run my fingertips along the hard muscle and trace the ink on his arm. He cupped my ass and brought me flush to his body, the new friction bringing me closer to orgasm than actual sex ever had.

I unzipped my sweatshirt and flung it behind me, revealing the flimsy almost see through tank underneath. My hands shook as I pressed them into Matteo's chest. Stripping for him wasn't against my better judgment because I had absolutely no judgment at that point. I was too high on the man below me, the one that looked at me with such passion in his eyes that nothing short of death could pull me away.

He glided his hand up and down my back before inching down one side of my tank, pulling it down along with the strap of my bra until I fell out of the cup.

"You're so gorgeous," he whispered before dipping his head down to suck on the nipple. It wasn't frenzied or mindless like our kisses had been up until this point. It was almost reverent the way he slid the rigid peak in and out of his mouth, worshiping it with his tongue. I lost myself in the pleasure of his warm wet mouth against my skin.

He raised his head, sliding his hand up my torso to cradle my cheek.

"Lay back."

I shivered at his low grunt. He lifted me off his lap and crawled on top of me, backing me onto the couch before I could comply. He kissed me again, this time slow and sensual before his hand skidded down my stomach to the waistband of my jeans.

"What do you want, Melanie?" his gravelly whisper triggered even more heat to pool between my legs. He'd asked me this once before, but I'd been afraid to reply, because I knew my answer.

Him. Without a single doubt. The fear of what could happen made me hesitate, but not change my mind.

"I want what you want," I finally breathed out. It was both an admission and a cop out. If he wanted to back off, I'd do it. If he wanted to take me on his couch right now, I'd do that, too. The only thing I didn't want was to lose him or his daughter, and I worried for the repercussions of our reckless actions.

His eyes held mine as he unbuttoned my jeans.

"I want you to come."

The minute his hand dove inside the wet silk of my panties, I almost did just that. His eyes fluttered as his fingers drifted back and forth, swirling over the near-painfully swollen bump that had taken over my brain for the past half hour.

My body shuddered when he slid a finger inside, his thumb still circling my clit.

"You're so damn wet. And tight. Jesus, I'm not going to survive you."

Every nerve ending from my head to my toes jolted alive as my orgasm crested over me all too quickly. Matteo pressed his mouth to mine, swallowing my needy whimpers as I gave in to it all.

His arms cinched around me as he dropped kisses to the top of my head. My eyes shut as I allowed myself to pretend that for a few minutes, this was all mine. That he was all mine. I had no clue what would happen next, but I was certain that it all changed from here.

"Did I mention how glad I am that you're here?"

I kissed him, giggling against his lips.

"I'm glad I'm here, too. I'm sorry Lauren is sick, but I'm always glad I'm here, with the both of you."

A satisfied groan erupted from his throat as he pulled me closer. I buried my head into the crook of his neck, savoring him while I could.

"What do *you* want, Matteo?"

"It's not obvious?" He laughed, grabbing my hand and resting it against his chest. "I want *you*. We'll figure it all out, okay?"

My head jerked toward the monitor after Lauren moaned something I couldn't understand, I pushed against his chest to leap off the couch when Matteo shook his head.

"She's talking in her sleep. She does that when she's sick or really tired."

"I've never heard her talk in her sleep," I mused, breathing a delayed sigh of relief that she hadn't decided to come downstairs and find us tangled up on the couch. We had to be careful not to be so into each other that we forgot we weren't really alone.

"She does. There aren't many times she *doesn't* talk." He lifted his head to glance at the screen before dropping it back on to the pillow.

"I actually don't think I can make it in. That hour of sleep didn't help much."

"You never miss a day and always stop by when you're not working." I propped my head on my elbow. "Take a day off." I pecked his lips and rested my head on his chest.

"You'll stay?"

I shut my eyes when he tightened his hold around me. I doubted I'd get much work done, but taking care of Matteo and Lauren for a night would be well worth the setback.

"There's nowhere else I'd rather be."

MATTEO

"You're in a good mood," Will noted after our staff meeting. Ty and I thought that given the extended shifts, new staff, and increase in live music nights, a little regroup in the office wouldn't be the worst thing before what we expected to be a busy Saturday night. We went over the staff rules for the new servers while I focused on not staring at Melanie the entire time.

"Why? Am I usually an asshole?"

"No, definitely not. Firm, but fair. You laugh, occasionally." He shrugged. "I don't know, you seemed almost happy going through all those boring rules." Will dropped a dramatic hand on my shoulder. "I'm glad whoever she is, or it is, is keeping you smiling."

Christ.

"Thanks," was all I could think to say when I came back onto the floor. Even when I wasn't near Melanie, the effect she had on me was obvious.

Now that we were together, or at least not skating around each other, we had to be careful. We were only at Speakeasy together one day a week, but we still needed to watch ourselves. Being friendly was one thing, but I couldn't scoop her into my arms for a kiss hello when she started her shift or show her any kind of affection that people would notice. At Speakeasy, I had to think of her as just another one of our waitresses, a beautiful waitress with a lush mouth, gorgeous body, and the sexiest moan when she came apart in my arms.

When my gaze had caught on hers earlier tonight as she zipped back and forth through the busy crowd, we shared a tiny smile. I wondered if the same glorious memories of the past week ran through her head as much as they did mine, but I wanted more for us than just fooling around on my couch when I came home from work. I kept Lauren's baby monitor hooked up in case she decided to come downstairs and surprise us. Our kisses still felt stolen, and I wanted one night when we could enjoy each other without having to look over our shoulders.

One reason I'd avoided dating was because actually dating beyond a drink and a hookup took a lot of time and planning on my part. I'd tried to ensure the women I saw were on the same page as far as fancy dinners and romance since I didn't have it in me and had no desire to plan anything. With Melanie, it was all I could think of. I needed to get her alone tonight, but all these eyes and ears around us made it difficult.

I pulled my phone out of my pocket when I couldn't find her in the crowd.

Matteo: *Let me know when you go on break. I want to talk to you about something.*
Melanie: *Am I in trouble?*
Matteo: *Do you want to be? I'm parked far enough on the end of the lot if I need to put you over my knee.*
Melanie: *What did I tell you about turning me on here?*
Matteo: *Spanking turns you on? Noted.*
Melanie: *I go on break in 10 minutes. I can meet you at the back entrance.*
Matteo: *You didn't answer my question.*
Melanie: *Don't you have a bar to manage? I'm a little busy.*

"Must be good news." Lily motioned to where I was shoving my phone into my pocket before she turned back to writing on the dry erase board.

Trying to think of a reason why I'd get such a kick out of looking at my phone screen, I fell silent. I was sure Lily would call bullshit if I said it was something with Lauren.

She smiled and shook her head, hanging the board back up. I hoped she'd let it go before she leaned in, dropping a hand to my elbow.

"I'm happy for you guys," she whispered before turning to speak to one of the waiters on the other side of the bar.

I had to laugh. No matter what we did, I guessed hiding us was a waste of time.

"So, tell me boss, what did I do?" Melanie asked when I came outside. She flashed a wide grin as she leaned against the wall.

"Does that mean you want to run to my truck for a minute?"

She narrowed her eyes when I laughed.

"I switched my night off with Ty this week, so I'm off tomorrow."

"So you don't need me tomorrow night. Everything okay?"

"No, I still need you. Carol is going to watch Lauren tomorrow night."

"So…why do you need me?"

I stepped closer, scanning the area around us to see if we were being watched before I leaned in. "Because I want you to go out with me. On a real date where I pick you up and we go somewhere. Not just make out on my couch when I come home from work."

Her eyes heated when they met mine, a sly grin playing on her lips.

"I like making out on your couch. Can't we do both?"

I huffed out a laugh, taking another glance around the parking lot before I snaked my hand around her waist.

"We absolutely can do both, I just want better for us. Any chance of you breaking out those leather pants again?"

"I'd love to go out with you. But," her smile faded as she chewed on her lip. "Where can we go? I'm not ashamed of us, but going out around here—"

I pressed a finger to her lips. "I found a nice restaurant in Burlington. We still may run into people we know but we wouldn't be as on display as we would in Colebury. I'm not ashamed of us either, but I'd like to enjoy each other without people gawking as we eat dinner."

"I thought you didn't take women out to dinner." She sifted the zipper of my jacket back and forth between her fingers.

"I don't. But I want to take *you*. I want a lot of things with you."

She grinned, chancing a quick glance behind her before getting closer.

"I want a lot of things with you, too. I probably should find out if dating my boss here breaks any rules, but I'm ready to be out in the open." The corner of her mouth tipped up.

"We're only here together once a week. We can find a way to control ourselves."

She tilted her head. "Then you shouldn't offer to spank me until my shift is over."

I laughed and yanked her closer.

"You also need to ignore what you may hear," I nodded at the back entrance. "Most probably already know and would be happy for us but one or two may be a dick about it. If anyone is, promise me you'll tell me."

"Most people ship M & M." Her smile grew as she ran her finger along my collar, still glancing behind her every couple minutes like I was. "I'm a big girl and can handle it, if it means I get to have you."

One quick kiss in the parking lot wouldn't be completely inappropriate, right?

I framed her face, her eyes fluttering as I ran my thumb up and down her jaw.

"You have me. No doubt about that."

She grabbed my wrists but didn't push me away. Tasting her hadn't taken away the hunger. I only wanted her more every time.

"It's so damn cold, but it feels *so* good."

We broke apart at the sound of Anne's voice. She didn't appear to notice our embrace as she swung the door open, more focused on speaking to Grace, one of our waitresses who also sang a few times a week, who was behind her.

"Oh hey," she said when she noticed us. "Grace and I were getting overheated in the crowd. I guess you guys were, too."

Anne looked between us without meeting our gaze. Melanie snuck me a wince before turning toward the door. That couldn't happen again. As much as I wanted her, I needed to somehow keep it in check during work hours.

Getting lost in each other was entirely too easy for both of us.

"Definitely." Melanie ambled over to where they stood. "What are you going to sing tonight, Grace?"

I rushed back inside, giving them both a nod hello and hoped that Melanie was successful in her change of subject.

I needed to keep in mind that I was a manager not a lovesick teenager, even though the sweaty palms and accelerated heart rate that sometimes seemed to sneak up on me whenever I came near Melanie made me feel like one.

When I woke up the next morning jumpy and nervous for a date with a woman I'd seen almost daily for months, I wondered again if I was seventeen or twenty-eight. I'd spent most of the day with a shit ton of nervous energy I had no idea what to do with.

"Daddy, why are you so dressed up?" Lauren crossed her arms and plopped herself on my bed. She was so used to me in jeans and T-shirts, I guessed black pants and a button down was dressed up to her.

"Because I'm taking Melanie somewhere nice. You can't wear jeans everywhere." I dug my shoes out of the bottom of my closet, trying to remember the last time I hadn't worn boots or sneakers. I couldn't recall, and didn't blame my daughter for looking me over with a confused gaze.

"If I don't wear jeans, can I come too?" Lauren brought her gaze to the carpet before lifting her puppy dog eyes to mine.

"Next time." I pressed a quick kiss to her forehead as I scooped my wallet and phone off of my dresser.

"Is it because it's a date?"

I stilled before I turned back to Lauren. This was a conversation we'd never had to have before because when I did see a woman, it just looked like I was heading out with the guys. She'd never seen me make a big deal over anyone. My chest deflated at the memory of the last time I'd made a big deal over a dinner.

It was before she was born with the mother she didn't know.

"Yes," I allowed, not wanting to lie to her. "I like Melanie a lot, and I wanted to do something special with just her. Like our nights at the diner when it's just us."

"Oh. I hope Melanie isn't sad when we don't bring her."

I stifled a smile at the concerned frown pulling down her lips.

"She understands. Like you understand. Next time we all go out you can pick the place, okay?" Like she didn't always pick the place anyway, but she liked it when I told her she could.

"Make sure you take her a place where they have cake. She likes cake *and* cookies, too."

My lips twitched when she leveled her eyes at me.

"I'm sure this place has both—"

"And don't take so long to kiss her." She glared at me with a hand on her hip. "You were *so* slow when she was a princess. Don't make her wait, again."

I waited until she headed downstairs before I laughed. I'd kissed Melanie a lot since that night, and taking too long was never an issue since we had to make the most of every minute.

Tonight, I'd make sure every second counted.

MELANIE

For most of the day, I'd been scrambling around my apartment trying to work off my nervous energy. I wasn't nervous really, even though my heart always kicked up whenever Matteo was around. It was a "too good to be true" type of nervous.

We'd had plenty of dinners together at his house, but going somewhere alone with him, without Lauren between us, was something completely different. Tonight, we were a couple—not a friendly manager and waitress, or parent and babysitter. We were just Matteo and Melanie. It was exhilarating and frightening all at once.

I glanced at the time on my watch as I zipped up my knee-high boots. Matteo requested leather pants, but this evening called for a dress. Last year, I'd bought a black and white knit dress with a flower belt buckle in the hopes of Chase taking me out somewhere special. I thought purchasing the dress would give off some kind of *take me out* vibes, but as I cut the tags off earlier today, clearly no vibes or night out had ever happened.

I'd dreaded coming back to Colebury to start over, but after a few months here, it felt right. Almost like a home it never had been even when I lived here. Matteo and Lauren had a lot to do with that, but I'd come here with a goal, and although some days were harder than others, I was still moving forward towards something *I* wanted. I was proud, happy, and thankful I'd gone through with what felt like the most reckless decision of my life at the time.

I was about to pick up my phone to check if Matteo had texted when a tap on the door startled me. The only one who ever came to the door for anything was Mrs. Evans, my landlord, when she'd let me know if she was visiting her grandkids for the weekend. Since I had a side entrance, I'd hardly interacted with her other than that.

I opened my door and found Matteo, looking so damn gorgeous it was painful. His hands were stuffed into the pockets of his jacket as a slow grin spread across his reddened cheeks.

"What are you doing here? Why didn't you just text me when you were outside?" I leaned against my door, wiggling the phone still in my palm.

"What kind of date would that be? Apologize to your landlord for me, I didn't know you had a side entrance and I rang her bell." Matteo's gaze swept back and forth over the small studio I called home. I'd reiterated how tiny it was, but I felt a twinge of embarrassment now that he was here to witness it.

"This probably shouldn't even be an apartment. I don't think this space was meant for anything other than storage." I winced as I glanced over my shoulder. "If you can squeeze yourself inside, come in. I just need to grab my coat."

When I closed the door behind Matteo, his chilled hand cradled my cheek before he brushed my lips.

"I don't remember the last time a date picked me up at the door." I said as I wrapped my arms around his waist. "I didn't realize you were so old-fashioned, Mr. Gallo."

"You would have had flowers, too. But by the time I got Lauren settled with Carol I couldn't find anything open on a Sunday." His hands drifted down my arms, giving me another shiver. "Now I really wish I'd left earlier. That dress deserves a garden full of them."

My cheeks flushed hot as my gaze dropped to the floor. "I know you asked for leather pants, but there's always next time, right? Are those dress shoes?"

"And a button-down shirt. Lauren didn't understand why I was so dressed up tonight." He grinned and unzipped his jacket.

"You clean up pretty nice, too." I pressed my hands to his chest, inching them down his torso, my fingertips itching to undo a couple of the buttons. "Did you tell Lauren that you were going out with me, tonight?"

He nodded. "She gave me instructions, too. I have to take you somewhere with cake *and* cookies, and don't take so long to kiss you like I did on the couch."

I burst out laughing and dropped my head to his chest.

"That little girl is pretty wise. Cake, cookies, and fast kissing works for me."

"I can promise dessert but," he rasped, grabbing my waist to pull me flush to his body. "We don't have to kiss fast tonight. I have a midnight curfew," I laughed at his crooked smile, "but for the next few hours, I can savor these lips over and over…"

He drifted his thumb over my bottom lip before taking my mouth in a slow but hungry kiss. I was tempted to ask if we could just stay here for the night. Easy access to Matteo and his lips without the chance of anyone interrupting us was my idea of a perfect date.

"Go get your coat before we never leave." He kissed my forehead and motioned to where my coat was draped over the folding chair by my desk.

When I picked it up, Matteo took the coat out of my hands before I could shrug it on and held it open.

"You're killing me with all this chivalry, tonight." I shook my head before slipping my arms through the sleeves, my smile so big it was hurting my cheeks. "Not that I mind, but I think you're the first man to do that."

My father putting on my coat when I was a kid didn't count.

"I shouldn't have been," he said, planting a quick kiss on my lips before taking my hand.

He was the first man for lot of things, and what I felt for him was growing into something I'd never had with anyone. I thought taking it slow would stop me from drowning in someone else, but with Matteo, all I wanted to do was jump into the deep end.

With each minute that passed as we drove out of Colebury, I relaxed a little more. I agreed about wanting tonight to be about us and not having to tolerate stares or whispers from anyone, but if we were going to be together, that was a fact of life we had to get used to. Still, I'd appreciate the escape for the night.

"You know what I was thinking?" Matteo asked after the waiter brought us menus. He'd taken us to an Italian restaurant off of Church Street in Burlington. Force of habit had me trailing the wait staff back and forth from the bar and taking an odd interest in how they carried the trays.

"What's that?" I smiled when he scooted his chair closer to the table to lean in.

"The bar and tables are packed, and I don't have to give a shit about anything but my own drink, my own food, and the pretty girl at my table. It's a beautiful thing."

"I will drink to that." I raised my honey cocktail and clinked the glass with Matteo's old fashioned.

"This is so good," I said around the rim of my glass. "Since being home, I'm hooked on Lyon's honey again."

"That's the first time I've ever heard you call Colebury home." Matteo leaned back in his seat.

"I guess that's an odd slip." I shrugged. "It's starting to feel like it more than it did when I was a kid. I think working at Speakeasy and getting to know the people in town more helps. Angie was probably right. I was my own biggest enemy back then."

"Why didn't you feel comfortable when you lived here? Other than Milo's asshole brother, did anyone bother you in school?" Matteo asked.

"No. Well, no one in particular." I shrugged. "I always felt lonely, but I guess I was really just afraid. Afraid to put myself out there or let anyone other than Angie get to know me. I guess now after a broken engagement and forced relocation back to Colebury, things like that don't scare me as much. You have to meet people halfway, and now that I've been making more of an effort, it does feel a lot more like home."

"What about a needy dude from New York and his relentless kid? Do they make you feel more at home too?" I laughed at his raised eyebrow.

"I'd say so." I slid my palm against his and squeezed. "I was pretty lost when I came here. Frazzled, pissed off at myself."

"Because of your ex-fiancé?" His grip tightened around my hand.

"He was part of it, but I shouldn't have given up everything to follow anyone. He was persuasive as hell, but in the end, the decision to put graduate school on hold to help him start his business was mine. I also ignored everything that was wrong between us and how little of a life I had." I rolled my eyes at the memory.

When I looked back on my short-lived engagement, it was the frustration at myself that still lingered. How many other things in my life did I settle for or cheat myself out of because of my shitty self-worth? My return to Colebury was my attempt to break that lifelong cycle.

"When Chase broke up with me, he said that we'd rushed into it, and I wasn't as special to him as he'd thought if he'd fallen in love with someone else so easily."

I could only shrug when Matteo gaped at me. "That's who I put everything on hold for."

"He said that?" Matteo's jaw clenched, and I couldn't hide my smile.

"Sure did. I'd internalized as I wasn't that special—period. It took a long time to shake, and I still haven't completely, but those are also residual feelings from high school coming into play, too."

"I hate that you felt that way." He skated his thumb back and forth over my wrist. "You're pretty damn special to *me*."

His eyes bore into mine, giving me both a rush of heat and a chill.

I glanced away for a moment to take a breath from the intensity.

"Anyway, that's why I'd rather work seven days a week toward something I want than put everything on hold for someone who would never do the same."

I took my hand from his and swirled the last drops of my drink in the glass.

"Let's not talk about him. We're supposed to be having fun. Tell me about your family in New York. I think you said you're an only child, too?"

"Yep," he nodded. "A ton of cousins, but no siblings. We're all scattered between Queens and the Bronx. My parents can't make it for Thanksgiving since my father has to work, but my cousin and his wife and kids are coming up. Not sure how I'll make a Thanksgiving dinner from scratch, but I'll figure it out.'

I cocked my head to the side. "You cook for me all the time, I know you'll figure it out, and it will all be amazing."

"Maybe if you helped me…I'll cook and you can bake."

My chest pinched from his sheepish smile.

"Are you asking me to come to Thanksgiving with your family?"

"Yes, I believe I am." The corners of his mouth quirked up. "I know you probably have plans with your own family, but I'd love it if you were there. Sorry, I didn't mean to spring it on you like I just did." He scrubbed a hand down his face.

I stifled a laugh at Matteo's frustrated sigh. Instead of dreading my solo holiday, I couldn't wait to be with them both.

"I would love nothing more than to be with both of you on Thanksgiving."

He dropped his hand from his face and tilted his head.

"You would?"

I replied with a slow nod. "I would. Although I won't be any help, so I don't want to get your hopes up."

"You'll be there, that's all I care about." He picked up my hand off the table and kissed the top of my wrist.

"Your parents must miss you both a lot."

His smile faded as he lifted a shoulder. "They do. I think they'll be here around Christmas time. After all of these months away from their only grandchild, my father is going to have to attach a trailer to the back of his truck to be able to transport all of her presents. We video chat a few times a week, but it's not the same. I was afraid they'd hate me for moving us so far away, but they understood."

"I'm sure they're proud of you and the amazing father you are."

His gaze broke from mine as he took in a deep breath.

"I appreciate it when you say that, but as weird as this is going to sound, it bothers me sometimes when people tell me that."

I jerked back, my stomach dropping from saying the wrong thing, although, I had no clue what it was.

"I know you're humble, and I'm sorry to make you uncomfortable—"

"No, that's not it. I know you mean it when you say how good a father I am, and I work hard for my daughter. But that's what I'm *supposed* to do. I'm her parent." He let out a humorless laugh. "Does it suck that I do this alone? Sometimes, yes. But some people don't get to do it at all. Fathers shouldn't be held at a lower standard. Lauren's mother leaving her is just as bad as if I'd left. When a mother abandons her kid, I guess it's worse because everyone expects her to stay, and the father to leave, right?"

"I guess I never thought of it that way. I'm sorry, Matteo. You're right. I think you're an amazing parent, period."

"I know you do." He picked up my hand again. "I didn't mean to make you feel badly about it. No one means anything by it, and I do wonder when she gets older how I'm going to handle it."

"Does she ask about her mom a lot?"

He cocked his head from side to side. "Not a lot. She never looks sad about it, more curious. But someday, that's going to change and I don't know how to protect her from it."

"You can't protect her from everything, as much as you exhaust yourself trying. As long as she has you, and you're honest with her about her mother when she asks, I think she'll be just fine."

His gaze slid to mine, a bashful smile curving his lips.

"There's a lot that I wish I could protect her from."

"You mean boys?" I asked, trying to lighten the mood a little.

I laughed when Matteo's head jerked up.

"No, I can't bring myself to think like that, yet. Even though she's already rating what Disney princes are cuter than others." He groaned and cupped his forehead. "I'm afraid of not being able to teach her everything she needs to know."

"You're teaching her how to be a good person. The rest, you'll figure out as you go. I'm sure of it."

He shrugged before the waiter placed our dinners on the table.

"I've been doing that for five years, I guess." A weak smile lifted his mouth as he picked up his fork.

I stilled before I cut into my Chicken Parmesan, wanting to ask the question that was always on the tip of my tongue. After he first told me about Lauren's mother leaving, I never pressed because it was none of my business. It still really wasn't, but if Matteo and I were more than just friends who worked together, whatever happened was an important part of his past. And judging by the tension drifting across his face whenever he mentioned Lauren's mother, it was a part of the past that still affected him in the present.

"Matteo, can I ask you what happened with Lauren's mother? You don't have to tell me if you don't want to, but—"

He set down his fork, taking a long pull from his glass before he answered.

"No, I actually do. I was with Callie for about a year before she got pregnant. I guess you could say we were each other's first serious love, although I was a few years older than she was." He fell back in his chair, blowing out a long breath. "We always seemed to be on a fast track. Before anyone could blink, she'd moved in with me, and I'd asked her to marry me. I didn't think there was anything wrong with it because we were happy, and we didn't care about what anyone said about slowing down."

I nodded. "I've been there. No one's opinions matter when you're that deep into it with someone."

"Right. She got pregnant, and obviously we didn't plan for it, but I wasn't upset. Shocked as hell, but it was what I wanted for us eventually. So, it was earlier than we'd thought." He shrugged. "Who cared? But looking back, that's when she'd started to pull away. An aunt told me at Callie's baby shower that she was the most unexcited mother she'd ever seen."

He smiled when my hand flew to my mouth.

"She actually said that to you?"

"Some of my relatives lack a filter. That's where Lauren gets it from."

I laughed, but otherwise stayed silent, hoping he'd continue.

"I..." He trailed off. "I loved her and wanted us to be a family. So, I'd kept hoping she'd come around. But when Lauren was born, she couldn't handle it. Between the crying and the long hours with no sleep, she was more miserable every day. She withdrew from me, and from us, completely. From the beginning, I took care of my daughter mostly by myself. I always made sure someone was around to help Callie when I wasn't there, either one of my parents, hers, or one of my aunts who lived nearby. I'd tell them that I wanted to give her a break, but honestly I was afraid to leave her alone with Lauren." His chin dropped to his chest. "That's the first time I've said that out loud."

"That's a lot for a new parent to handle." My voice shook, my heart breaking at the pain etched on his beautiful face. I wanted to climb onto his lap and cover his face with kisses right there in the restaurant. Anything to take away the lost look in his eyes.

"One morning, she packed her bag and told me she was going

to visit her sister in Florida for a few days to figure things out. She said she was too young to be a wife and mother and felt pushed into all of it. She handed me my engagement ring and walked out the door." He took another sip of his drink before he continued. "She was supposed to only go for a long weekend, but she never came back and wouldn't respond to any of my calls. The last I heard, she was living in Tampa. One of my friends was there on business a few years ago and ran into her in a bar. He said she'd noticed him and said hi, but she never asked about the daughter she abandoned."

"I'm so sorry, Matteo." I reached across the table and ran my hand up and down his arm, hating myself for bringing any of it up in the first place.

"It's still hard to talk about honestly, but it actually feels good to get it out. Again, you're the only person I've wanted to tell. Since then," he covered my hand with his, grazing his thumb slowly back and forth across my wrist, "I kept both of us in a bubble. I'd see a woman here and there, but nothing even close to serious, and I *never* brought them around my daughter. Callie's rejection of us only lives in *my* head, Lauren remembers nothing. Her mother could be Belle for all she knows. I didn't want her growing attached to someone who was only temporary."

"Understandable." I lifted my chair to bring it next to Matteo instead of across from him and slid my hand over the nape of his neck. "Thank you for trusting me with all of that."

"I trust you with a lot, in case you haven't noticed." His hand dropped to my thigh and squeezed. "You always have a way of pulling me in and making me forget everything else. Even on your first night at Speakeasy I had trouble staying away from you."

A lump in my throat kept me from replying for a minute. "I'm sorry you probably had beer splattered on you when I took a dive."

"Worth it," he whispered before pressing his lips to mine. It was a closed-mouth but sensual kiss with heat, comfort, and a little relief. "I liked taking care of you, even if I didn't understand why. I should thank Yvette for knocking Ted into you that night."

"Thank her?" My jaw dropped in mock horror. "I still have a scar from the scrape on my arm."

Matteo smoothed my sleeve up to my elbow and dipped his head to paint tiny kisses over the small, thin line. My body rolled with a sigh as heat pooled between my legs. I pressed my thighs together to relieve the sudden ache.

"Better?" he asked, his voice low and husky. "Are those goosebumps I see?" He trailed his finger along the raised flesh down my forearm.

Heat rushed up my neck. "Maybe. It's cold in here." I lifted a shoulder, stifling a laugh at Mattco's wide grin. "I'm glad I fell, too," I whispered.

And I was, but not on the beer-slicked floor at Speakeasy. I was glad I fell for Matteo, although that night was probably the start of it. It was still messy and complicated, but oddly enough, that's what made it so perfect.

MATTEO

"I don't like the idea of you coming in and out of this side entrance at night."

Melanie craned her head over her shoulder and flashed a smile as she unlocked the door. Other than a flickering light, it was dark and desolate, with the closest neighbor more than a block away.

"It's fine, really," she said as she threw her keys in the bowl on the small table next to her bed. "The only thing I have to worry about are the chickens escaping from Mr. Mullins's yard up the road." She slipped off her coat and kissed my chin. "Still thinking like a New Yorker, I see."

"Always." I kissed her forehead. "That won't change no matter how long I live here. But crazies live everywhere, so please promise me we can at least get a better light over the door so I don't have to worry about my girlfriend fumbling around in the dark for her keys."

It wasn't until Melanie froze as she hung up her coat that I realized what I'd said.

"Does that bother you? What I just said?"

The night I'd planned for us had taken an unexpected turn. Instead of enjoying the time alone, we'd ended up trading sob stories. I'd never actually told anyone about what happened with

Callie because everyone important to me back in New York was there to witness it. I had no inclination to tell it to anyone new, and I especially never wanted to bring it up here.

Melanie was important to me now, and if we were going to have a real shot, I had to be honest about everything. Hearing words come out of my mouth describing some of the happiest yet darkest days of my life was like ripping off a years' old Band-Aid. It hurt like hell but felt lighter and freeing at the same time.

"No, it doesn't bother me at all. Just felt…significant, I guess." She met my gaze with a wistful smile curving her lips. "I don't mind being yours."

"Damn right, you're mine." She laughed when I grabbed her waist and pulled her to me.

"How long before curfew? I don't have anything to offer you other than a cup of coffee, but I'd love it if you stayed a little while."

"You don't have to ask me twice." I peeled off my jacket. "I liked having you all to myself, tonight. Not ready to give it up just yet. And I have about an hour and a half."

I kept my arms around her as I took a quick glance around the apartment. There was a bed, bookcase, small counter with a coffeemaker and toaster, mini-fridge, and two doors that I assumed led to a closet and a bathroom.

"For a small place, you have a lot of books." I nodded to the bookcase on the other side of the room taking up a quarter of the space.

"That's not even all of them. I have two shopping bags of books in the closet. When Mrs. Evans offered the bookcase to me, even though it really doesn't fit, I took it." She shrugged. "Something that makes it feel like me."

"It definitely feels like you here. I see a lot of romance books." I smirked, pulling her closer. "I didn't know that was your thing."

Her smile faded before her lips pursed. "Why? You thought I only read books like *The Velveteen Rabbit*?" Her eyes narrowed. "I read other genres too, but romance was always my favorite.

Reading about love is a comfort when real life gets complicated. Boys are always better in books." Her hand drifted down my chest. "Or, at least, they used to be."

She cinched her arms around my neck and pressed her lips to mine before reaching for the coffee maker, turning her back to me as she plucked two mugs out of a small cupboard. My daughter had more space in her bedroom than Melanie had in her entire apartment.

"I'm a romance hero?" I wrapped my arms around her from behind. "Sounds like someone is trying to sweet talk her way into my pants, which I assure you is completely unnecessary." I brushed the dark waves of her hair off her shoulder and trailed light kisses down the side of her neck, smiling at the rapid beat of her pulse against my lips. "I'm all yours if you want me."

"I do want you," she whispered as she lolled her head to the side. "It feels good to just say it instead of talking myself out of it all the time." She leaned into me with the sweetest moan.

"It does. *So* good." I dragged my lips over the nape of her neck. I smiled against her skin when she shivered in my arms.

"I keep expecting to hear someone stomping down the stairs. Ah, right there …" She slumped against me when I ran my tongue over the sensitive spot behind her ear.

This wasn't the first time I'd touched her, but this was the first time I wouldn't have to stop.

She reached back to loop her arm around my neck and pulled me in for a kiss. It was slow and hungry, both of us savoring each other for the little time we had left tonight. I slid my hands down to her thighs and pressed her body into mine, her sweet ass grazing against my cock. I grew harder with every sway of her hips against me.

She broke the kiss, panting against my lips. "This still feels like a dream." She met my gaze with a breathless chuckle. "All the times I'd thought about you here."

Melanie invaded my every thought, no matter how hard I

tried to push her out of my head. Touching her like this, being with her tonight, was still surreal.

"I know you don't have much time," she murmured against my lips, "but—"

"Shhh." I covered her mouth again, swallowing her whimper when my tongue curled around hers.

"We'll make it work," I whispered, nudging her legs open with my knee and slipped my hand under her dress. "We'll *always* make it work." She slumped against me when I cupped the mound between her legs, the sexiest groan escaping her when I squeezed.

"Open wider for me, baby," I rasped. She quickly complied, steadying her hands on the counter. I dipped my hand inside the waistband of her tights, my own knees almost giving out at the wetness coating my fingers.

"I love you in a dress," I grunted, swirling circles around the swollen little bump. "You're so beautiful. So beautiful and so *mine*," I growled. "I love how wet you always are. I could do this to you all day. Would you like that, Princess?"

She nodded before folding, dropping her head onto the counter with a soft thud. I tightened my grip around her waist so she'd stand up.

"Come here. There's my girl." I teased her clit with a slow, wide circle before I slid a finger inside her. When she gasped and pulsed around me, I pulled it out and shook my head.

"Not yet, baby."

I turned her around and dropped to my knees. I peered up at her hooded eyes, loving her swollen lips and flushed cheeks. I dragged the zippers down the side of her boots, lifting one leg at a time to slide them off. Hooking my thumbs into the waistband of her tights, I pulled them down her legs along with her panties, kissing my way down her thigh until everything pooled at her feet.

"I hope your landlord is a heavy sleeper," I told her before hooking her leg over my shoulder and swiping her clit with my tongue. Melanie cried out and gripped the back of my head as I sucked harder, alternating with tiny kisses and bites.

When she dripped down my chin, I grabbed her hips and brought her closer, licking inside her while her thighs trembled against my face. Every drop of her on my tongue made me lose it that much more. She was even sweeter than I thought she'd be, and the taste was driving me out of my mind.

"Matteo, I can't. It's too good, I..." She clenched around my finger, hard this time. I still didn't let up, my mouth and hands going faster until she begged me to stop.

When I lifted my head, Melanie draped her hand over her eyes as her chest heaved up and down. "I never thought you could feel an orgasm in your toes," she finally said.

I chuckled against her damp thigh.

"I never thought anyone could taste as good as you do." I stood and kissed her hard. She fell against me on shaky legs, probably still feeling the aftershocks. "Come to bed with me." I murmured against her lips.

I pulled her dress over her head, my eyes drinking in her creamy skin and the black lace of her bra, the swells of her breasts spilling over as she still chased her breath.

She plucked the buttons on my shirt open one by one and dipped her head to trail kisses down my chest. I speared my hand into her hair, weaving my fingers around a fistful and pulling harder as she inched lower.

"I want to make you feel good." She sank to her knees, fumbling with my buckle and inched my zipper down once she unbuttoned my pants. "I want to take care of you."

I smiled, my hand still in her hair. "Yeah?" I cupped her chin and swiped my thumb over her bottom lip. She parted her lips and sucked it into her mouth, and any breath I had left me in a rush.

"*Fuck.*"

The sight of her inching my thumb in and out of her mouth, holding my gaze as she hooked her fingers into the waistband of my pants and dragged them down my legs, was definitely going to end this before I wanted to.

She nodded, her hooded eyes glassy as she peered up at me.

"You deserve that. You deserve everything."

"So do you," I whispered. "So fucking special." I ran my thumb along her jaw.

A bashful smile played on her lips for a minute. She ran her tongue along the tip of my cock right before swallowing me whole.

"Fuck," I groaned again, grabbing a fistful of Melanie's hair while resisting the urge to pull her to me and go deeper. I grabbed her wrist and pulled her up to standing.

"I love your mouth, but I need inside you." I reached behind her and unclasped her bra, inching the straps down her shoulders before I sucked a nipple into my mouth, groaning when it pebbled on my tongue. "And I don't have much time."

We stumbled onto the bed while I reached into my back pocket for my wallet, palming the foil packet I was looking for. I kicked off my pants, rolled on the condom and settled between her thighs. My hands shook from the rush, but I couldn't wait another second. Holding her gaze, I slid inside her slowly, inching out once I was fully seated inside her.

"You're so damn perfect," I cradled the back of her head. "I knew I wouldn't survive you." Her eyes were wide, a wince of pleasure drifting across her face whenever I pushed deeper.

"I can't come back from this," she said, her blue eyes hazy as they bore into mine.

I never thought I'd be here again. This wasn't my first time having sex since Callie left, but my soul and my heart hadn't been involved before. As much as I'd fought it from the beginning, Melanie had both.

"We're not going back. I can promise you that."

My clumsy mouth found hers as our lips came together in a kiss that felt both desperate and reckless.

"Please, Matteo," she panted. "I need…" She trailed off and mewled into my shoulder.

"What do you need, princess? Tell me," I whispered as I moved faster.

"I need to come again. Please," she begged, her voice a breathless whisper.

"Your wish is my command." I slid a hand between us and pressed on her clit, circling it fast with little pinches in between. Her eyes went wide at the same time the lower half of her body went rigid, pulsing around me. I was done and finally let go, spilling all I had into her.

"I hope I can move my legs to walk you to the door when you have to leave." She burrowed her head into the crook of my neck, the gust of her long exhale tickling my shoulder.

I lifted my head and pressed a soft kiss to her lips.

"You're okay?"

"I'm so much better than okay." She wiped the hair from my sweaty forehead.

"That was even more amazing than I thought it would be. And I've thought about it a *lot*."

She shut her eyes, a contented smile drifting across her lips.

"So did I." Her hand feathered down my cheek. "So, you love me in a dress, huh?"

She giggled, but I didn't laugh with her.

"I love *you*." All the mirth faded from her face, but I wouldn't allow myself to panic. "I do, Melanie. Maybe it's too soon to tell you, but it's too much of a miracle to ignore it."

After spending so long closing myself off from anyone other than family and my daughter, what I felt for Melanie was magical. I wanted to celebrate it not bury it or play stupid games.

"I love you too, Matteo. So much." She met my eyes with her watery gaze. "What time is it? You have to get back to your other girl." She shot me a sleepy smile as she sifted her fingers through the dusting of hair on my chest.

"My other girl is going to want to hear *all* about tonight." I turned on my side. "I think I did everything she told me. We had cheesecake for dessert, and I kissed you fast." I snaked my arm around her naked waist. "Fast, slow, deep, but I'll only tell her fast."

"You both take such good care of me." She cuddled into my chest and kissed my cheek.

"That's because we love you," I whispered into her hair, the gravity of being with Melanie finally hitting me. I'd done exactly what I swore I'd never do. I'd fallen in love with a woman and allowed my daughter to know and love her just as much. I prayed this was the happy ending everyone assured me would come, because I didn't know how either of us could let Melanie go.

23

MELANIE

This was supposed to be a good day.

Even though I'd had a late start because I couldn't drag myself out of bed to get to school—Matteo's scent on my pillow made it impossible for me to get up—I managed to get to the library before classes started and almost finish the paper due before Thanksgiving break. Focusing was difficult, as memories of last night distracted me. Matteo and me against the wall, on my counter, in my bed. He was the lover I'd always known he would be—passionate, deliciously aggressive at times, and full of love.

Ty had asked a few of us to work an extra shift tonight since there was a big event scheduled in the upstairs space. They'd anticipated an uptick in the usual lowkey Monday crowd, so Matteo asked Carol to work for an extra night this week so I could help out.

I was so high on us since he'd left last night I forgot about all the silly complications that had prevented us from being together sooner. Until Mrs. Evans knocked on my door as I was getting ready for work and told me that she needed to replace more of the pipes, and it would probably take up to a week. Unless I wanted to give myself sponge baths with bottled water, I had to find somewhere else to stay.

Angie would take me in with no problem, but with two babies and a husband with crazy work hours, I'd only be in the way. When I'd met Sheila at the bar by school a few times, she always told me I could stay in her dorm room for a night. But one night was different than a whole week, and commuting to Matteo's house and Speakeasy from school would be too long of a trek to make at night.

The logical solution was to stay with Matteo, my boyfriend—which, even after all that happened last night, was an odd notion to think about. Why was I hesitating? Sleeping in his bed, having breakfast with Lauren, it all sounded like heaven—a heaven I was afraid to get used to.

As I drove to Speakeasy, already dreading packing for a week when I came home, I figured out the root of my stress. As silly as it was, staying with Matteo felt a lot like moving in with Chase. We hadn't done it all the way at first. Weekend here, couple of nights a week there, until I had no clothes in my apartment because they were all at his place.

Matteo wasn't Chase, but I didn't want to be the Melanie that I was back then. I wanted to be with Matteo, but I also wanted to keep the small piece of independence I'd gained since moving back to Colebury.

But soon, I'd be independent with no running water or working bathroom, and I had a night to make some kind of decision.

"Hey girl," Anne greeted me as I came into the breakroom. "How's our favorite grad student?"

I laughed at her greeting. "I'm fine. Tired as usual." And sore in places I didn't know you could be sore, but I couldn't tell her that. The dull ache between my legs had put me in a great mood until I had to prepare to be homeless.

"Hey, at least we're both off on Thanksgiving. My next paycheck will suck, but I can't wait for two days off in a row."

"Good for you." Troy huffed as he opened the locker next to mine. "I need every shift I can get." He shoved his jacket into his locker and closed it with a loud slam. "Unfortunately, not everyone is close enough to management to make their own hours." He shot me a glare before he headed inside.

Troy was always this side of miserable with an ever-present chip on his shoulder, but my presence seemed to agitate him all the more. I'd heard his huff more than once behind me whenever I chatted with Matteo by the bar.

If we started rumors just being in the same space too often, staying at his house would set the gossip mill on fire. Even if I claimed live-in nanny, most people would know we were full of it.

But at the end of the day, what did it matter? None of these people paid my tuition or paid my rent. We were in love and happy, and life was too short to factor in the opinions of people who'd never mattered in the first place.

I went to work, taking a few orders and trying not to think of my new and old problems.

"Hey," I greeted R.D., one of our bartenders, who was the opposite of Lily. Instead of chatting me up, he usually greeted me with a nod and handed me my order without a word.

My gaze caught Matteo's on the other end of the bar. His lips curved into a small but quick smile before he turned to huddle with Ty about something. We couldn't kiss hello, but his eyes on me for that minute was enough of an intimate greeting to heat my cheeks.

That was my only interaction with Matteo for half the night as the crowd wouldn't give any of us a break. When I was finally able to plop down on the couch in the breakroom, my phone buzzed in my pocket as soon as my ass hit the cushion.

Matteo: *Not kissing you or touching you is driving me up the goddamn wall right now. Just wanted you to know that.*
Melanie: *Same. I haven't even gotten a chance to talk to you. This night is insane.*
Matteo: *Stay with me tonight.*

I leaned forward, resting my elbows on my knees as I stared at Matteo's invitation.

Melanie: *Do you have a few minutes? Can you meet me in the back?*

Matteo: *Go, heading there right now.*

I shrugged on my jacket and made my way to the back door. When I pushed it open, I found Matteo, a crease evident in his forehead as he approached me.

"Talk to me, what's wrong?" He leaned his hand on the wall next to me, his searing gaze all too familiar. Even with my ridiculous inner turmoil, memories of what he'd done to me against my own wall played in my mind.

"Nothing's wrong."

He tilted his head to the side. "You ignored my question and asked to talk. You don't want to stay with me tonight?"

"I do. Really I do." I rubbed my eyes before I peered back up at him. "Mrs. Evans told me today that I need to leave my apartment tomorrow. The plumbing has always been bad, and it will take a week to fix whatever is wrong this time. So, I need to stay somewhere else."

I studied him, awaiting his reaction.

"Somewhere *else*." He quirked a brow. "You couldn't just ask to stay with me?"

"I could, it's just…" I let my head fall back on the wall as I shut my eyes. "Lauren will get used to seeing me every day. I'll get used to being with both of you." I turned back to Matteo, biting his bottom lip as if he was fighting a smile. "I have moving in anxiety thanks to…before." I shrugged, not wanting to say Chase's name. "I know it makes no sense, and *I* make no sense right now.

"You're afraid if you stay with me, you'll never want to leave." He shot me a wide grin.

"Something like that. You think I'm crazy, don't you?"

"No, I don't."

I exhaled and leaned into his hand when he cradled my cheek.

"I'm learning how to love someone again, too. As much as I want to rush in, it's still a little scary." He shrugged. "Why don't we just enjoy the moments instead of worrying what they mean in the future? We did that already, and it sucked."

I nodded, smoothing my hand down the front of his jacket. Not touching him after the amazing night we'd had had been torture for me, too.

"It sure did."

"So, you'll come home with me tonight. Tomorrow, you'll head home to pack and then stay with me as long as you need to. Okay?"

"If you insist." I lifted my shoulder and fought the twitch of a smile.

I laughed when he groaned and pressed a quick, chaste kiss to my lips.

"Isn't this cute?"

Our heads jerked toward Troy as he came up behind us. The parking lot had appeared empty, but he could've come from anywhere. And he could've been watching us for who knew how long.

Matteo dropped his hand from my face, but Troy had already seen enough.

"Going over your schedule?" He huffed out a laugh.

Matteo straightened and glared right back at Troy, but neither of us uttered a word in reply. What could we say? It was our fault for getting cozy at work and being caught.

Troy looked us over and shook his head before stalking back inside.

"I don't want you to worry about that," Matteo told me. "I'll talk to Ty and—"

"And what? Say that we're seeing each other and Troy saw us being a little too affectionate in the workplace and is probably going to make an issue. It is what it is. I'd like to think most won't have a problem, but the minute someone thinks I'm getting any kind of special consideration…" I shrugged. "The best thing is to just get back to work."

Matteo grabbed my wrist when I shifted to go back inside. "Tell me if anyone gives you a hard time tonight—"

"No."

He reared back as if I'd hit him.

"I'm a big girl, and I can handle it." I turned and pushed the back door open, trying to shake off what had happened and get it out of my head until tonight's shift ended.

I stood straight and held my head high as I bussed tables and passed out drinks, feeling extra eyes on me the entire night. No one was standoffish, but they all looked like they were holding in a question. As tough as I'd attempted to sound to Matteo, I wasn't sure how I'd answer yet. I welcomed the awkward silences.

When I gathered my stuff from my locker at the end of the night, my phone buzzed before I stuffed it into my bag.

Matteo: *I'll wait in the parking lot. You can follow me home.*
Melanie: *I do know where you live. The offer for an escort is appreciated but not necessary.*

I waved goodbye to everyone before I made my way outside, rushing to my car to escape the cold. Sure enough, Matteo's truck was still in the lot, now parked next to me. Once I started the engine, I punched out a text.

Melanie: *You didn't have to stay.*
Matteo: *I wanted to. Let me do things for you when I can.*

A smile pulled at my lips as I watched him peel out of the spot. This was Matteo from the first night we met. Kind, considerate, protective, and irresistible. We'd pay for our lack of resistance tonight, but like he'd said, I'd try to enjoy the moments without worrying about the future.

For the next few nights, I'd enjoy slipping under the sheets with the man I loved instead of sleeping around the lump in my mattress.

After I parked my car behind his in the driveway, I found Matteo sitting on his front steps.

"Did you think I'd forget where the front door was?" I asked, dangling my key as I approached.

I spied his sad smile as he stood.

"I'm sorry. Tonight was my fault."

I sighed out a long white puff into the frigid air.

"I didn't swat you away or step back. We knew someone would catch us being overly friendly one day and confirm all the suspicions people have had about us for months."

I draped my hand over the back of his neck and brought our foreheads together.

"Stop blaming yourself for a misstep we *both* made or thinking you have to protect me from any jerks who want to give us a hard time. Talking to Ty may not be a bad idea, and if I know Alec, as long as I do my job and I don't blow you in the breakroom or something, he'll most likely be fine with it."

His brow popped up. "Thanks for the visual. Now, I'm never going to be able to be in the breakroom with you again."

I wrapped my arms around his waist and rested my chin on his chest. He peered down at me with a sexy smile and wicked glint in his eye.

"That would be a shame. I have nice memories of us in the breakroom. Sitting on the floor complaining to each other about our problems, and that first night when you bandaged me up." I smoothed my hands down his jacket collar. "I think I started falling in love with you back there." I kissed the corner of his mouth. "It's going to get a little messy, but nothing we shouldn't have expected. Learn to roll with it, babe."

He took my face in his hands and pressed his lips to my forehead.

"You're right."

"Yes, I am. Same as you were right when I freaked out earlier tonight. We'll talk each other off the ledge. It's what we do." I pulled him closer. "We're good together."

"We are," he said, pressing a slow kiss to my lips that warmed me all the way to my toes. "And we can be good together all night long."

I laughed at the growl escaping his throat.

"Well, let's be good together all night long inside. It's a little chilly out here."

When he unlocked the door, I was surprised to hear Lauren's voice.

"Cookie, what are you still doing up?" Matteo asked her on an exasperated sigh when we got to the kitchen.

Carol held a large glass of what looked like juice by the bottom as Lauren gulped it down.

"She woke up a little while ago and said she was thirsty."

Matteo shook his head when he met my gaze. "She did this last night, too. That's why I told Carol to put a cup by her bed tonight."

"But I wasn't thirsty for water, Daddy." She wiped her mouth with the sleeve of her night shirt and gasped when she noticed me.

"Melanie!" She ran to me and tackled my thighs with a hug. "I thought you worked with Daddy tonight."

"I did," I smiled at Carol as I thought of the right way to phrase why I was here. "I don't have any water in my apartment so Daddy said I could stay here with you for a little while." I snuck a grimace at Matteo.

"So, you're sleeping over?" she asked before her eyes bugged out. "I'll get my sleeping bag out of the closet. Goodnight, Carol." She hugged Carol quickly before racing up the stairs.

"I don't think she'll go back to sleep very quickly. Just a hunch." Carol chuckled, looking between us before she picked up her coat from the hook. "Good luck, and goodnight."

Matteo opened the door and waited by the window for her to get into her car, just like I knew he always did with me.

"My sexy protector." I kissed between his shoulder blades. "Can I borrow a T-shirt and shorts to sleep in?"

"Who said you needed clothes to sleep?" He craned his head, cocking a brow at me.

"Melanie, I couldn't find the sleeping bag, but you could fit in my bed." The words rushed out of Lauren's mouth in her excitement as she came up behind us.

"She does," I whispered in his ear, holding in a laugh when his shoulders fell.

"Daddy is going to give me some pajamas, and I'll be right in." I rested my head on Matteo's back, his groan vibrating against my cheek.

"Oh, great. Go get them, and come in my room." She tore back up the stairs.

"Come on," I said as I pulled Matteo toward the stairs. "I'll tell her it's a one-time thing. She's too excited."

Matteo grumbled as he trudged up the stairs behind me.

"I don't think I've ever really been in here." I said as I swept my gaze around Matteo's bedroom. "This is nice." I ran my hand along his plush gray cushioned headboard.

"Lauren picked that out." He opened a drawer and rummaged through it. "When we have movie night in here on my nights off, she likes to lean on it."

He handed me a Yankees T-shirt and a pair of boxers, flashing me a wry grin.

"You're right, she's too excited. I should be used to sharing you by now."

He made every single decision with someone else in mind, but no one kept *him* in mind. I wanted to be that person—the one who took care of Matteo while he exhausted himself taking care of everyone else.

I shut the door behind me before taking the clothes from him then stripped. Heat singed my skin from the path of his gaze as it traveled up and down my body. I took my time on purpose. First smoothing my jeans down my legs and folding them up before pulling on his boxers, then peeling off my shirt, sliding the straps down my shoulders before reaching behind me to unhook my bra and slowly slipped the T-shirt on.

"Smells like you," I said, inhaling his scent off the collar.

"You're being mean." His words were strangled with need before he pulled me onto his lap and kissed me, shoving his hands inside the shirt and lifting it over my breasts.

"Maybe you should wear my clothes more often." His husky whisper fanned hot against my skin as he dipped his head to drag kisses over my collarbone and across the swell of my breast. I squirmed when he sucked a nipple into his mouth and grazed it with his teeth, giving it a quick bite before it popped out of his mouth.

"Now, *you're* being mean." I pressed on his chest, panting as the echo of my heart pounded in my ears. If Matteo could rile me up that much in the little spurts we were able to steal, imagining what he could do for an entire night almost made me combust.

"Good," he whispered before sucking my bottom lip into his mouth. "We have a few more seconds before we hear a knock." He tapped my thigh. I kissed him one more time before I climbed off of his lap.

He opened the door and nodded toward Lauren's room. "I'll be a minute," he said before leaning against the wall and motioning to the erection tenting his jeans.

I laughed to myself all the way to Lauren's room.

"I found a quick Disney cartoon." Lauren pointed to the TV with the remote. "Daddy won't let us watch a whole movie." She lifted her Belle comforter for me to climb in.

"I think it's late enough, and you have school tomorrow." I took the remote from her hand, holding in a laugh at her deep frown when I turned the TV off.

"It's nice of you to let me sleep in your bed. But I can only do it tonight, okay?"

She nodded before rolling toward me. "I'm glad you're here."

My chest always pinched whenever she said that. I was just as happy to be with her, too. She was a tough little cookie as Matteo always said, but she had the same pure and considerate heart as her father.

"Me too, Laur." I tucked a lock of hair behind her ear. "But again, I can only sleep in here tonight."

"That's right. Just for tonight."

Matteo leaned against the doorway, shaking his head at us before walking over to his daughter's side of the bed. "Go to sleep. I love you, Cookie."

"I love you too, Daddy." Lauren settled on her side and snuggled into my shoulder. Matteo and I shared a smile over her head.

"I love you too, Princess," He kissed me on the lips, chaste and quick but enough to liquify my knees against the mattress.

"I love you, too." My reply was gruff due to the scratching at the back of my throat. I loved him more every day, for so many reasons. Maybe tonight didn't turn out as we'd planned, but when Lauren looped an arm around me in her sleep, there was nowhere else I wanted to be.

My fears were spot on, because I already knew I never wanted to leave.

MELANIE

My eyes fluttered open at the loud buzzing under my pillow. I reached for my phone and squinted at the screen to decipher who would be trying to contact me so damn early. Mrs. Evans, probably the only woman I knew her age that could text, had sent a message a little after six a.m.

> **Mrs. Evans:** *Apologies for the early message, but I wanted to let you know right away. The issue with the pipes is more extensive than we thought, so the apartment still isn't ready. I'm so sorry for the inconvenience. Let me know if you need help finding another place to stay in the meantime.*

I shook my head and set my phone on Matteo's nightstand, groaning into the pillow. I was annoyed but couldn't deny the relief I felt. It was too early to ponder any of that, so I settled back on my side and tried to catch an extra fifteen minutes of sleep. An arm tightening around my waist followed by a sleepy grumble vibrating against my back told me that wasn't in the cards this morning.

"Don't get up yet." I smiled at Matteo's gravelly whisper before he pressed a warm, wet kiss to the nape of my neck.

"I wasn't. Mrs. Evans texted me to let me know I still can't go home, and she'd help me find another place to stay if I needed one."

My body jerked when he yanked me back.

"It's a good thing that you don't need one." He weaved a hand into my hair and swept it off my neck, dragging open mouthed kisses down my back. I melted into the mattress as his lips and hands traveled down my body, giggling when the scratch of stubble tickled my hip.

"I'm that annoying houseguest that you can't seem to get rid of—ahh don't stop."

His hand landed between my legs, his finger running back and forth over my already drenched flesh. The more sex I had with Matteo, the less prep time I needed. He tortured me with long strokes and tiny circles as his mouth inched closer to where his fingers were, my lower half going rigid already from anticipation alone.

Early mornings did *not* suck at Matteo's house. In fact, they made the idea of going back to my apartment all the more dreadful. I'd have to find a way to live without the late-night cuddles, early morning orgasms, and everything in between that made staying here feel like heaven.

I was too used to our glorious but temporary arrangement.

"Don't tease," I chided, inching my legs open so he'd get the hint.

I felt his smile against my skin before his hand landed on my ass with a loud smack.

As it turned out, spanking was a huge turn on. Especially, when Matteo dragged his lips over my skin after to make it all better.

"I could say the same to you, making me sleep next to that beautiful naked body. Like your plan isn't to drive me fucking crazy every night."

"I was too tired to put clothes on, and so were you…"

I trailed off when his mouth wrapped around my clit, sucking and letting it slip out of his mouth slowly with a graze of his teeth. I grabbed a pillow and whimpered into it as Matteo worked me over with his mouth and fingers, all the nerve endings in my body firing at once. I threw the pillow off the bed once my legs started to shake.

"Condom, please," I begged.

Matteo dove to his side of the bed, sinking his teeth into his wet lip as he felt around his nightstand drawer. His body sagged with relief as he tore open the packet and rolled it on, climbing on top of me right before plunging inside.

"I love waking up like this. With you," he said as he moved faster, taking my mouth in a hungry, desperate kiss. The good thing about his plush headboard was that it absorbed most of the impact and so we wouldn't wake Lauren by pounding against the wall.

"Me too." I wrapped my arms around his neck and held on. A knock on the door during sex was often inevitable, so while I wished we could go slow sometimes, the unknown time limit over our heads forced us to go fast, which somehow made it that much hotter.

"I'm close, Princess. I need you to come."

I dug my nails into his backside and pulled him in even deeper, the shock making his eyes bulge and sending me right over the edge. He pulsed inside me right as the shaking subsided.

"Let's hear it for old plumbing systems and shitty pipes." He kissed the tip of my nose before rushing into his en-suite bathroom to get rid of the condom.

I couldn't stay here forever, at least not yet, but I loved this game of pretend as much as I loved Matteo.

A smile curved my lips as I buried my head into his pillow, right before my phone buzzed again across his nightstand.

Who would be calling this early in the morning? I scooped up my phone and froze when I read my mother's name on the screen.

"Mom? What's wrong? Is Dad okay?"

"He's fine. Why didn't you tell us that the plumbing at your apartment is broken? Where have you been staying?"

"H-how did you know that?" I stammered, caught so off-guard it was hard to force sounds out of my mouth.

"I sent Gloria a fruit basket for Thanksgiving to thank her for giving you an apartment, and when she called last night, she told me that she had to shut your water off and ask you to stay somewhere else for the past week. We would have sent money for a hotel if we'd known."

As I tried to figure out a way to explain where I was staying, Matteo strolled out of his bathroom, gloriously naked from the waist up and regarding me with a deep crease in his forehead.

"My mother," I mouthed, my heart pounding in my ears as I grabbed at the sheets to cover myself as if she could somehow see me.

"I don't need a hotel, Mom. I'm fine."

"Well, I'm paying for your plane ticket, and you can come with us to California. Bad enough we were leaving you alone in that tiny apartment, but I don't want you sleeping on someone's couch on a holiday."

"I have plans for Thanksgiving, and I'm not sleeping on anyone's couch."

"Well then, maybe you can enlighten us since you never seem to give us any details about what you're doing up there."

My heart kicked up again, stuttering in my chest at the long and deafening silence. When my gaze found Matteo's, he leaned against the wall, his arms crossed, waiting on my answer along with my mother.

"Well," I repeated, squaring my shoulders in preparation for impact. "I'm spending Thanksgiving with Matteo, Lauren, and their family, and I'm staying at his house until the plumbing in my apartment is fixed."

My mother took so long to answer, I glanced at the phone screen to see if the call had dropped.

"That's very generous of him to offer his home to you and

invite you to Thanksgiving. Is there something else you'd like to tell me?" I could almost hear her finger tapping against something as she waited for me to give the answer she already knew.

"Matteo and I are together. Yes, I know how it looks. I work for him at the bar, and I take care of his daughter. I'm aware of all you're thinking and what you want to say because I'm sure it's nothing that hasn't crossed my mind a time or twelve. But I love him, and I'm happy. So, even if you don't agree with what I'm doing, I hope you can manage to somehow be happy for me."

I inhaled after dropping all the words in one breath.

"I'd be happier if I wasn't afraid of you getting hurt again. This is...messy—to put it lightly. But I'm so relieved that you aren't sleeping on a floor in someone's dorm room, I'm willing to concede that you're happy and leave it at that. For now."

"When you come in for Christmas, you can meet him and Lauren, and you won't worry anymore." I lifted my head and returned Matteo's wide grin.

"Just, please be careful. That's all we ask."

An ache bloomed in my chest at the desperate tone in my mother's concerned voice. I honestly couldn't blame her, because I'd worried about the risk involved from the beginning. But I was too far into it with Matteo to back out now.

I hung up, wiping an imaginary drop of sweat off my brow as I stood up with the sheet still wrapped around me.

"I'm almost twenty-four, so telling my mother I'm temporarily living with my boyfriend shouldn't have been this taxing." I huffed out a nervous laugh, but Matteo didn't laugh with me. "I always intended to tell her, and I'm in no way ashamed of us, but you have to admit, it's a little tough to explain. But I love you, and I don't care if she or everyone between here and New Hampshire knows."

I shrugged and headed into the bathroom before Matteo pulled me back by the arm.

"Do I really make you happy?"

I narrowed my eyes at his smirk.

"Yes. Very happy. And I love you. You know that." I jabbed his side. "In fact, I'm thankful for old plumbing and shitty pipes, too." I wrapped my arms around his waist, my sheet already drooping down my torso. "I'm enjoying these moments a lot." I brushed his lips with a light kiss.

Matteo framed my face, his eyes leveled on mine.

"It's crazy, but what if we," he started before his gaze darted away for a minute. "What if I asked—"

"Daddy! Melanie! Do we have time for pancakes today?"

His forehead fell against mine as Lauren pounded on the door.

"One second, Cookie," he called before he plucked the T-shirt and shorts I'd been using as pajamas off the floor and handed them to me.

He pulled on a T-shirt before pulling me in for a quick but passionate kiss.

"You make me happy, too. So damn happy." He tapped my chin with his knuckle and unlocked his door.

We might be a risky mess, but I couldn't worry about my heart after I'd already given it away.

MATTEO

"I'll be happy for a day off tomorrow," Lily said as she retraced the lines on a chalk sketch of a turkey next to the list of what we had on tap. "This place is crazy tonight."

The Wednesday before Thanksgiving bar crowd was always insane no matter where I worked. Alec said the kids from Moo U combined with the skiers starting to trickle into town would keep us busy tonight. As every table was taken, and the patrons were almost shoulder to shoulder in here, his prediction had been right. The restaurant customers were light, but the bar area was packed. College kids were great customers, but they hated to go home and would most likely close the damn place along with me tonight.

"I don't really have a day off since I have family to cook for, but yes, I'm glad to have a break from this place tomorrow through Saturday."

Dominic and Thea were driving up tonight and would be at the house any minute now—if they weren't already. As tired as I was, life felt awesome. I wished I could bottle the feeling or stop the nagging in the back of my mind that it was only temporary.

"That's great. I bet Lauren is excited for…everything." Lily's hesitation was loaded. *Everything* included Melanie staying with us. People knew, but no one commented on it. I tried to ignore the whispers and snickers when we'd work together.

Between my cousins' impending visit and Melanie's extended stay, my daughter wouldn't sit still. Each morning, Lauren woke up bouncing with excitement and stayed that way until bedtime. I felt every bit of the happiness that radiated from her, and every day it was on the tip of my tongue to ask Melanie to stay with us permanently. The plumbing issues at her apartment had lasted longer than anticipated, and every time some kind of delay popped up, a happy wave of relief washed over me.

It was too soon, and I knew that, but somehow it didn't feel that way. I'd only known her for a few months, but once we agreed to stop the exhausting pretense and be together like we both wanted, everything had moved quickly. To my initial surprise, that didn't scare me one bit.

I loved having her around so much I dreaded when she'd have to go back to her apartment. She was already gun shy about staying in the first place, and I didn't want to push her. Still, the entire house, especially my bed, would feel empty as hell when she left.

As I surveyed the crowd, making sure the wait staff had a clear path across the tap room floor, Melanie's name drifted across my phone screen. I jogged out to the front entrance to take the call outside. I didn't grab my jacket because it was sticky enough inside to welcome the cold. As much as I loved beer, the stale stench of it among all the warm bodies made me a little nauseous.

"Hey Princess, everything okay?"

"Hey! Yes, just wanted to let you know that Dominic and Thea are here. Oh my God, their twins are *adorable*. Poor Luca got dragged into Lauren's Disney princess game."

I laughed. The twins had just turned seven, a couple of years older than Lauren, but when Lauren and Lyndee got together, they always ganged up on the poor little guy.

"Yes, neither Lauren or his sister give him a break. I'll try not to be too late, tonight, but—"

"It's fine. The Wednesday before Thanksgiving is a drinking holiday so I certainly didn't expect you home early. Dominic is telling me all these stories about when you were kids, and I'm enjoying the hell out of it."

"Of course he is." I grumbled, now feeling the chill as my skin cooled off. "I'd better get back inside. I'll try not to be too late. I love you."

"I love you, too, *Matty.*"

My shoulders shook with a chuckle before I ended the call and shifted to go back inside. A couple of waiters lingered by the entrance which was against the rules. That was why we had employees come and go through the back. I shouldn't have been out here either, but I was about to shrug it off and go back inside when I stilled at the mention of Melanie's name.

"She's living with him now, but they aren't saying anything. Not that everyone doesn't know. I mean, it's kind of obvious."

I bristled at their shared snicker. I tried to keep what Melanie said in mind. We had no control over what people said, and when I'd spoken to Alec and Ty, they'd been mostly okay with it as long as it didn't become an issue here.

Exhausting myself worrying about gossip I had no control over was pointless, but something about, "She's living with him now," not "they live together," had a connotation I didn't care for.

"I wonder how they work out hourly rates." I recognized Troy's voice. "Maybe she makes overtime when she baby-sits on her back."

"Excuse me."

They both went rigid as I approached, squaring their shoulders before they turned around. Louis, one of the waiters I'd trained over the past month, had the decency to look a little contrite. Troy glared at me with a hint of a smirk that made me want to punch the audacity off of his face.

"I can't control what you all gossip about, but that is the last time I ever hear you talk about Melanie like that. She's done nothing to you and works her ass off when she's here. If you have an issue, take it up with Alec, who already knows about us or Ty. I'm not sure if you know, but Melanie is a family friend of Alec's, and he's pretty loyal. And busybody douchebags are one of his peeves."

Troy's eyes widened as I stepped closer. I had six inches of height and about twenty pounds of muscle on him, and in my early days as a club bouncer, I could pull off scary and intimidating when I needed to. I had to be professional and figure out a way to let comments roll off my back if we didn't want to call attention to ourselves. However, regardless of the consequences, I'd still lay him out before he ever insinuated that my girlfriend was a whore again.

"You got what you wanted." Troy said nothing as I went on. "Longer hours, more shifts. Why don't you leave her alone? Are you trying to deflect from anyone noticing what a shitty waiter you are? Management here cares more about that than what anyone does when they leave. So, unless you want me to point that out, don't push me."

"Matteo, I…" Louis stammered but quickly shut up when he met my glare. My jaw was clenched so tight a sharp pain shot down my neck. He nodded and put his hands up.

That five minutes sucked my good mood right out of me. I couldn't beat up everyone who talked about us, which I guessed was most of the staff here and some of the town. The single dad dating the babysitter was perfect fodder for gossip, and I should've been like Melanie and just taken it in stride. But anyone thinking that way about her made rage bubble in my veins. Not being able to fix it made me want to shove my fist into a wall.

By the time I closed up and headed home, it was after midnight. When I pulled into my garage the downstairs lights were still on. My cousin was probably calling up every embarrassing story from my childhood, and there were enough to keep Melanie entertained through the holiday.

When I unlocked my front door, I thought of what my mother had said—when I met someone important to me, the first thing I'd want to do was introduce her to Lauren. My daughter loved Melanie as much as I did, and I couldn't wait for my whole family to meet her. I went from keeping women at a distance to holding myself back from wanting it all with this one. Even I had whiplash at my huge change of heart.

Melanie and Thea's laughter wafted out from the kitchen as I hung up my jacket. Dominic always had jokes but was a lot more serious than he let on. I was sure he'd pull me aside later and drag everything out of me like he'd always been able to.

"Hey, there he is." Dominic stood from his seat at my kitchen table to walk over and pull me into a hug. He clapped my back before he pulled away. "You look good, kid. Country life suits you."

I shook my head at his wry grin.

"Good to see you, too." I dropped a hand on his shoulder. "Did you have a good time making my girlfriend laugh at my expense?"

"For sure. I didn't cover everything, though. I figured I'd pace myself through the weekend."

"You know your cousin is relentless." Thea came up behind him and wrapped her arms around my neck. "Good to see you, Matt. You look great." She stepped back, squeezing my arms. "A little tired, but great."

"It was a madhouse tonight. I'll be happy to give that place a rest for a few days." I spied Melanie over Thea's shoulder and grinned.

The sight of her in leggings did things to me. Maybe it was because of the way her perfect ass looked—along with the promise of easy access—or that she was comfortable enough to make herself at home in my home.

I was the one who said we should enjoy the moments and not look too far ahead, but lately the future was all I could think about.

I went over to where Melanie sat at the table and bent to press a light kiss to her lips. She cupped my neck and leaned into me.

"Hi," she whispered, her crystal eyes bright and beautiful.

"Hi, yourself. Please tell me all the kids are in bed."

She nodded slowly. "Luca is in a sleeping bag on the floor of Lauren's room, and Lyndee is sharing Lauren's bed."

"Lyndee won't sleep without Luca in the same room," Thea said, shaking her head. "We're trying to keep them in their own beds, but she keeps sneaking in."

"I think my son would like a break, but he takes care of his sister, like it should be." Dominic looped his arm around Thea's shoulders. "Melanie told us that you guys picked up a wild turkey for tomorrow. Do you cook it or do we chase it around the yard with a fork?"

Melanie chuckled into my side.

"He's not going to stop with the Vermont jokes for a while, is he?" I sighed, shooting a glance at Thea.

"Aw dude, come on, I've been holding these in for months," he said on a yawn. "Now that we saw you I'd like to get some sleep. We had a long drive from Jersey, and Melanie already settled us in, so you kids have a good night." Dominic smirked at me before leading his wife upstairs.

I dropped into the chair next to Melanie with a groan.

"Thank you," I said, grabbing her hand.

"Thank you for what? I just pointed them to the room next to yours. Thea is so sweet, and Dominic is hysterical." She stood and planted herself on my lap.

"Yeah, he's a riot." I rolled my eyes and cinched my arms around her, resting my heavy head on her shoulder. I held her tighter as the awful words I'd overheard about her tonight angered me all over again.

"Hey, are you okay?" She rubbed light circles on my back. "Did something happen tonight?"

"No, I just missed you." I lifted my head to kiss her cheek.

"I missed you, too. I'm surprised you aren't sick of me yet. I've been squatting here for a while now."

"You aren't squatting. I love having you here." I slid my hand over the nape of her neck and brought her in for a kiss. "I love coming home to you at night."

I'd love to come home to her every night, but telling her that would send her into a panic. Since the morning I almost slipped, I had to make a conscious effort to not bring it up again. Instead, I kissed her, swiping my tongue along her bottom lip before licking inside her mouth with slow, lazy strokes. She whimpered and squirmed until I picked up her leg and moved it to the other side of my lap.

"Much better," I rasped, grabbing her ass as she straddled me.

"We have a house full of people," she whispered as her head fell back. I dragged kisses over her throat, slipping my hand inside her sweatshirt. She shivered when I grazed a rigid nipple with my thumb.

"Ready for bed, Princess?"

She nodded before our mouths fused back together, my cock aching every time she squirmed in my lap.

She stood and pulled me by the hand and dragged me up the stairs. When we stepped into my bedroom, I closed the door behind us with my free hand, clicking the lock I'd never used until the first night Melanie stayed in my room.

"You like to push our luck," she said on a breathy whisper as I backed her against the bed, loving the giggle that escaped her when I gave her a gentle push onto the mattress.

"I can't help it," I rasped before dragging my lips down her neck. "You make me want crazy things, Princess."

She had no idea all she made me want, all that I never thought I'd even consider. I'd gotten so used to ending my days with her in my house, in my bed, I wasn't sure what I'd do with myself when she left. But I'd have to deal with it, no matter how much I wished I didn't have to.

A blush crept up her cheeks as she turned to my gaze.

"Like what?"

"Like maybe when you're on a break from school, you and I can get away for a couple of days. My parents would stay with

Lauren for a weekend, and I can take you wherever and however I want and not worry about getting interrupted." I slid my hand down her thigh and hooked her leg over my hip.

"That sounds like heaven." She looked up at me with a wistful smile. "Not that I'd ever want to get rid of Lauren, but I'd love more time alone with you."

"After the new year, we'll think of something. Somewhere warm with a lot of sand." I drifted the back of my hand down her cheek. It was hard to focus on the here and now when all I wanted was more of the future. More of a future with her.

Melanie rolled us over, propping her elbow on my chest and resting her head on her hand.

"Still don't want to tell me what's wrong?"

I didn't want to ruin tonight with Troy's ugly words or my fear of how much I felt for her and how fast, or my yearning to just say fuck it all, and ask her to permanently move in with us. I wanted to bask in her love tonight without worrying about how's or what if's.

"Nothing's wrong. I just wanted to get to this part of my day a hell of a lot faster."

"Maybe you need to relax." She brushed a light kiss against my lips before peppering tiny kisses along my jaw. I grabbed at a fistful of her hair when she nipped her way down my throat, dragging the hem of my T-shirt up, her nails tracing the ink across my ribs.

I arched my back off the bed when her lips moved to my stomach, reaching to help her as she fumbled with my belt buckle. A growl erupted from deep in my throat when she took me in her mouth, bobbing her head slowly as she worshipped every inch of me. She pressed against my chest every time I tried to sit up, and the vibrations ricocheting down my legs every time she moaned around my cock made me want to both beg her to stop and grab the back of her head to go deeper.

"I'm going to come hard, baby. Please…" My eyes clenched

shut as I trailed off. Melanie's only reply was a shake of her head as she sucked harder.

My head fell back as I bit the inside of my cheek to hold back a roar as I spilled down her throat.

I chased my breath as I waited for the feeling to come back in my legs.

She chuckled as she climbed back up my body. I was still nothing but a wet noodle against the sheets.

"Sometimes, I just like taking care of you. You've waited too long for that." She kissed me, close-mouthed but slow, my neck jerking up as my lips wanted more of hers.

"Maybe I waited too long for you."

I rolled back on top of her and kissed her slowly, my erection coming back to life before either of us expected it. I went slow, despite how desperate we were for each other. I took my time to taste and touch every inch of her, making us both insane with need until we collapsed onto the mattress. Melanie cuddled into my chest, murmuring, "I love you," before her breathing slowed with sleep.

My eyes were still wide open as I threaded my fingers through her hair. A woman I'd only known for a few months had turned me inside out after I'd spent years of making sure I was as detached as possible.

Maybe I needed to focus on the quality not quantity of time and forget my impatience for wanting more.

MELANIE

The howling wind woke me from a dead sleep. It took my tired eyes a minute to register the blur of white through Matteo's bedroom window. I laughed to myself, guessing Matteo and his family had never experienced a Thanksgiving snowstorm. I couldn't remember a Thanksgiving growing up when there hadn't been snow on the ground, but my college friends from New York were all so shocked at how early snow appeared in New England. I'd bet all the kids would be begging to head outside to play in it right after they woke up.

When I sat up to check the time on my phone, an arm around my waist pulled me back.

"Where do you think you're going?" Matteo's grumbly whisper in my ear sent a trail of goosebumps down my neck.

Despite knowing it was probably later than we should be getting up, I cuddled into him and the morning poke into my back I'd gotten all too used to.

"We need to get up. There's a lot to do, and I'm sure the kids want break—"

I trailed off when Matteo's hand traveled up my shirt—his shirt. I still hadn't put on my own pajamas since I'd been here as I was high on wearing his clothes, along with being high on him in general. He traced a slow circle around my nipple with his finger before gliding his hand down my torso, slipping it into the pair of boxers I'd stolen from him that first night.

"Already wet, Princess? You must have been dreaming about the same thing I was." His lips drifted down my neck while my legs fell open. With Matteo's mouth and hands on me the time of day and anything else about reality faded away. Nothing had ever been this good.

It was so good, it almost made me forget my worries from last night. Something was weighing on Matteo even though he'd denied it. He'd made love to me slowly, almost making me scream in anticipation, but there was a desperation to it. It seemed as if he feared I'd vanish in his arms. I knew the feeling, since my new problem was being afraid to get any closer to him and yet scared he'd slip away. Both urges were ridiculous but they gnawed at me, often at the same time.

Our lips came together in a deep, needy kiss as he yanked the boxers off of me so quickly, I thought I'd heard them tear.

"We need to be fast."

His lips curled in a dirty grin, pulling away from me to reach inside his nightstand. By the time he rolled back over, his shorts were off and the condom was already down his length.

"If we need to be fast, Princess, you drive."

He flipped us over so that I was on top.

"Door's still locked?"

I sank down on him the second after he nodded, his teeth digging into his bottom lip as I moved up and down, quickly and softly, trying not to make the mattress creak.

"That's my girl," he rasped, sitting up and wrapping his arms around my waist as his hips bucked off the bed, the new angle of friction hitting a spot that brought a guttural moan out of me. I went faster while covering my own mouth in case a scream that I couldn't hold in escaped.

"I'll give you something to do with that mouth," Matteo whispered, cupping my neck and dragging my mouth to his. The rushing combined with the intensity sent me over the edge fast, my legs going rigid as I dug my nails into Matteo's muscular shoulders for balance. He grasped my hips and groaned into my mouth as he pulsed inside me.

We sat still for a long moment, trying to be as quiet as possible while getting a hold of our rapid breathing.

"That's a good start to a holiday." He gazed up at me with a throaty chuckle. "Happy Thanksgiving." He pulled me in for a soft kiss. "I'm so glad you're here."

There was that look again, adoration mixed with fear. No man had ever viewed me as if I was his lifeline and he was afraid to let me out of his arms. He should know how much I never wanted to be anywhere else.

"I'm glad I'm here, too." I sifted my hand through his damp hair and dropped my forehead against his. "We need to get up."

As if on cue, two loud knocks pounded on the other side of the door.

"Daddy, are we still making pancakes today?"

Before Matteo could answer Lauren, another little voice asked, "Could I have French toast, too?"

"She's got backup." Matteo chuckled, rubbing his temple.

I laughed at the shake of his head as I climbed off of his lap. I pulled on his shorts and a bra from the drawer as Matteo quickly cleaned himself up. It had taken me a few days to unpack my suitcase and use the space he'd cleared out for me, and I still was afraid to move beyond two drawers.

If only my torturous brain took holidays off.

"Lyndee, honey, this isn't the restaurant." Dominic's stern voice drifted in from the hallway. "Matteo isn't one of the cooks who works for Daddy and can make you whatever you ask for. You and Lauren can choose one thing for breakfast, and that's it."

"What about bacon?" I heard Dominic's son, Luca, ask on a yawn.

"I guess the long trip didn't make anyone want to sleep in," Matteo sighed before he opened the door.

"Good morning, everyone." He bent to kiss Lauren's forehead. "French toast and pancakes aren't a big deal. Happy to accommodate our guests." He tapped Dominic's arm before heading downstairs with all three kids running behind him.

"My cousin is going to wear himself out before the turkey," Dominic leaned against the doorframe with a smirk.

"He's great like that. Always tries to make everyone happy." A wide smile stretched my lips as I walked toward Dominic because of how happy Matteo always made *me*. "I'm here to help in case he gets overwhelmed."

"I'm glad you are," Dominic said, his smile fading before following everyone downstairs.

While everyone was distracted, I headed to the bathroom to give myself a quick once over. After smoothing my hair back into a ponytail, I splashed some water on my face before changing out of Matteo's clothes and into leggings and a hoodie. I'd been having breakfast in his T-shirt and shorts all week, but with his extended family here it seemed a little too intimate. On the inside, where it was only us, it felt so right, but I could see how others might perceive it as wrong and too fast.

I'd only known this man since the end of August, and he and his daughter had become the nucleus of my life. It should've set off panic, but it didn't. The only sense of dread I experienced came when I thought about going back to my apartment. This was a glorious long vacation, but it would come to an end before I knew it. And to hold on to some semblance of self-preservation, it had to.

Matteo already had breakfast going when I came into the kitchen. The kids congregated at the dining room table with Dominic and Thea, Lauren's voice the loudest, of course.

"You even have coffee going." His cheeks lifted with a smile when I kissed the back of his neck. "How can I help?"

"Ask the monsters to get the toys off of the table so we can eat." He slid a spatula under a pancake and added it to the pile on the plate next to the stove. "I only need a few more minutes." He caught my gaze before he flipped the French toast, a tiny smile drifting over his lips. "I like seeing you like that."

"Like what?" I chuckled, crossing my arms before I leaned back on the counter. "A mess?" I laughed as I reached back to tighten my ponytail.

He lowered the heat on the stove before stalking over to me. "Comfortable. Beautiful." He cradled my cheek, drifting his thumb over my lips. "Mine."

"Is the coffee ready?" Dominic trudged into the kitchen, bending to peer into the almost full coffee pot. "I need to wake up before I can enjoy all this country living. Don't stop on my account." His lips curved up when he glanced back at us. "Where are your mugs?"

"In the cabinet on top of the coffee maker," Matteo answered with his arm snaked around my waist. "If the coffee is ready, feel free to take it to the dining room. Breakfast, in all its forms, is almost ready."

"Can I have sausage too, Matteo? Or is it too late?" Luca ran into the kitchen, shooting his father a sheepish look.

"Already covered, little man." Matteo laughed. "Are the girls giving you any trouble?"

He shrugged. "The sleeping bag was cool, even if it was for girls. I wish Lyndee would let me sleep by myself." He leaned his head on Dominic's hip.

"You're a good brother," Dominic said before he bent to kiss his cheek.

The more I looked at Luca, the more he reminded me of both Dominic and Matteo. The same thick, deep brown hair, olive skin, and soulful chocolate eyes.

"She has Lauren this weekend, so you can hang with Matteo and me if they get to be too much."

Luca nodded and moped back into the dining room.

"Poor guy." Matteo sighed and shook his head at me. "Our two girl cousins used to do that to me *all* the time. Dominic was older, so he'd walk away for me to deal with it." Matteo shot him a glare.

"But think how well all that Barbie training paid off. I did you a favor." Dominic poured the coffee into a mug and quickly took a sip. "You're welcome."

Dominic and Matteo seemed more like brothers than cousins. When we sat down to breakfast, my stomach hurt from laughing at all their jabs back and forth.

"I need to give Aunt Netta a call," Matteo said around a mouthful of bacon. "She called when I was at work this week, but I never got back to her. Have you spoken to her lately?"

"I have. She's fine. Call her tomorrow," Dominic said.

Thea's smile faded as she poured Lyndee some orange juice.

"Not call her on Thanksgiving?" Matteo's eyes narrowed before he turned to me. "Aunt Netta is this sweet at first, little old Italian lady. She knows everything about everyone and can take down any of us with one sentence."

"She's basically Lauren in support stockings," Dominic muttered around the rim of his mug.

"I know better than to not call her on a holiday, especially with the lecture I got from the whole family before I moved up here about staying in touch."

"Guys, why don't you go play in Lauren's room for a little while. Maybe we can play in the snow a little before dinner," Thea said to the kids.

"Okay, I'm full." Lauren said. "Let's play the princess story game!"

Lyndee squealed while poor Luca grumbled as they pulled him off of his chair.

Matteo glanced back and turned to Dominic when the kids were out of sight.

"What don't you want Aunt Netta to tell me until tomorrow?"

Dominic and Thea shared a tense look before Dominic took a deep breath.

"Netta was shopping in your old neighborhood and ran into Callie last week."

My stomach dropped as Matteo's jaw went slack.

"Callie? That doesn't make any sense. The last I heard she lives in Florida."

"She's back and looking for a job."

"She told Netta all this?" Matteo's body was rigid as he waited for Dominic's reply.

"No, she didn't get the chance." Dominic snickered. "Netta approached her in the store, berated her for leaving her baby without a word and told her she was a disgusting human being."

"You've got to be kidding me," Matteo said, still squinting at Dominic.

"My father was with her and gave me the play by play. She drew a little bit of a crowd. I'll be honest, usually I pity anyone unfortunate enough to be on the receiving end of Netta's wrath, but this time I wish I'd been there to applaud. Anyway, she called your parents to tell them, who then got in touch with Callie's parents, who confirmed that she was back." He let out a long sigh and turned to me. "Our family is spread out, but we all connect the dots quickly when we have to."

Matteo was unreadable as he crossed his arms and leaned back in the chair.

"And my parents didn't say a word." He sat stoic, his eyes on Dominic. "And you wouldn't have either."

"They would have, Matty. But why ruin your first holiday up here? I'm actually glad you guys moved and won't risk running into her," Dominic said.

Matteo didn't reply as he dug into his pancakes. An eerie silence fell over the table, a big contrast to how boisterous it had been only minutes earlier. I studied Matteo's face, trying to decipher what he was feeling. Right now, I guessed he was pissed off that his family had kept this from him. But he was so affected by how Callie left them both, he still had trouble talking about it.

"Hey, I'm sorry." Dominic set down his fork and leaned his

elbows onto the table. "I guess we didn't want you to worry about it until you had to. Netta forced our hands, but we should have been honest from the beginning. We all hated what she put you through and didn't want you to relive any of it. Forgive us. Please."

Matteo lifted his coffee mug to his lips, the room so quiet we could hear him swallow.

"I'm just impressed you managed to keep your mouth shut about something." Matteo turned to me, the side of his mouth curled up. "That isn't his thing," he told me in a loud whisper.

Thea fell back in her chair with a relieved smile.

"We *are* sorry, Matt. I wanted to tell you, but after seeing you so happy when we got here, I didn't want to ruin it, either."

"You didn't. I get why you didn't say anything. And I'm glad I'm spared from seeing her on the street and having to explain to Lauren who she is. I may have to eventually, it's not like we'll never set foot in New York again. But who knows if she'll even stay. As far as my daughter and me, we've moved away and moved on." He stood and lifted his plate and mug from the table. "And I have a turkey to kill for dinner, so if you'll all excuse me." He snuck me a grin before heading into the kitchen.

I smiled back despite my heart fluttering against my ribcage. The past couple of weeks we'd spent playing house were just that —playing. We both still had our own demons to slay, and I feared his was haunting him more than he let on.

MATTEO

"I love it," Dominic mused as he peered out my back door as all the kids ran back and forth through the snow in my yard. Melanie and Thea tried to help them make snow people, but all they cared about was throwing the fresh white snow back and forth and diving into it.

"Love it?" I laughed as I shoved the last of the dishes into the dishwasher. Dinner had been a group effort, but all I wanted for the rest of the day was to sit on the couch with a beer and watch whatever football game was on. "They're going to come back in filthy and soaking wet."

"And exhausted." He shut his eyes and smiled before leaning against the glass. "I once told the twins there was a fly in the house and made buzzing sounds so they'd run back and forth. They napped for two hours that day."

"Where would I be without your great parenting example?" I reached into the fridge and pulled out two beers, handing one to Dominic and gesturing toward the living room.

"My God, even the beer is better here." He eyed the bottle in his hand after he took a sip. "This is local?"

I nodded. "We serve it at Speakeasy. If you guys want to stop there for lunch tomorrow, we can. The menu is sick, I think you'd love it."

"We'll see. Lauren keeps talking about these amazing pretzels on every video call, so I thought we'd take the kids to that place."

"Busy Bean? Yeah, we can stop there, too."

"So," Dominic set the bottle on one of the coffee table coasters before leaning forward. "How long has Melanie been staying here?"

"A couple of weeks. Her apartment has plumbing issues, so she hasn't been able to go back." I turned back to the TV screen, ignoring Dominic's narrowed eyes in my periphery.

"You guys seem close."

"We are," I said, noting the defensive edge to my voice. "I know it's fast."

"Matty, I didn't think you'd ever be close with anyone, at least while Lauren was still little. I'm not judging you at all. In fact, I'm happy as hell for you. Maybe we're all a little too protective of both of you and don't want to see you guys get hurt."

"I know, and I appreciate that. Melanie is…" I trailed off, trying to put into a few words all I felt about her. "Neither of us went into this lightly. There's a lot of risk. She works for me here and at Speakeasy. Although, since I told them about us, she reports to the general manager now."

My gaze drifted outside to where Melanie stood with Luca.

"It's just…I never thought life would be this good. I was happy with only my daughter, but Melanie just makes it all better. I can't explain it any other way. Loving someone after what happened to us isn't something I thought could happen again. But once it did, I would have been an idiot to ignore it."

"All true." Dominic's lips curved up. "Is she on the same page as you are? I know she's a little younger."

"That crossed my mind at first, too," I admitted. "But she's the opposite of Callie. She knows what she wants and is getting her master's in education. She loves kids, and Lauren fell in love with her on sight."

I took a long pull from the bottle, trying to quell the fluttering of nerves every time I thought of Callie back in New York. She hadn't spoken to her parents since she left, or so I'd been told. And it made me uneasy when I thought of her finding out where we were. I couldn't see her having any kind of interest in Lauren now, but the truth was, I didn't know anything about her now. Maybe I never did.

"I should have tried harder to make Callie sign over her rights," I blurted and ran a hand down my face.

"This is why none of us wanted to tell you, yet." He heaved an audible sigh. "How could you make her sign if you couldn't find her?"

He let out a heavy sigh as he leaned back. "I'll be honest, even before she split on you guys, I was never a fan. It was always obvious to me that she was all about herself, so while I hated when she left you and Lauren, I wasn't surprised." He downed the rest of his beer before pushing off the couch.

"She's probably home because she ran out of money and will be back on the road to wherever soon. I know it's hard, but try not to think about it, at least for today. You're surrounded by people who love you, one who loves you so much that she's helping take care of extra kids." He nodded toward the backyard with a chuckle. "And now, I'm getting a second one." He held up the bottle and walked back to my kitchen just as the screen door opened and everyone rushed back inside.

"That was fun!" Lauren was about to charge at me before Melanie pulled her back to take off her boots.

"Yes, it was a blast. But how about we head upstairs first and get all those icky wet clothes off, Laur? The twins are doing the same."

I laughed at both Lauren and Melanie as I headed toward them. The bottoms of their pants were soaked from running in the snow, even with boots on. The sight of them giggling with the same red cheeks and big smiles made my chest swell.

"Lauren is going to need a whole outfit change." Melanie

peeled off Lauren's hat, the wet ends of Lauren's hair now sticking to her sweatshirt sleeves. "Come on, girlie." They rushed past me to climb the stairs.

Melanie and I hadn't had a minute alone since this morning. I hoped that she wasn't jumping to a ton of conclusions after watching the blood drain out of my face at breakfast.

I followed them up the stairs, laughing at Lauren's request to go back outside later as she let out a loud yawn.

"I think we've all had enough snow for today. We have lots of dessert and hot chocolate. Maybe we can watch a movie in the living room if the twins are up to it."

I stepped into Lauren's room just as Melanie pulled Lauren's Belle sweatshirt over her head. Lauren's brow furrowed as she looked down.

"Does your friend Belle at work have a Belle sweatshirt? She should have one if that's her name."

Melanie and I shared a laugh over Lauren's shoulder.

"I don't know but if we go to Speakeasy for lunch tomorrow, you can ask her yourself. I'm sure she'd come out of the kitchen for a minute."

Belle was one of our chefs, and the reason why Ty had been so amiable about taking over Melanie's schedule when I told him and Alec about us. He knew how getting tangled up with someone you worked with caused a slew of complications.

"Tell you what, Cookie." I crouched down in front of Lauren. "Why don't you go downstairs and ask the twins what movie they want to watch?"

"Can we pick two?" She folded her hands under her chin.

My daughter had a future as a lawyer, always negotiating for a mile once she got an inch.

"I think you guys will be lucky if you make it through one." I kissed the top of her head. "I want to talk to Melanie for a second."

"Oh." She shrugged and scurried off.

"I better go change," she said, giving me a quick kiss before scooping Lauren's wet clothes off of the floor. "Give me a minute."

I followed her into my bedroom and caught her hand when she tried to close the door before I could enter.

"Are you sure fooling around with all the kids awake is a good idea?" She shot me a playful grin that didn't quite make it to her eyes before wrapping her arms around my waist.

"That's why doors have locks, Princess." I delved my hand into her hair. "Everything okay?"

Her gaze broke from mine as she gave me an unconvincing nod.

"Come on, talk to me. I'm sure you have questions about the bomb Dominic dropped at breakfast."

"I don't have questions, it's just…" She lifted her eyes to mine, biting her lip. "I'm worried about you."

I shook my head and grabbed her hands.

"There is nothing to be worried about. I promise."

She tilted her head, a frown pulling down her lips.

"You went pale the minute Dominic said Callie's name. Knowing she's this close has to be bothering you."

"It's more of a shock than anything else. I doubt very much she came back to the Bronx for either of us. But you're right, I don't like knowing she's back, even though she's still far enough away from us." I drifted my hand up and down her back, air escaping my lungs again as I tensed up thinking about it.

I searched Melanie's gaze, looking for any signs that she believed what I said. The last thing I wanted was doubt between us. As much as I'd tried to keep our life here a new, separate beginning from all of that, I should've known the past would catch up to us eventually.

"I love you," I whispered as I framed her face. "You know that, right?"

"Of course, I do. I love you, too. You can talk to me about this, you know. I won't go crazy jealous or anything."

"Really?" I cocked my head to the side. "That's kind of disappointing."

I kissed her again when she shoved my shoulder.

"So," I began, backing Melanie up against the mattress and settling on top of her when she fell. "We have cake and cookies, tired kids, and no work or school tomorrow. I want to celebrate the rest of my first Thanksgiving in my new house with my family and the woman I love, which is you."

She peered up at me, her eyes hazy as a slow grin stretched her lips.

"This has been the *best* Thanksgiving I've ever had." She reached up to wrap her arms around my neck.

"Wait until later." I hooked her leg over my hip. "When everyone is asleep, we'll make it a fucking *spectacular* Thanksgiving." I flicked the seam of her lips with my tongue so they'd open for me. She moaned into my mouth and tightened her leg around me.

This had been my best Thanksgiving, too. I'd meant it when I told Dominic that I never thought life could be this good. I only hoped it stayed that way.

MELANIE

"Who needs a gym?" Grace laughed next to me. "From the kitchen to the bar to the tables, I'm spent!" She let out a long exhale, tucking a stray blonde wave behind her ear.

I nodded as I leaned against the bar waiting for my drink order. Weekends were getting crazier, and I expected Speakeasy to be packed all the way to New Year's. My shift seemed to whir by faster each night.

"You better not get too tired, you have to sing later, right?"

She shook her head. "Ty is going to DJ until open mic night starts. So, I get a break." She smiled back at me. "Unless no one volunteers. If you can sing, feel free to head up there."

She laughed at the slow shake of my head as I lined up my drinks on the tray.

"Um, no. Not even a little. I only sing in my car or the shower where no one can hear me."

"You're not so bad." My head jerked to Matteo's husky whisper. "Although, that one time I was in there with you, I remember a high-pitched scream, not a song."

His lips curled in a wry grin as he leaned his elbows onto the counter.

I swiveled to make sure Grace was out of earshot. My cheeks

flushed hot as his head fell on the counter, the bastard's shoulders shaking with a laugh.

We still attracted lingering looks whenever we chatted at work, but I didn't feel the need to avoid him anymore when we had the same shift. We were a confirmed rumor, and I guessed when you removed the speculation, gossiping about an established couple wasn't as much fun. The interest in M&M seemed to wane now that we weren't such a scandal.

"Just because management knows doesn't mean you can get all cute with me at the bar," I scolded in a loud whisper.

"Cute?" His smile grew wider. "All I am is cute to you?"

"No, now you're annoying. Keep it up, and I'll tell Ty and Grace you play guitar."

His brow pinched when I gestured to the stage.

"How do you know I play guitar?"

"Lauren told me you used to play but haven't since you moved here. She showed me where you keep it hidden away in the basement." I dropped a hand on my hip and narrowed my eyes. "Maybe I'll volunteer you, anyway."

"You play the guitar? Seriously?"

I turned toward the deep chuckle next to me. A tall, burly man with a buzz cut settled into a bar stool beside me, cracking a grin and rolling his eyes in Matteo's direction.

"Because looking like *that* isn't enough? I'm Oz, and I'm guessing by that little exchange I couldn't help but overhear, you must be Melanie."

I laughed and took his extended hand. "I am, nice to meet you."

"For someone who works in a bar, you come here enough." Matteo grumbled but didn't hide the twitch at the corners of his lips. "Oz usually stops by on weeknights."

"It's a different experience when you aren't a customer and can just drink and people watch." He shrugged before turning back to me. "I work at Vino and Veritas in Burlington, but my boyfriend and I like a change of scenery." Oz glanced at his watch.

"He's a little late, so I can annoy the hot rock star back there to pass the time. You should meet Reeve when he gets here. He works at the bookstore, and Matteo told me you're a big reader. He's excited about this classics section he's working on, and talking about it with someone like you would be nicer than someone like me who wants to listen but doesn't appreciate it enough to pay attention."

"That would be awesome. Come find me when he gets here." I nodded a thank you to R.D. when he set the last glass of wine on my tray. "I better get going. Nice to meet you." I glanced at Matteo's beaming smile one more time before I headed back to my table, my cheeks aching with my own wide grin.

When my break finally came, I was grateful to fall into one of the chairs and read a book for pleasure for a change. As I dug out my e-reader, I groaned when my phone buzzed in my back pocket. The groan turned into a wince when I read Mrs. Evans's name on the screen.

"Hi, Mrs. Evans. Everything okay?"

"Hi, sweetie. I wish I had better news for you, but we still can't get the plumbing to work upstairs. The plumber told me it's something to do with the way the pipes burst, but I'm not smart enough to follow what he's saying. All I understood was that he had no way of knowing when it would be fixed, or if it could be. I hate to put this on you, but it may be a good idea to start looking for another place to live."

My stomach leaped then plummeted. The apartment wasn't the best place to live, but it was mine. And now I had to figure out if I wanted to hunt for a place that was in my price range, which was next to impossible, or stay put.

My head fell into my hands as my throat almost closed with panic.

My light mood dissipated in a rush as I tried to get lost in work for the rest of the night. I caught Matteo's concerned gaze a few times as I zipped back and forth, not stopping to chat as I usually did.

I didn't see him again until he waited for me by the breakroom at the end of the night. I gave him a weak smile as we headed to the parking lot and climbed into his truck.

"Are you okay?" Matteo asked, reaching over the console as he drove to grab my hand and lace our fingers together.

"Just tired. Once finals are over I can relax. Sort of." I tried to force a smile.

"Stop worrying." Matteo shot me a quick glance as he drove, his dark eyes swimming with love and concern. "You're going to ace every class this semester, and you know it. Don't stress yourself out, Princess."

I nodded. Despite my current crippling panic, warmth always flooded my chest whenever he called me Princess.

"Are you sure that's it?" He let go of my hand and squeezed my knee. "You're not yourself."

I leaned my heavy head against the car window, watching the bare trees filled with snow whir by.

"Mrs. Evans called me earlier. She managed to get the house plumbing up and running, but for some reason, the water still won't work in my apartment, and they can't figure out what's wrong. She suggested looking for another place."

"Well, I can't say that I'm surprised. I don't even think that was supposed to be an apartment in the first place."

I nodded. I shouldn't have been this upset when I'd been expecting this call. Losing my apartment put Matteo and me in a place I'd been trying to avoid. While staying with him indefinitely made my life easier, it also made it a hell of a lot more complicated.

I'd had my eyes shut for so long, I didn't realize we were back at Matteo's house until he stopped the truck and shut off the engine.

"So, what's on your mind? Are you afraid I'll throw you out?" He quirked a brow when I turned toward him. "I told you that you could stay with me as long as you needed to. I haven't been that unbearable to live with, have I?"

I huffed out a laugh and shook my head.

"No, that's the problem. I think I've—*we've* gotten too comfortable. We'd barely gotten together, then I basically moved in right after. For two people so damn gun shy about relationships, I'm not sure if that was the healthiest thing to do."

His smile faded into a frown before he stepped out of the truck. I almost wished I could take back what I'd said, but it was the truth. I both wished he'd seen my point and hoped he disagreed with me. I followed him inside, waving a hello at Carol before I headed upstairs. I hadn't wanted to be rude, but I didn't have energy to chat. And I couldn't quite look Matteo in the eye yet.

I checked on Lauren and smiled. If I left, I'd miss her early morning greetings. She always had so much to say before she even ate breakfast. And I'd miss how she'd climb into bed with us on weekend mornings to watch TV. I loved it here and didn't want to leave, but I couldn't help the nagging feeling that I should.

I got ready for bed, pulling on the shirt and shorts I still hadn't given back to Matteo and climbed in. I yanked the covers up to my nose, breathing everything in. If I wasn't supposed to be here, why did it feel so much like home?

I didn't turn around when Matteo's side of the bed dipped. Where would I go? If I moved anywhere else, I needed to find a roommate, and I'd had less than stellar experiences in college with anyone I had to share a dorm room with. The only person I was able to live with without issues was the gorgeous man I'd just hurt about twenty minutes ago.

I jumped when he slid his arm under me and rolled me over to face him.

"Do you want to leave?"

My breath caught when his eyes bore into mine. I wanted to look away, but there was no way I could.

I dragged a hand down my face and heaved out a frustrated sigh.

"Don't you think this is too soon for me to live here? Shouldn't we—"

"I don't give a shit about what you should do or what I should do. I'm asking what you *want* to do." He ran the back of his hand down my cheek. "So, I'll ask you again, do you want to leave?"

That stupid lump popped up in the back of my throat again. I should've said, "Yes, I do," because it made the most sense. Yet, I could only shake my head.

He peered down at me, a slow smile lifting his lips.

"And I sure as hell don't want you to leave. So, why are we both moping around?" He settled on top of me, my legs falling open for him as they always did.

"I agree that it's fast, especially since we took so long to figure everything out at the beginning. But now that we have…" He cupped my cheek and dragged his thumb across my lips. "I don't want you to go. Ever. I was rooting for Mrs. Evans to condemn the damn place."

I shoved his shoulder and tried to squirm out from under him when he pressed his lips to mine. Our kiss caught fire, his tongue making long sweeps inside my mouth as my knees liquified against his mattress.

"Matteo," I groaned and bucked my hips off the bed when his hand slid inside my panties.

"Doesn't feel like you want to leave, either. Stay with me, Princess," he hissed, his eyes hooded and glazed with want.

With every swirl of his finger around my clit, my vision clouded, along with my judgment. Yes, it felt amazing to be here and, yes, I loved him a very short time after swearing I wouldn't fall so hard and so fast again, but as safe as he always made me feel, I couldn't shake the fear.

My heartbeat kicked up to match the throb now pounding between my legs. I fisted the comforter next to me as I fell, coming hard against his hand.

He broke away from me to peel off his shirt and yank down my shorts and panties in one swoop. He crooked his finger at me to sit up, and I straightened, reaching my hands in the air for Matteo to get rid of my shirt.

"Christ, you're beautiful," he whispered, holding my gaze as he felt around his nightstand drawer and grabbed a foil packet.

He slid inside me as soon as he rolled the condom on, moving faster and harder than he usually did at first. Our lips were unco-ordinated and sloppy as we pawed at each other to get as close as possible. I threw my arms around his neck and held on, his fast pace and deep thrusts making me gasp, my toes already curling as he hit that spot no one had seemed to be able to find before him. It felt like a promise and a claiming at the same time, and I was powerless to refuse either one.

My legs went rigid a second time as I mewled into his shoul-der, the second orgasm barreling over me faster than the first. Matteo stiffened above me, collapsing into the crook of my shoulder as he tightened his hold around me.

He rained kisses down my face, across my eyelids and cheeks before coming back to my lips, brushing them gently before climbing off the bed.

When he came back, he cinched his arms around me from behind and pulled me back.

"I love you. More than you know, Princess. Relax and sleep," he whispered, pressing a kiss to the nape of my neck before his breathing slowed behind me.

"I love you, too," I said, running my fingers back and forth over where his hand rested against my stomach.

How could I sleep anywhere else and give all of this up?

I couldn't, and that was the scariest part of it all.

MATTEO

"We should discuss rent."

The fork of eggs in my hand stilled right before it got to my mouth at Melanie's request.

"Seriously?"

She set her coffee mug on the table, shooting me a glare that was as funny as it was hot. But I'd only piss her off if I let out the laugh I was holding in.

Lauren sat across from us, slurping her milk and stabbing at her tablet screen with the tip of her finger, oblivious to anything else.

"Yes, seriously. I'm not getting a free ride here if I stay."

"If?" I put my fork down and sat back. "Are we back on this, again?"

The most adorable growl escaped her as she glowered at me.

"I will contribute somehow. Groceries, utilities, you cut my pay, something."

"You need that for tuition. Aren't there live-in baby-sitters or nannies who have room and board included? There, all settled."

"Live-in nannies have their own room. They don't sleep with —" Her gaze flicked to Lauren before she rubbed her temple. "Let's just say no, that's not the answer."

I bit my lip to stifle a laugh.

"If it makes you feel better to buy groceries sometimes, go ahead."

"You're not listening to me." She shot up from the chair. "To feel comfortable staying here, I need to give you something. It's important to me, so stop laughing it off!"

"I'm not laughing it off. Come here." I stood and pulled her into my arms. "I'm sorry." I kissed her cheek when she turned away from me. "We'll work something out that you can afford. I don't want you to struggle just to prove a point." I raised my hand when her nostrils flared. "But it's important to you, so, we'll figure it out." I dipped my head to meet her gaze. "Okay?"

I tightened my hold around her, her arms still at her sides. Her eyes narrowed, but I caught the beginning of a smile.

"Okay. But I mean it."

"I know you do. And I want you to be as comfortable as possible here. So tonight we'll work out how. I promise."

I'd take the money she'd insist on giving me and set it aside for her. I understood her need to contribute, and I loved that about her, but I didn't need the money. And I knew she did, even if she fought me.

She brushed my lips and carried her dishes to the sink. I watched her as she walked, biting on my bottom lip to stop the huge smile that wanted to break out. My girl was here to stay. I'd agree to whatever semantics she wanted.

"Someone's knocking on the door," Lauren said, still not looking up from the screen.

"I didn't hear anything."

Sure enough, the doorbell rang. I found it a little strange that someone would knock before ringing the bell. When I peeked through the side window, all I saw was the back of someone's head.

"Can I help you?" I asked as I opened the door. When the woman at the door turned, my stomach dropped as her big brown eyes met mine.

"Hi, Matteo."

"Callie?"

I blinked a few times, sure I was hallucinating. I'd been afraid of this ever since I'd heard she'd come back to New York but tried to brush it off as ridiculous because why would she search for us after all this time?

She looked exactly the same. Maybe a little tired and worn out judging by the dark circles around her eyes as she stepped back and forth, as if she was unsure whether to stay or run.

"How?" was the only word I could force out. *Why* was the stronger question, but my brain was struggling to catch up.

"My parents gave me your new address, but I don't think they expected me to come here."

"That makes all of us." I closed the door behind me, praying that whatever video Lauren was watching held her interest long enough for me to get her mother to leave our front porch. Callie's parents stayed involved in Lauren's life, and from what I'd known, until recently, they hadn't been in touch with their daughter since she'd left. I bristled at their inconsideration. If they'd given Callie our address, a heads-up on one of our weekend calls would have been nice.

"I know you're angry, and I have some explaining to do—"

"Some? It took you five years to *clear your head*, I guess?"

I crossed my arms over my chest, trying to slow my breathing as I remembered finally getting a hold of her sister when Callie stopped returning my calls, only to have her tell me that Callie wasn't coming back to either of us.

So why the hell was she here now?

"Look, you don't owe me anything. But I want to see her. I don't deserve it." Her voice cracked. "Can we go inside and talk at least? Ten minutes." Her lip quivered as she lifted a sheepish shoulder.

I exhaled a slow breath, rubbing my eyes and wishing it were five minutes ago.

"Give me a minute. Stay here."

I closed the door behind me before jetting into the kitchen. Melanie spotted me as she was loading the dishwasher and rushed over.

"What happened?" She clutched the sides of my face. "Who was at the door?"

"Callie is on the porch," I told her in a shaky whisper, fighting to keep my voice even. "She wants to talk for ten minutes, but I don't want Lauren to see her. Can you take her up to her room and distract her for a little while?"

Melanie's eyes were wide as she nodded.

"Did she say what she wants?"

I shook my head. "Just that she wants to see Lauren, but I'm not ready to agree to that yet, or ever. I want her out of here, and I think talking to her is the only way."

Melanie's brow furrowed as she nodded, a flash of concern ran across her face and only made me feel worse. I'd deal with that in fifteen minutes after I'd hopefully had convinced Callie to go and never come back.

I watched Melanie whisper something in Lauren's ear and hold out her hand. My daughter had no clue who was on the other side of the door. She followed Melanie upstairs without a worry or care, and it sickened me to think how that might change.

Callie jumped when the door opened, her face crumpling as if she'd start crying with gratitude.

"Ten minutes," I said as I held the door open. "Lauren is upstairs, but she's staying up there until you leave."

Her shoulders drooped as if she were about to argue, but she only nodded and came inside.

"This is a nice house," she said, sweeping her gaze over the living room before she took a tentative seat on the couch. "I heard you're a bartender up here."

"Bar manager," I corrected. "But it's not important, and I'm sure you didn't drive five hours to make small talk with me." I sat on my recliner, leaning my elbows on my knees as I studied her.

Lauren had always resembled her mother, but seeing Callie

again highlighted what were almost overwhelming similarities. Lauren's brown hair had shades of red when the light hit it just right, and her long lashes grazed her eyebrows just like Callie's did. Her eyes lifted to mine and then darted away, just like Lauren did whenever she thought she was in trouble or was trying to ask for something she knew she wouldn't get.

"I've been thinking about you both and the awful way that I left. I was messed up for a long time. It was all…too much for me back then." Her voice cracked as she wiped at her nose with a tissue.

Too much. Lauren and I had been too much for her—her fiancé and her daughter. The anger I'd done my best to bury all these years threatened to boil over, my insides already churning as I watched Callie squirm on my couch.

"I'm not the great parent you always were, and I will never be worthy of her."

"It's not a question of being worthy of her." I fell back, holding in the frustration now exhausting me. "It's doing right by her because that's what you're supposed to do. The best gift you gave her was leaving early enough so that she wouldn't remember you. And now you want to take that back? I won't let you hurt her."

She shook her head, still sniffing into the crumpled tissue.

"I wouldn't…I don't even want visitation rights."

"Good, because you wouldn't get them."

Her eyes shut as she nodded.

"I just want her to know me a little. Maybe we could talk on the phone sometimes. I could see her for a bit when you go home to visit your family. I know it's terrible to even ask that, but I'll take whatever time you'd let me have."

She pulled a piece of paper out of her purse and scribbled something.

"I checked into the Motorlodge in town for a couple of days. That's my cell phone number. I'll accept any decision you make."

She dropped the paper on the table, sliding her purse on her shoulder before standing and heading for the door. I followed, almost ramming into her when she stopped short at Lauren's school picture.

"Oh my God," she gasped, her quivering hand covering her mouth. "She's beautiful. My parents had some photos, but this must be new."

I nodded. "Her kindergarten school picture. She's gorgeous, smart, and sweet."

"Of course she is. She has you." She glanced back at me and then turned back to the photo. "She's a really good combo of us. Me from the eyes up, you from the nose down."

An unexpected smile snuck across my lips.

"She is," I whispered, cringing when I heard her laugh with Melanie.

Callie's eyes drifted toward the staircase. I'd guess she was registering the two different laughs coming from upstairs. I expected her to comment, but she just nodded and headed out the door.

I trudged over to the staircase and collapsed onto the bottom step. My instinct was to tear up the paper on my coffee table and try to forget about this morning. I could protect my daughter now and take the chance of her being angry with me later when she was old enough to understand that I'd sent her mother away the one time she'd tried to see her.

"Daddy!" Lauren called down the stairs, her eyes big as she plopped next to me. "We need to go shopping. Like right now. Melanie and me just watched a Christmas cookie show, and we have no cookie cutters. None. And Christmas is in two weeks. I'll go get dressed, and you can drive." She stomped up the stairs before I could answer. I turned my head and found Melanie laughing behind her.

"It was the first thing I found." She tiptoed down to where I sat. "I was relieved when it held her interest."

"What happened with Callie?" Melanie sat next to me and leaned in, dipping her head to meet my gaze.

"She's staying at the Motorlodge for a few days and wants to see Lauren for an afternoon. She says she doesn't want visitation or anything, just wants to know her." Saying it out loud made the anxiety rise all over again.

"Well, what are you going to do?"

My head whipped to face her.

"What I'm *not* going to do is introduce her to a mother she'll probably never see again." Melanie reared back after I snapped at her. "We can go into town for cookie cutters. I'll get dressed, and we can leave in a few minutes."

I didn't meet Melanie's watery gaze, just patted her knee before I stood and headed up the stairs.

Protecting my daughter was the single most important priority in my life, but this was the first time I didn't know how.

MELANIE

Matteo was a zombie for the rest of the day, even drawing odd looks from Lauren when we went shopping. I tried over and over again to get him to talk, but all I'd gotten were one-word grunts. This wasn't the sweet, confident man I'd grown to love over the past few months. Callie had rattled him in more ways than just asking to see Lauren, and I wondered if he'd ever be able to face that.

When we arrived back home, Matteo camped out on the recliner, watching football but not appearing to be focused on whatever was happening on the screen. It broke my heart to see him so listless and distant.

His love for Lauren fueled everything he did, including bringing her here to have a better life. While I never doubted that was his main reason, running from a painful past also came into play more than I thought he was able to admit. Now that the past had followed him here, he had no idea what to do with himself. And I didn't know how to reach him.

"Why is Daddy so sad?" Lauren asked me as we finished decorating the cookies. As hard as I tried to wipe up all the edible glitter, I'd be finding bits of it for days.

"Why don't you go cheer him up a little." I nodded toward the living room.

"I can do that." She left the cookie on the table and padded to the living room. I watched as she climbed into his lap and wrapped her little arm around his shoulders. A hint of a smile ghosted his lips before he rested his chin on the top of her head.

The poor guy had an impossible decision to make, but there was more to it. Callie had left them both and hurt them both, and it was harder for Matteo to ignore it now that he'd seen her. He often tried to blow it off, but he was holding in so much anger and resentment, and now that Callie was back, he couldn't ignore it anymore.

I grabbed the hoodie Matteo always kept on a hook by the back door and snuck outside. After I'd just made what felt like the huge decision to move in, it didn't feel so right anymore.

Feeling lost, I called the only friend with enough context to maybe point me in the right direction.

"Hey, Melanie. Are you okay?"

My stomach twisted at the concern in Angie's voice after I'd only said hello.

"Not really. Do you have a few minutes?"

"Yes, of course. Tell me what's wrong."

I went through a shortened version of the story. Agreeing to move in, Callie coming back and asking to see Lauren, Matteo's catatonic state since. I felt guilty telling her his personal business, especially since he'd never shared it with anyone, but I needed to talk to someone about the mess I was suddenly in.

"That poor guy. I can't even imagine what it was like for him back then. No wonder he's rattled. But why are you upset—other than being worried for him and Lauren?"

"I think," I sucked in a gasp of cold air as I leaned on the deck, "I think he needs to face whatever Callie did to both of them while she's here and before we make this kind of commitment. He could barely speak about her to me after knowing each other for months. He needs to figure it out, and he needs to do it alone."

"Are you saying you want to break up?"

"No. God, no." I swallowed a sob before I continued. "I love him, Angie. I know it's only been a short time, but I love him and Lauren so much. There's nothing I want more than to stay here. But I think we need…a break. Take me moving in out of the equation for a little bit while he figures out what to do about Callie. Is that terrible?"

"No. He's not thinking clearly, and maybe this will force him to. Milo made himself a man cave downstairs in the basement with a couch, TV, and his own little bathroom. You can stay there as long as you need to."

"Are you sure? I hope it wouldn't be for more than a few days." A tear escaped before I could help it. Matteo let me in more than anyone else, and I hated the thought of him believing I was throwing it back in his face.

"I'll put fresh towels downstairs now and let Milo know. Just text when you're on your way tomorrow."

"Thank you. I'm so sorry to put you out like this—"

"You aren't putting me out. Truly. This will all be fine in the end. I know it."

I wished I could be so sure as I dipped my nose into the collar of Matteo's hoodie, his scent intoxicatingly familiar and comforting. It was why I slept in his clothes every night even while I slept next to him. As dramatic as it sounded, tearing myself away for just a few days would be the most painful thing I'd ever do, especially if I couldn't get him to understand why.

When I came back inside, Lauren had already gone back upstairs, and Matteo was in the same position I'd left him in the living room. I sucked in a shaky breath, hoping I wouldn't lose my nerve as I climbed onto his lap.

"Can we talk?" I asked as I cuddled into his chest, getting the most out of being this close to him before I said what I needed to say.

He wrapped a weak arm around me and shook his head.

"I'm not good for conversation today." He rubbed his eyes, exhaustion evident in every move he made.

"That's because all of this has been weighing on you since before I met you. You've just never had to face it like you did today."

He squinted his heavy eyes at me. "I don't understand what you mean."

I sat up, sliding my arm around his shoulder.

"In the entire time I've known you, you've talked about Callie maybe twice, and both times, it was a struggle for you. The way she left you both is something that has eaten away at you for years. You even said it was part of why you moved, to not have to think about it."

"I wanted a new start for us. Without all the shit we went through, or that I went through without Lauren being old enough to realize it. What's so wrong with that?" His back stiffened against the chair as his jaw ticked.

I winced, already hating how badly this was going.

"You have a lot to unpack. Now that Callie is here, I think it's time to finally do it." I cradled his cheek, rubbing my thumb along his jaw as if it would somehow make him absorb what I was saying, even though he'd turned away from me. "And I think all of this talk about me moving in needs to take a back burner for a little bit until you do."

His body jerked as if I'd shocked him back to life before he turned his head toward me.

"What are you saying, Melanie?"

I grabbed his face and rested my forehead against his.

"I'm saying, I love you. I'm saying that all I want is to be with you and Lauren. Both of you are *everything* to me."

I swallowed the tears threatening to spill over and pushed my lips into a smile.

"I love the moments, but I *really* love the idea of a future with you. We may be fast and crazy, but we're real. I know that, and I want to move forward with you more than anything. Even if I know any rent I give you, you'll just sneak back to me later."

The side of his mouth curved a tiny bit, offering me a sliver of hope.

"I think you should call out for the next two days while Callie is here. Ty has been after you to take all the days you have piled up. Tell him it's a family emergency or something."

I thought I spotted a tiny nod as he looked away, so I continued.

"I know you said you wouldn't let her see Lauren, but her number is still in the same place she left it this morning. Something is holding you back from ripping it up and throwing it away. Whether she sees Lauren is your decision alone, but I think your little girl is more resilient than you may be giving her credit for."

He shrugged before leaning back in the chair with his eyes shut.

"So, you're leaving me?"

"No, I'm giving you some space to figure things out for a few days. I'll stay in Milo's man cave while you finally push the monkey off your back, as the old saying goes."

I choked out a sad laugh. Matteo's hand dragged lazy strokes up and down my back as his glassy eyes bore into mine.

"Don't look at me like that," I whispered.

"Like what?" he asked, his voice raspy as he tightened his hold around me and rested his head on my shoulder.

"Like I'm breaking your heart."

He raised his head and cradled my cheek, a sad smile tilting the corner of his mouth.

"That's because you are, Princess."

His hand threaded into my hair before he pulled me to him and kissed me. He slipped his tongue past the seam of my lips, making long, slow strokes inside my mouth as if he were drinking up all he could. I was doing this for him, for us, so we could have a real chance. Why did I feel like the cruelest and stupidest person alive for separating from this man for even a minute if I didn't have to?

But I did have to, even if he didn't understand that, yet.

We broke apart, his head falling against my chest as more tears snaked down my cheeks.

"Either way, you don't have a head to manage anything tonight, so please stay home. I'll make us dinner. I think I can sorta manage that, and I'll pack tonight and head to Angie's before school tomorrow morning. I'll tell Lauren that it's finals week and I have to study at school. I'll be back before we even miss each other."

Another lie, since I already missed them both so much it hurt.

Matteo didn't answer as I climbed off his lap and headed into the kitchen in search of something quick to make that I wouldn't screw up.

I wanted this to be a beginning for us. And I hoped that when I left in the morning, it wouldn't be an end.

MATTEO

I was used to being alone in the house at this time of morning. With both Melanie and Lauren off to school, I had nothing to do and nowhere to be until I had to get Lauren off the school bus at three p.m. Today, being by myself was pure torture.

I made my daily workout twice as long and tried to make it painful. Anything to distract me from the shit show that my life was right now. I collapsed in a pile of sweat, still unable to escape the fog that settled into my brain and the ache pulling at my chest after my "break" from Melanie.

The last time I'd felt this lost had been when Callie first left. Looking back on it, I'd known from the beginning she wasn't coming back. I'd accepted that *I* lost her, but I never got over the fury and hurt when she'd left us both without so much as a word. It would be easier for me to cut off a limb than to separate from my daughter, yet she'd taken a five-year vacation, Lauren's existence only meaning something to her now.

Back then, I didn't have much time to dwell. I had an infant to take care of and a life to figure out. I hadn't done a bad job of either, and I was happy. We all were, until Callie's return upended it all. Melanie was right, it was hard for me to think about Callie much less talk about how she'd left us, or remember the shame of how I'd held on for months when she'd started slipping away.

I was about to force myself to eat something when my phone buzzed across my kitchen table. My chest deflated in relief when I saw my cousin's name drift across the screen. Just like when I was a kid, my first instinct was to go to him with any kind of problem, and after an excruciating goodbye with Melanie this morning, I'd texted him asking to talk before I realized what I was doing.

"What's going on?" Dominic asked as soon as I accepted the call. "A text at seven a.m. on a Monday is never good news."

"I didn't want to wake anyone by calling the house."

"Thea goes to work early, and the school bus comes at seven-thirty. The time to wake us up was hours ago. Spit it out. You sound like shit."

"Callie showed up at the house yesterday."

I heard heavy steps and a door slam.

"Are you fucking kidding me?"

"I wish I was. All of a sudden she wants Lauren to know her. She's staying up here for the next couple of days waiting for me to decide."

"And." Dominic prodded. "I mean, that's heavy, but I get the feeling there's another reason for this call."

I understood why Melanie left but even though she swore she was coming back, I was terrified she wouldn't. We were moving fast, but it all felt right to me. Wrong was watching her drive away, possibly losing my future because I'd never dealt with the past.

"Melanie left. She was supposed to move in, but she said she wanted to give me space to deal with what happened with Callie because she thinks I've been avoiding it. She said when I'm ready, she'll come back."

I wished I knew what *ready* meant to her. When she'd stuffed her suitcase in her trunk this morning, it was all I could do to not grab her by the ankles and beg her to stay because I had no clue how to convince her to come back.

A long moment of silence lingered between my cousin and me.

"Go ahead, tell me how we moved too fast, and now my life is fucked because of it." I ran my hand through my damp hair, dreading what would come next. I'd taken off from work the next two days, but if Melanie didn't come back, I'd need to search for another babysitter. And Lauren would be just as devastated as I was.

"I think Melanie is right. I was happy to see you get close to someone after you kept every woman at arm's length for all these years. It doesn't sound like you guys broke up. She's just letting you figure it out. And after five years, it's finally time. Did you tell Callie about all you went through after she left?"

"What good would it do?" I spit out.

"I really don't know. Maybe the act of telling her will get enough anger out of you to prevent the ulcer you're going to eventually give yourself. She left Lauren in a horrible way, but she left you, too. And you've *never* dealt with it. That's the real reason you never wanted to get serious with anyone. Melanie *is* a miracle for making you snap out of it."

I wanted to tell him he was wrong, but when I opened my mouth to argue, nothing came out.

"And, this may shock you, I think you should let her see Lauren."

"What?" I yelled before I popped off the couch. "No way, Dom."

"You know how I feel about Callie. But she's still Lauren's mother. My baby cousin is smart and tough. If you explain well enough, I think she can handle it. And years down the road, if you keep her from meeting her mother, and she finds out, you know as well as I do that she'll resent the shit out of you."

"And if meeting Callie hurts her, then what?"

"Then," he exhaled, pausing for a second. "Then, she has a good dad who will help her understand that some people aren't supposed to be parents. That doesn't mean they're bad people or that anything was wrong with her, or you, to have made her mother leave. Maybe explaining that to yourself would help, too."

I fell back on the couch, eyeing the piece of paper with Callie's number still on my coffee table.

"For an asshole, you're sort of wise."

"I'm a *very* wise asshole."

A real laugh slipped out of me for the first time since Callie rang my doorbell.

"I'm always here, Matty. Call Callie. Do what you need to do. Then go get your girl back."

I ended the call, my gaze still lingering on that stupid piece of paper.

As much as I loved my daughter and worked my ass off to give her everything, I always felt like I wasn't giving her enough because she didn't have a mother. As much as I might have wanted to, I couldn't change history or biology. Callie was Lauren's history, and Lauren had a right to know who she was.

Before I lost my nerve, I punched the numbers into my phone and shot Callie a text.

Matteo: *Can you be here at 2? Lauren gets off the bus at 3, but I think we need to talk first.*

She replied not even a minute after I put the phone down.

Callie: *I can do that. Thank you, Matteo.*

I tried to keep busy for most of the day. I was almost tempted to stop by Speakeasy to work a few afternoon hours, but that would be avoiding my problems. If I was really going to give us the life out here that I'd set out to, I needed to break my years' old habit of distraction and avoidance.

When my doorbell rang at a quarter of two, I braced myself before heading to the door. There was a time I'd dreamt of this moment. Callie coming back and wanting to see Lauren and all three of us would be the family I thought we should've been. But she was a stranger, now. She was then, too, although I didn't want to acknowledge it at the time.

"Hey!" Callie's greeting was still tentative but not as skittish as when she'd stopped by yesterday. She gave me a nervous smile, clutching a gift bag so tightly I could see the white of her knuckles. "Thank you for this."

"Come in," I told her, holding the door open for her to enter.

"My parents told me she loves *Beauty and the Beast* and loves books, so I picked up a book for her." She held up the bag. "It feels a little crazy being so anxious to talk to her after I carried her for nine months." She choked out a nervous laugh, and I almost sympathized with her.

Almost.

She'd carried Lauren then split before her daughter cut her first tooth. The thought made me want to open the door again and tell her to see herself out, but I forced myself to move forward with the decision I'd made.

"So, um, you said you wanted to talk first?" She settled on my couch, still keeping a tight hold on the bag handle.

I sat on the other end of the couch, pinching the bridge of my nose as I tried to articulate what I'd gone through for the past five years.

"I get that you were done with me, but not one phone call, card, or contact with your daughter in all that time?"

"Matteo, I told you." Her eyes darted from mine. "I was messed up."

"You've said, and that's a shit excuse. There *is* no excuse or explanation for leaving your baby without even checking up on her."

"I knew you'd take care of her. I just couldn't be a wife and a mother. I was only twenty-one. I got wrapped up in us and all the new passion and when I was locked in—"

"Locked in?" I scoffed out a laugh. "I made you feel locked in?"

"Maybe not on purpose, but yes. You were full steam ahead

with baby supplies and wedding plans, and I was suffocating." Her voice cracked as she brought a quivering hand to her temple. "You were ready for it all, and I couldn't breathe."

"I wasn't ready for a baby, either," I admitted. "Not yet, anyway. You thought I was? I did what I had to do for my family."

"I know." She gazed at me with a sad shake of her head. "You were always good like that. Putting everyone else's needs before yours. I… I couldn't do it. I couldn't be what you both needed me to be. I didn't plan on never seeing her again, but the longer I stayed away, the more shame I felt about coming back. You're right. There is no excuse." She set down the bag in front of her, regarding me with an almost wistful gaze.

"You deserved someone who appreciated your dedication instead of feeling smothered by it. I wished I was that person, but I couldn't be. I'm sorry for that too, Matteo."

My mind went to Melanie. I'd always been drawn to her in a way that transcended passion, although we had plenty of that. Talking to her made me feel good, better about so many things that I couldn't open up about to most. *She* was that person, the one who appreciated everything I did for her but never tried to take advantage of it.

I'd told Dominic that Melanie made life better but hadn't known how to describe exactly how. She loved me and made sure I knew it. Memories of Callie and me drifted through my brain, drastically contrasting with what I had with Melanie these past few months.

Looking back on my time with Callie, it seemed more like an overwhelming infatuation rather than love. Even when I'd been with her, we weren't really together, at least, not how I'd romanticized us to be. My pride had been hurt more than my heart, but I'd been too distraught over being left alone with Lauren to know the difference.

Maybe it was time to admit that I'd been going through the motions with Callie towards the end, too.

She flicked her wrist over to glance at her watch.

"Two-fifty," she noted as her gaze drifted out the window.

"So, about that, how is this going to work?"

She squinted at me before she reared back.

"How is it going to work? I'm not asking for shared custody or anything, I just wanted to know her and let her know me."

"Right, but is this a one-time thing, or are you planning to stay in touch? At this point, it's up to you. But if you plan to keep talking to her, it needs to be consistent. The second you ghost on her, you don't get another chance."

"Noted." She nodded, her eyes still fixed on my front window. "Like I said, it's probably weird having to get to know your own kid, but I want to."

Our heads jerked toward the loud hiss of the school bus brakes. My stomach fluttering a little, I headed out to greet Lauren.

She waved to me from the window before stepping off and running into my arms when I met her at the bus. When I scooped her up, I held her extra tight as if that would create some kind of protective layer around her when I put her down. As much as I wished I could, I knew I couldn't safeguard her forever.

"You're getting so tall, I'm not going to be able to lift you much longer." She giggled when I tickled under her arm.

"Are you still sad, Daddy?" She touched my cheek and then recoiled back. "Why is your cheek so scratchy? You look like Mason's dad. He's a farmer. Only he wears a plaid shirt."

"I skipped shaving for a day, Cookie. But I don't think I'm a lumberjack farmer, yet." She squealed when I buried my head into her neck and rubbed my stubble against her cheek.

I set her down on the porch and crouched in front of her.

"There's someone inside who wants to meet you. Her name is Callie."

She scrunched up her nose as she looked toward the window.

"That's my mom's name, right?"

I was taken aback for a second. All the questions she'd asked about her mother, I couldn't remember her asking what her mother's name was.

"Yes, Callie is your mom. How did you know that?"

She shrugged. "Grandma Terry showed me pictures. She said I have my mom's eyes and her hair." She twirled a strand around her finger. "She told me my mom was traveling, and that's why I hadn't met her yet."

I closed my eyes for a moment, shaking my head. Traveling was one way to look at it, a nice spin that Callie's mother had put on her daughter's abandonment, but Lauren didn't seem bothered by it. From what I could tell, to Lauren, Callie was simply another family member who lived somewhere else. I should have been the one to tell Lauren about Callie years ago instead of just quickly answering whatever she asked and changing the subject.

"Well, she stopped in Vermont to see you." I held out my hand to lead her inside. "She's in the living room."

Lauren took my hand and followed me inside. Callie met us in the hallway, her hands clasped under her chin as a wide smile broke out on her tear-stained face.

"Hi, Lauren," Callie squeaked out as I helped Lauren pull off her coat. "It's so nice to see you."

Lauren's eyes narrowed a little, but she seemed curious, not bothered.

"Hi," was all my daughter said as she padded over to her.

"I'm Callie." Callie didn't have to bend much since Lauren came up to her waist. Somehow, I hadn't recalled how small Callie was. So many details of us blurred as I looked back on them.

"You're my mom. Grandma Terry told me. When did you stop traveling?"

Callie blinked and lifted her gaze to mine for a moment.

"Um," she stammered, "a few weeks ago. I brought something for you. I heard you love *Beauty and the Beast* and love to read. I do, too! Do you want to come with me to the couch?" She dropped a tentative hand on Lauren's shoulder.

Lauren went with her with no issue. She dug into the bag and pulled out the book, eyeballing the cover.

"Thank you. This is cool. It won't take me long to read since I read chapter books, now."

I laughed to myself as Lauren stood straighter.

"Oh really? What books do you read? I'd love to see."

"Melanie and me are reading *The Velveteen Rabbit*. We already finished it, but this time, I'm reading it to her. But I don't read as fast as she can, so it takes longer." Her nose crinkled before she shook her head at Callie. "I don't want to show you, because my special bookmark from Daddy's friend Lily may fall out. When Melanie comes home, we'll finish."

"Oh." Callie's gaze dropped to the floor as I rubbed away the pesky ache in my chest. I was waiting for Melanie to come home, too.

"But there are other books that I can show you when I have time. I have *lots.* That's my only chapter book."

"When you have time?" I raised an eyebrow at Lauren. "Why are you so busy today?"

"You said this morning that if I didn't have any homework we can go to the Busy Bean and get a pretzel. And I don't have any. I want to put on my pendant, and we can go." She turned back to Callie. "It's a mood pendant, but Daddy won't let me wear it to school because he said I'll change my mood too much and not pay attention," she explained.

The corners of Callie's mouth twitched when Lauren raced toward the staircase.

"When did I say that we were getting a pretzel?" I called after her.

She stopped, shifting toward me with her very first eye roll.

"This morning before the bus came I asked you if we could get a pretzel after school if I had no homework. You said sure. Which means yes. Callie can come, too."

I was practically a zombie this morning, worried about what to do about Callie, missing Melanie, and had zero recollection of anything she'd asked before I put her on the bus. I fell back against the wall and rubbed my eyes. My kid was always a step ahead.

"I'm guessing you've had your hands full."

I nodded slowly. When I opened my eyes to meet Callie's gaze, a real smile spread across her lips.

"You could say that." I peered up at the staircase and shook my head.

"If you're uncomfortable, I can head back to the hotel and stop by later." Callie stood from the couch. "Trust me, I realize how generous you've been already."

"No, she knows who you are and invited you along. The Busy Bean isn't far, and she devours those pretzels in minutes. You can take a ride with us."

Callie's chin quivered as she pushed off the couch.

"Thank you."

"I'm ready!" Lauren called before tearing down the stairs. She stopped at the last step, studying Callie for a minute.

"Your skin isn't that white," she said with pursed lips.

"What do you mean her skin isn't that white?" I asked.

"I heard Grandma Rose and Aunt Netta talking about you, and they said you were always a flake. But you don't look like a snowflake." She shrugged and strolled past us.

I held in a laugh as I helped Lauren with her coat. My little girl was relentless and resilient in ways that I never could have imagined.

My tough little cookie.

MELANIE

Two finals down, three to go. All tomorrow.

I wasn't sure if I'd make it, especially when every moment I wasn't throwing myself in a book, I was thinking of Matteo. I didn't consciously think stepping away from him so he could face how his ex had left him and their daughter would throw him back in her direction.

Consciously, I knew that.

But that silly voice in the back of my head, the one that always held me back from putting myself out there or believing that I was worthy of anything, kept reminding me of how they shared a child. And while Callie had been gone for a long time and had badly hurt Matteo, a child was a strong and permanent link between two people. Doubt took root, and along with that, fear that Matteo would never forgive me for leaving in the first place.

Before I headed to Angie's to study for the next few hours, I decided that carbs would be the solution for my stressful week and battered heart. Plus, I felt terrible taking away Milo's sanctuary until I figured out my next move, so I thought muffins and pastries would be the best way, or at least *a* way, that I could afford to convey my gratitude.

I yearned for the day I had a solid and decent place to live that was independent of my love life.

"Hi, Melanie!" One of the baristas I knew greeted me with a beaming smile. "Let me guess, pretzels for the little lady."

"No." I forced a smile, pretending that didn't punch me in the gut just a little. "It's finals week. I'm here for provisions. Please give me four banana muffins and five baked goods of anything chocolate. Surprise me."

"I got you." She winked. "I'll be right back."

I leaned against the counter, realizing that an extra-large coffee would be needed if I was going to keep my eyes open until midnight. Just as I was about to ask to add that to my order, something barreled into me from behind and took hold of my thighs.

I looked down and found Lauren, her arms wrapped around my legs in a death grip. I'd only left her this morning, but seeing her again brought a lump into my throat as if it had been years. I knelt down and let her pull me into a tight hug, cinching my arms around her. I'd done a good job of not crying in front of her when I'd left, but if I didn't pull away in the next few seconds, I'd fail.

"What a surprise!" I gasped, grabbing her hands. "How did you get here on a school day?"

A devious smile lifted her lips to match the glint in her eyes.

"I asked Daddy this morning if we could come here if I had no homework. I don't think he heard me when he said sure, but a promise is a promise."

He probably didn't hear her because he'd been just as catatonic today as he was when he'd gone to sleep last night. Still, I had to laugh at Lauren's devious scheme to get a pretzel.

"What are you doing here? I thought you were staying at school?"

Shit.

"I came here to buy some study snacks before I went back to Burlington."

I paid for my order with a shaky hand before turning back to Lauren, afraid to search the Busy Bean for her father. After pulling myself away from him this morning, I'd hoped for a little recovery time until I saw him again. In fact, I wanted the next time I saw him to be our happy reunion, but I wasn't sure what needed to happen between now and then.

"Where's your dad?" I asked before I locked eyes with Matteo over her shoulder. He hadn't shaved, his stubble already long after a day away from his razor. But God, he was so beautiful. I was tempted to launch myself at him and tell him to forget the whole damn thing before my gaze drifted to the woman sitting next to him. She was petite with dark hair and eyes, but I noticed her resemblance to Lauren right away.

I took in a quick breath through my nostrils to shake it off. This was good. Matteo had agreed to see Callie and hash it all out, and since they were all out together, it appeared to be working. This was what I'd asked him to do. For us. I'd ignore the irrational burning sting of jealousy poking at my gut.

"He's over there with Callie. She's my mom, and she's visiting before she goes back to traveling." Before I could absorb everything she'd said, I was pulled by the hand toward their table.

"I found Melanie!" Lauren announced before jumping back into her seat.

"I see that," Matteo said as his gaze slid to mine. I couldn't decipher the expression in his eyes. He looked sad and shocked, and something else I couldn't pinpoint.

"I'm Melanie, you must be Callie. Nice to meet you." I held out my hand, my jaw hurting from pushing the smile across my mouth.

"Nice to meet you, too." Callie stood and took my hand. "I've heard a bit about you." She was gorgeous and looked good next to Matteo.

Shut up, voice. Just shut the hell up.

"When are you coming home?"

In my periphery I spied Matteo tense up and Callie's eyes widen at Lauren's question—both of them focused on me.

"It's finals week, Laur. As soon as I'm done, I'll be back." I tucked a stray lock of hair from her barrette behind her ear.

"When is that? You can study at our house. I promise I'll be quiet."

I smiled when she brought her little voice down to a whisper.

"She'll come home when she's ready, Cookie." Matteo said to Lauren, his gaze locked with mine, bringing all the guilt I'd tried to bury all day up to the surface.

"Soon. I mean it." I didn't say "promise" because I didn't know if I could keep it. I meant it, though, so it wasn't a lie. I bent to give her another hug and kiss on the cheek.

"Don't study all night," Matteo said, his glossy dark eyes still pinning me where I stood. "Get some sleep."

"I won't. I promise," I croaked out in a scratchy whisper.

Everyone else at the table faded away. Even though I'd probably hurt him, and he was as upset as when I left him this morning, he still worried about me.

"I better get going. You guys enjoy. It was nice to meet you, Callie."

When I turned to leave, I still felt Matteo's eyes boring into my back.

She'll come home when she's ready.

I *was* ready. Despite how strongly I felt that he needed space, I was ready to come back to him now, fall asleep in his arms tonight, and forget the whole thing.

But it didn't matter if I was ready. I needed to make sure that he was.

MATTEO

Lauren rambled on the entire trip to and from the Busy Bean Café, telling Callie about school, about her cousins coming to visit for Thanksgiving, and all about Melanie. I'd spied Callie nod as Lauren went on about how pretty and smart Melanie was, how she'd taught her how to bake, and how I always smile more whenever she was around.

If Callie had any question of who Melanie was to us, Lauren answered it and then some before we pulled back into my garage.

"So, I have time to show you my books now." Lauren said after she shrugged off her coat and kicked off her boots by the door. "Come on."

She grabbed Callie's hand and pulled her up the stairs. I followed, keeping a distance as to not look like I was hovering, even though I was. Lauren's reaction to Callie brought me a ton of relief, but Callie hadn't earned time alone with our daughter. At least, not yet.

Callie offered to send letters back and forth to Lauren while we'd sat at the Busy Bean, and Lauren thought the concept of getting her own mail would be fun. When we left and piled into my truck, I pulled Callie aside before she got in and told her she could send Lauren letters, but she should know I'd be reading every one. And if she tried to twist anything and mess with our daughter's head in any way, Lauren would never see the letters or her ever again.

I may have been a little bit of a dick about it, but while Callie appeared to be contrite and seemed to want to be in Lauren's life, until I was sure of her intentions, she'd always have to go through me.

"Wow, you do have lots of books." Callie let out an exaggerated gasp as Lauren led her to the bookcase.

"Yep," Lauren nodded, full of pride. "Oh, that's the book we're making for Daddy," she told Callie in a loud whisper, pointing to a binder nestled into the corner of the bottom shelf. "I can't show you that either, it's his Christmas present. Melanie thought of it."

"Melanie thinks of everything, I see," Callie said, her smile not so wide this time.

Melanie *did* think of everything. Of me, of Lauren, of us. Now, I had to think about sleeping without her tonight. I doubted I'd get any real rest after a night of laying in sheets that still smelled like her. But changing them would make me feel even worse.

"I think I'm going to head back to my hotel," Callie said when we came back downstairs. "I have to leave super early tomorrow morning so Grandma Terry and Grandpa Frank won't worry about me coming home too late. I can't wait to tell them all about our visit."

Callie's watery gaze darted to the floor before she looked up again.

"I think you are the coolest kid I've ever met. And I can't wait to learn more about you."

"Me too," Lauren chirped before she cinched her arms around Callie's waist. At first, Callie was too shocked to know what to do with her own arms but eventually hugged Lauren back. If Callie turned out to be the flake that Lauren heard my mother and aunt say that she was, at least Lauren would remember one good afternoon with her mother. For that, I was grateful.

We walked Callie to the door, Lauren waving to Callie as she stepped into her car and drove away. Dusk was setting in, and the days were getting shorter and colder as we headed toward our first Vermont winter. The house already seemed dark and depressing without Melanie, and all I wanted to do was head to Angie's and drag her back here. And I would. But I needed to figure out what to say to convince her that I was ready for her to come back and never leave my life ever again.

I was about to make dinner for us, even though the last thing I wanted to do was eat, when my phone buzzed with a text. Hoping against hope that it was Melanie saying she decided to come back, I swiped the text notification on the screen.

> **Oz:** *Where are you tonight? Reeve was able to score that present you asked him to find.*
> **Matteo:** *You're kidding. He found it?*
> **Oz:** *Of course he did. My man rocks. They said you were off tomorrow too, we could just leave it here.*
> **Matteo:** *No, that's a little too valuable to leave in a locker in the breakroom or behind the bar. I'll come meet you.*

My stomach churned with excitement. Melanie was going to flip out, and I wasn't going to wait until Christmas to watch. I remembered that night she'd told me all she wanted was to be real, but she was so damn real, everything else was fake compared to her. No one ever had compared to Melanie, and she'd never doubt it again.

"What's for dinner, Daddy?"

"Phoebe's soup in a pretzel bowl."

I laughed at Lauren's gasp before I grabbed her coat and helped her shrug it on.

"We get to have dinner at your work? Will Melanie be there? Will she come home with us?"

"No, Cookie. But I'm working on it."

I zipped her coat and planted a kiss on her forehead.

When we first arrived at Speakeasy, it took a long time to make it to where Oz sat at the bar with Reeve. Lauren had her own little fan club with the Speakeasy staff, and the social butterfly that my daughter was couldn't help stopping to chat with them all.

"Well, who is this little lady? A new waitress?"

Lauren giggled at Oz. "I'm Lauren, and I'm too young to work. I wish I could, I'd spend all my money on more books."

"You're my kind of girl," Reeve said. "You know, if I liked…" His eyebrows lifted when he met my gaze. I shook my head, biting back a smile as Oz snickered next to him. "I'm Reeve, and this is Oz. I work in a bookstore with *lots* of books."

He reached into his inside jacket pocket and pulled out a bag as my daughter gaped at him.

"Do you know what a first edition book is?" Reeve stood and crouched in front of Lauren.

She shook her head, eyeing the bag in his hand.

"The books we read can change covers many times, but this book is a first edition copy of *The Velveteen Rabbit*. It has the same cover and inside as the original book, and that makes it very valuable. Do you know that book?"

Her head bobbed up and down in a boisterous nod. "I read it one and a half times."

"Wow, one and a half? A first edition copy of their favorite book is the best gift that you can give to a reader." He grinned, lifting his gaze to mine. "Melanie is a lucky woman."

"Thank you," I mouthed, handing Reeve an envelope with the payment I'd had set aside.

"My pleasure," he said, placing the book into my other hand.

"When are we giving it to her? I can't wait until Christmas." Lauren pulled at the hem of my jacket.

"Tomorrow night. When we bring her home."

34

MELANIE

"Can I get you anything?" Angie asked as I lounged on Milo's couch.

As man caves went, not that I was familiar with any, he had a pretty nice setup in the basement. The black sofa was a soft leather and would have been easy to sleep on if my frazzled brain would've stopped giving me such a hassle every time I tried.

"It's been a long day on no sleep. I can't muster the energy to sit up right now." I rubbed my eyes as my mouth fell open with a yawn. Maybe the pure mental exhaustion would allow me a nap.

"You have no more studying to do, so why don't you finally get some rest? Milo said when he went to work early this morning, he saw the light on down here. Please don't burn yourself out." She leaned over and squeezed my shoulder.

"I don't have any other speed than burn out." I said through another yawn. "I need a win, Angie. If I did well this semester, maybe this all wasn't such a bad decision."

She tilted her head, lips pursed as she glared at me.

"I know you're sad and displaced at the moment, but do you really believe that? It's actually made me very happy to see you putting yourself out there, finally. Only took years for you to listen to me."

I grinned at her tapping foot. Shaking the fear and taking risks had made a big difference. For the first time, I could say that my life was mine and headed into the direction I wanted it to go, with the exception of whatever I was going through with Matteo right now.

"I'm ordering pizza in a little while. Sleep, and I'll let you know when it's here."

I nodded, closing my eyes before I could watch her head back upstairs. Just a few minutes of sleep would make a huge difference, yet every time I tried, my heavy eyelids wouldn't stay shut. I peered at my suitcase in defeat before I pushed off the couch and pulled out Matteo's T-shirt. It had ended up in my bag by accident when I packed all the clothes I had laid out on his bed. Or maybe I'd taken it on purpose, and my pride wouldn't let me admit it. But I was too exhausted to ponder any of that.

I buried my face in the cotton and inhaled, his scent still so strong, it was as if he was here. I hadn't seen or heard from him since the Busy Bean, although I'd typed and deleted about ten texts. We were taking a break, but I guessed our rules of communication were fuzzy, or he just didn't want to speak to me. I'd purposely left some of my stuff at his house to prove my intention of coming back, but I was already worried I'd only return to clear it out.

It was borderline obsessive and unhealthy, but I bundled his shirt into my arms and rested it on top of one of the couch pillows. Regardless of how desperate and pathetic cuddling with Matteo's shirt made me, when I closed my eyes they finally stayed shut.

Once I succumbed to sleep, all sorts of scenarios played out in my dreams. I was serving Goldenpour in class, eating dinner in a library, and refreshing a computer screen that went blank every time I'd try to see my grades. One dream took me back to Matteo's house, in his bed, his lips grazing my cheek as he kept telling me to wake up.

When my eyes fluttered open, and I swatted away a tickle on

my cheek, I swore I heard a deep chuckle behind me. I was in that limbo when you first wake up, but a dream is still fresh in your head. I sank deeper in Milo's pillow, and into Matteo's shirt, trying to will myself back to slumber.

"Wake up, Princess."

My eyes popped open and landed on Matteo's. He crouched on the floor in front of me, running his thumb back and forth along my jaw.

"So that was the tickle," I muttered in a scratchy whisper, pinching the inside of my wrist to make sure the beautiful sight of him wasn't a cruel figment of my imagination. "What are you doing here?"

"Didn't I say not to stay up all night?" The side of his mouth quirked up as he cradled my cheek.

"Yes, but I never listen." I reached up to grab his wrist, leaning into his palm as ridiculous tears threatened to spill down my cheeks. I'd left him to sort out the feelings he'd never wanted to deal with, all the while terrified I'd never get him back.

"No," he whispered, resting his forehead against mine. "No, you don't."

Unable to take it anymore, I grabbed two fistfuls of his T-shirt and hauled him on top of me, pressing my lips to his in a relieved as all hell kiss. Yes, we still had to talk, but he was here, and right now, that was all I cared about.

We were a mess of lips and tongues, muttering I love yous and I miss yous between heated kisses. I wouldn't take my mouth off of his, still a bit afraid it was a dream. We broke apart and fell into each other, Matteo's head burrowing into my neck as his arms tightened around me.

"God, I missed you so much." He groaned as he came back to my lips. "I'm so fucking gone for you."

"I slept with your shirt," I nodded to where I still rested on his T-shirt draped over the pillow. "If you're gone, so am I. But before we revel in how pathetic we both are," I tapped his shoulder and nodded to the end of the couch for him to take a seat. "I want to hear what's been going on with you—all of you."

Matteo breathed out a deep sigh, nodding as he settled next to me on the couch.

"How are things going with Callie?" I asked. "You guys looked at least a little friendly when I saw you."

"I don't know if I'd say friendly. We worked up to amiable, I suppose. She's on her way back to New York, and Lauren knew who she was before I had to tell her. Her other grandparents filled her in on enough details for her to figure it out."

He shut his eyes and rubbed his temples.

"Callie promised to write letters to Lauren, but we'll see. She's not a big mystery to Lauren anymore, but Lauren seemed to think of her more as a new relative rather than a parent. What I mean by that, is that she was her friendly, unfiltered self but didn't expect Callie to stay." He leaned back and smiled. "For that, I was relieved. In fact, she name dropped you the entire time." He grinned as he nudged my knee. "It was Melanie this and Melanie that for most of the afternoon, especially after she saw you."

"She's my little bestie." I lifted a shoulder, a wistful smile pulling at my lips from maybe liking the fact that Callie heard about me nonstop while she was here a little too much. "And I think my biggest fan."

"I wouldn't say that. There's someone else who couldn't think of anything else except when you were coming back and spent the last couple of days worried and scared to death that maybe you wouldn't."

He scooted closer, cupping the back of my neck.

"I told you I was coming back. I just thought you needed time to sort everything out—"

"And you were right."

I blinked when he actually agreed with me.

"I'd never wanted to talk about Callie and how she left us, but Lauren had a right to know about her mother. It's her history and mine. I should have faced it head on years ago, not waited until it almost ruined everything because I couldn't deal with it."

"Did Callie say where she's been all this time?"

"It doesn't really matter." He shrugged again. "You can't force someone into a life they don't want, and I think towards the end, I was trying to do that without realizing it. That doesn't excuse her, and I told her that, but Callie leaving isn't the giant hole or trauma in our daughter's life that I'd always been afraid of. I'd managed to give Lauren enough love to be able to see her mother at face value, I hope." He winced and dropped his gaze to the carpet.

"You give her more than enough." I squeezed his knee to make him look up. "She's a tough, smart little girl. Too smart, since she told me how she tricked you for a pretzel."

"Yep," he sighed. "I was too blindsided by Callie and heart-broken over you to realize what she was asking me. She could have gotten away with a lot worse. I'm thankful all it cost me was a pretzel."

He slid an arm under my legs and lifted me onto his lap.

"When Callie left us, it hurt, but I was angrier that she'd left *us* alone more than she'd left me." He pulled me closer. "I was mad at you when you left."

"I know." I nodded. "I'm sorry for that, but I'm not sorry I left."

"I'm not sorry you left either, because it was either finally figure my shit out, or lose you, and I wasn't going to let that happen." My eyes fluttered when he sifted his fingers into my hair. "I lived in that house for months without you, but when you left, it was empty and quiet."

"It was quiet with Lauren?"

He chuckled at my raised brow.

"I'm not me without you, not anymore." His smile faded as his hand drifted up my thigh.

"That explains the long stubble." I scratched my nails over the bristles dusting his chin.

"I thought you'd think it was hot." His fingers hooked into the waistband of my leggings, sliding his thumb back and forth along my hip. A moan escaped me before I could help it. We'd only been apart for a couple of days, but since I'd spent most of that time afraid I'd lost him, I was high off his simple touch.

I felt his smile against my skin when he dragged his lips over the shell of my ear.

"Come home with me, Princess," his words fanned hot against my neck. I leaned into his lips as they trailed kisses along my throat.

"If we make out on Milo's couch, we'll ruin his man cave." I snaked my arms around his neck, lolling my head to the side to give him better access.

"Then, maybe we should leave and make out on our own couch."

His brows jumped before he nipped at my chin.

I pressed my hands against his chest.

"We still need to talk about rent or something."

His head slumped before he nodded.

"You can pay me whatever you want if it makes you stay. And I have a welcome home gift for you. It was supposed to be a Christmas present, but I can't wait. Lauren wanted to be there when you opened it, so she's probably going to be mad at me."

He reached behind him, flashing a wry grin as he handed me a white bag. When I looked inside, I saw the bottom pages of a hardcover book but let out a Lauren-like gasp when I pulled it out and recognized the image on the front cover.

"Matteo, how did you…" I ran my finger down the front, over the rabbit ears before my jaw dropped again as I gently opened it. "This is a first edition! This is too much, I can't—"

"Yes, you can. I love you." He framed my face, the pure love in his eyes coaxing out the last of my relieved tears. "You made me real, Melanie. Please come home."

My chest rose and fell with shaky breaths as I remembered the confession I'd made to Matteo that night about doing something with my life so that I could be real. Being loved by Matteo felt more real than I ever could have imagined.

"I need a bookcase," I squeaked out. "Maybe a couple."

His beautiful lips broke out in a wide smile before they were back on mine, this time slow and sweet but full of intention.

"I'll build you one myself in every room if you want me to."

"Well, in that case…" I smiled, cuddling into Matteo's chest. He was the best dream I'd ever had.

"You have a deal."

I lifted my gaze to his. "I love you. Take me home."

MELANIE

"I love Christmas parties!" Anne mused as she helped me string more lights around the bar. "Especially ones where we get to eat the food instead of serve it." Her brows rose as she held the cord in place while I plugged it in.

Speakeasy employees came in a few hours before we opened to the public for a staff only party. I wasn't sure how I felt about drinking beer before noon, but as Anne mentioned, it was nice to enjoy what Speakeasy had to offer rather than serve it. This party was a welcomed, perfectly-timed distraction as this semester's grades were due to post today. If I were home, I'd just be staring at my phone or telling Matteo to hide it somewhere.

In fact, said phone was already buzzing in my back pocket, but instead of checking who was trying to contact me, I took the cowardly route and ignored it. Either Sheila was telling me our grades were up, or my mother was texting me with questions about Christmas Eve tomorrow night.

My parents were coming to Colebury later than planned, which I was ashamed to say I was grateful for. I loved the life I had with Matteo, and I had zero desire to defend it to anyone. His parents were coming in later tonight, and I was nervous enough to meet them, never mind worrying about my parents' reaction to everything.

My father was quiet by nature, his only comment at my living situation was, "As long as you're happy, sweetheart." My mother often told me the same, but the sour pull of her mouth as she said it made it come across far less sincerely.

An early morning beer, or any kind of alcohol, suddenly sounded lovely.

Anne reminded me to skip one stool while I was decorating. When I'd first started, I'd been told the spirit of Hamish, the original owner of Speakeasy, inhabited that stool. It was a ridiculous yet creepy notion, especially when I'd hear stories of things becoming mysteriously lost and then found. Some people even claimed to trip over things that weren't there.

I wasn't a big believer in ghosts or the supernatural. But just in case, on the off-chance Hamish was really the one who'd knocked me over on my first night here and led me to Matteo, I'd sometimes whisper "thank you," when I'd walk by.

I swept my gaze around the room, most of us gravitating toward the buffet table in the back. Ty played a mix of contemporary and holiday music. Some of the wait staff dancing in the front seemed like none of them had an issue with morning beer. Before I indulged in anything fun, I needed some air.

I leaned against the wall by the bar and took a deep breath before I dug my phone out of my pocket. It was only Angie sending a picture of the twins in the outfits I'd bought them for Christmas. Carter reminded me of what Lauren must have been like as a baby, beaming at the camera with his chubby fist in the air. Crissy was more my speed, crouching away and clinging to her mother.

For Crissy's sake, I hoped it wouldn't take her almost twenty-four years to step out into the light.

"Did your grades come in?" Matteo asked, joining me against the wall.

"No, just a picture of the twins from Angie. I'm too scared to check for my grades." I clenched my eyes shut.

He frowned, tilting his head.

"You did great, and you know it." He squeezed the tight muscles in the back of my neck. "Relax, Princess."

"It's like you don't even know me." I heaved an exaggerated sigh. "I'm nervous about meeting your parents, and about your parents meeting my parents and thinking I'm like them." I dropped my head on his shoulder.

"You've met my parents. Granted, it was over video." He rubbed my back. "But they love you already. You're beautiful and sweet and keep their son and granddaughter ridiculously happy. Your parents…" He trailed off and shrugged. "They mean well. It'll be a great Christmas, even if I have to force people to cooperate." I laughed at his attempt at a menacing glare.

"We better get some food before they run out." I grabbed his hand and pulled him toward the buffet table.

"Wait," his eyes drifted to the speaker on the wall above us when the beat slowed. I recognized the first few chords of "Crazy Love," surprised an older slow song had snuck onto Ty's playlist.

"Dance with me a minute." He slid an arm around my waist and pulled me close, lacing our fingers together and bringing our joined hands to his chest.

"Here?" I scanned the space around us.

Everyone knew we were together, but swaying to a slow song like we were at a school dance felt a little too on display. Still, his hopeful gaze and wide grin made it impossible for me to refuse.

I melted into him as we glided back and forth, burying in his neck as he sang softly in my ear.

"You're not half bad. I bet they'd still let you volunteer if you wanted to go on stage," I teased. "That poor guitar is left abandoned in the basement just waiting to be played."

His chest shook against my cheek.

"I took guitar lessons when I was a kid, but never did anything with it. I kept the guitar and used to sing to Lauren when she couldn't sleep. Dom is the singer in the family. At best, I'm a step behind amateur, so I'd hate for you to get your hopes up."

I lifted my head, catching his gaze. "You sang to Lauren? Oh, my God, stop being so damn swoon-worthy. It's irritating."

He reared back, squinting at me. "Is that a real word? Let me guess, from one of your romance books?"

He laughed when I shoved his shoulder.

"Maybe the next time I can't sleep you can break out the guitar and see if it works on me."

He rested his chin on my head.

"If it helped you relax, I'd play for you every single night."

I smiled but tensed up, my skin crawling from the feel of a dozen sets of eyes on me, on us. I was about to ask Matteo to cut the dance short when I noticed Anne's wide grin as she pointed up to the ceiling.

"Mistletoe," I groaned when I glanced up. "Are you kidding me?" Bunches of green with red ribbons were spaced out by a few feet all along the ceiling. I had no idea how long they'd been up there. No one had taken advantage and made out on the tap room floor, or at least any more than usual.

I backed away from Matteo and took his hand, but he wouldn't budge.

"It's bad luck if we don't kiss."

I tensed at the playful smile lifting his lips.

"What? I've never heard that." I pulled him again, but he still wouldn't move. "We can't kiss here. You know that."

"Why? There are no customers here, and everyone knows that we live together and sees us come and go in the same car." His gaze shifted up to the ceiling for a moment. "You can ask my aunt when you meet her about not messing with the evil eye."

"Are you serious?" I narrowed my eyes. "Between the ghost at the bar and now the curse of the deserted mistletoe I've had enough weird superstition—"

Matteo cupped my neck, his mouth covering mine with a kiss

that robbed me of all words. I stiffened at first but went limp when his tongue curled around mine as I savored the taste I still couldn't get enough of. Even through all the whistles and catcalls, I was too captivated by his kiss to stop. I moaned into his mouth as his hand skated up my back and weaved into my hair.

I was boneless when we broke apart, my lips sore and tingling as I peered into Matteo's eyes, heated with intentions too dirty for a public place, a public place we both worked at.

"Relaxed now?" he asked, a wicked glint in his eye as he feathered his hand along my jaw.

"Uh huh," was all I could say as I pressed my hands against his chest for balance.

Matteo burst out laughing as I tried to grab my senses back.

"Did I kiss you speechless, Princess?"

I tried to scowl but dropped my head against his shaking chest and groaned.

"M&M forever!" someone yelled, but Matteo and I only laughed.

"Merry Christmas, M," Matteo whispered and kissed the top of my head.

"Back at you, M." I played with the collar on his polo shirt. "What other powers does mistletoe have?"

"Oh, well, if you kiss the girl long enough," he drew me closer, flashing a lopsided grin, "she comes home with you. Forever."

A wide smile pulled at my lips despite the sting in my eyes. Even though I felt every drop of his love, it still shocked and surprised me in all the best ways.

"I guess it's important to choose wisely, and make sure she's who you want."

A slow grin lifted his cheeks before he cupped my chin and brought my mouth back to his.

"She's all I'll *ever* want."

36

MATTEO

One year later

"My girls are home from school!"

Lauren giggled as she climbed up our front steps with Melanie shaking her head behind her.

"So, tell me Cookie. How was first grade?"

"Great!" Lauren wrapped her arms around my waist and peered up at me. "No naps, but I hated naps anyway. And Melanie's second grade classroom is two doors away from mine!"

"Well I *help* teach three times a week. Not really *my* classroom, Laur." Melanie smoothed Lauren's hair away from her face as the breeze blew stray locks in front of her eyes.

My gaze lifted to Melanie's wistful smile. She wore a black dress with a short cardigan sweater and heels. I wasn't aware of my hot teacher kink until I'd seen her at the breakfast table this morning, looking so gorgeous I was tempted to crawl between her legs and make her late on her first day of student-teaching at Colebury Elementary. But I'd never do that. Melanie had worked hard to be where she was right now, and I was so damn proud of her. I'd cash in on all the fantasies she'd unleashed later on tonight.

"How was your first day?" I asked before brushing her lips.

"Good," was all she said before following Lauren inside.

I made my way into the kitchen as Melanie reached inside the fridge for a bottle of water. I was a little concerned about the vacant look in her eyes, like she was there but a million miles away.

"Everything okay? Did something happen?"

"No, everything is fine," she answered quickly, shaking her head. "The second-grade teacher is great, the kids seem adorable, but most do on their first day, I suppose."

She shrugged, meeting my gaze for a second before a tiny smile teased her lips. "I passed Lauren's class in the hallway, and she screamed, 'Hi Melanie!' Her teacher told her that in school she needs to call me Ms. Thomas, and she said…" Melanie played with the water bottle wrapper, her face crumpling as if she was about to let out a sob. "She said, 'But she's my mom.'"

I raised a brow and leaned against the wall.

"Does that bother you?"

"No, of course not. It's just, I can't describe it. I never knew she thought of me like that. But I couldn't pull her into a hug and cry since I had my own class to worry about." Her head dropped to her chest as she breathed out a long sigh. "It made me emotional in a way I didn't expect. I love that she thinks of me like that, but I never thought she would."

"Lauren's sun rises and sets on you. That's not clear to you after all this time?" I grinned and met her by the kitchen counter, wrapping my arms around her arm from behind.

"No, I know that. But I thought since she speaks to Callie…" she trailed off, lifting a shoulder.

"She hears from Callie once a week and only sees her a few times a year. She's not the one Lauren runs to when she's excited or when she's sick. You're more Lauren's mother than Callie ever was."

Callie still kept in contact with Lauren, and we'd see her when I'd make a trip back to New York to see family. She never pushed for more or came up to Vermont again, but she stayed somewhat consistent with Lauren, so I'd let it continue. Callie was more like a pen pal than a parent. Everything my daughter looked for and needed came from us.

"Can *I* call you Ms. Thomas?" I swept her hair off her neck and painted tiny kisses up to her ear. "I didn't do my homework last night, Ms. Thomas." I drifted my hand under the hem of her dress and glided it up her thigh. "How can I earn extra credit?"

She elbowed my ribs when I bit her earlobe.

"I know you said you only help teach, but how does it feel?"

She cocked her head from side to side before craning her head to look at me.

"Great." Her mouth split in a huge grin. "Like I'm finally where I'm supposed to be. I still have a year to go until I get my degree and become official, but I'm excited to be this close. Which sounds a little strange to say about work and school, but it feels good."

Melanie's student-teaching job came with a small salary, and she'd pushed me to accept more rent from her from now on. I agreed but knew I'd just put it away in the same envelope with all the other payments she'd insisted I take.

"Do you really want to have a romantic dinner at Speakeasy on your night off?" She pursed her lips at me. "Don't we both see enough of that place?"

"It's your first day of teaching. We should celebrate."

"At the place we both work?"

"Exactly." I tapped her nose and gave her a quick kiss before I left the kitchen. I couldn't tell her the real reason why I'd chosen to go to Speakeasy tonight, or why we weren't bringing Lauren. For what I had planned, we couldn't go anywhere else.

I wasn't nervous when we arrived at Speakeasy, but as dinner went on, it was hard to make small talk. We kept getting visits from the wait staff every time I worked up the nerve to do what

I'd come here for. But by the time dessert arrived, I'd given up trying to do it during dinner. I needed to get her out of here before I lost my damn mind.

"Hey guys!" Phoebe caught my arm on our way out. "How was dessert?"

"So good!" Melanie gushed. "You're a genius."

"Glad you enjoyed it." Phoebe's gaze stumbled to mine, and I replied with a tiny shake of my head. I'd mentioned my plan for tonight and knew that was the reason for the complimentary dessert she'd sent over. She'd assumed, as I had, I would have been able to do it by then.

"Melanie!" Lily waved her over to the bar.

"I'll be right back." Melanie said before jogging over. I'd bet Lily was about to ask to see Melanie's hand, which would confuse the shit out of her. Lily and Melody, our flair bartender who entertained customers while mixing drinks, were the only ones here tonight besides Phoebe who knew what I was going to do.

"Another night, I guess?" Phoebe looked me over with a sympathetic gaze.

"No, I'll explode. I thought I'd walk her over to the water. Every time I tried, someone kept coming by." I rubbed my eyes.

"Happens when you both know everyone." She laughed. "Good luck." She kissed my cheek. "Not that you'll need it."

"That was weird." Melanie came back over to me with a furrowed brow. "Lily said congratulations and Melody teared up and offered me a special celebratory cocktail. When I asked for what, they clammed up and asked how my first day of school was."

"Have a good night." Phoebe said, biting back a smile and holding my gaze a moment before she turned to head back into the kitchen.

I wrapped my arm around Melanie's shoulders and led her toward the parking lot.

"Babe, you're acting a little weird." Melanie squinted in my periphery as I tried to figure out where to take her. I exhaled a relieved breath when my eyes fell on a spot near the river behind the parking lot. Not exactly my plan, but how it happened was a moot point. I needed to ask Melanie before I had a tantrum like my daughter.

"I appreciate you wanting to celebrate my first day of teaching, but you look like something is bothering you."

"Nothing is bothering me." I laced our fingers together and gave her a smile. "Come take a walk by the water with me."

"What? Why?" Her nose crinkled when I pulled her by the hand.

"Because I want you all to myself for a minute before we go home. Is that all right with you?" I quirked a brow at her as we walked.

"Yes," she whispered and squeezed my hand. "It's all right with me."

"Pretty isn't it?" I said as my gaze drifted toward the setting sun. The air was still humid but had a cool enough breeze to tease the fall.

"It is," she said, resting her head onto my shoulder. "I've never really looked at it before. Sorry if I seemed ungrateful. This was nice." She kissed my cheek and wrapped her arms around my bicep. "Perfect end to a great day. It's a little strange having little people call me Ms. Thomas. I keep looking around for my mother."

I laughed, turning to kiss her forehead. "I can see that. What if they called you something different?"

"I think Lauren is the only one who may get away with calling me Melanie." She burrowed into my side. "What else could they call me?"

"What if they called you Mrs. Gallo?"

I met Melanie's widened eyes when I dropped to one knee.

"I wanted to do this today because," I paused to dig the ring box from where it had been burning a hole in my back pocket for hours, "I thought the same day your dream came true could be the same day mine did, too."

"It's my dream, too. God, Matteo I—"

"Shh, let me get this out, Princess." I tapped her leg. "Holding this in for a minute longer is going to make me lose it."

She sniffled and nodded.

"At this point, it's probably just a technicality, but I want it all with you. I always have. Maybe I should have proposed in the breakroom where it all started."

A laugh slipped out through her tears.

"Before you, I never thought I'd ever love anyone this much. I just wanted safe, easy, no risk. But I guess there's no such thing as safeguards, and I'd risk it all to be with you. I loved you from day one, and if you let me, I'll love you forever. Melanie, will you marry me?"

She dropped to her knees in the dirt in front of me and grabbed my face, kissing me so hard I almost fell back.

"Is that a yes?" I murmured against her lips before we broke apart. "If it is, I need your finger."

"It's a big yes." She wiggled her finger at me. "I want to love you forever, too. And now, this all makes a lot more sense." Her eyes followed my hand as I slid the ring up her finger. "I feel bad for Lily. She looked so disappointed."

"You can show her next time." I kissed the top of her wrist. "So, you really want to marry me?" I speared my fingers into her hair and rested my forehead against hers.

"More than I've ever wanted anything." She glanced at the Speakeasy entrance. "Are you sure you don't want to go back inside and put them all out of their misery?"

"Yep. Totally sure." I stood and pulled her up by the hand. "I've been thinking about getting a hot teacher naked all fucking day. I'm ready for my extra credit, now."

I grabbed her hand when she swatted my chest and pulled her in for another kiss.

It was a rocky road to get here, but I agreed with Melanie. For the first time, it truly felt as if I was finally right where I was supposed to be.

T H E
E N D

ACKNOWLEDGMENTS

Thank you to Sarina Bowen for giving me the privilege of writing in the World of True North. It's special and surreal to write in the world of one of your favorite book series.

To my betas: Jodi, Bianca, Lisa, Rachel, Malene, Michelle, Lauren, and Julia. Thank you for always helping to bring out the best in me.

To Christine, thank you for always teaching me new things each time you edit one of my books and always making me strive to grow and be better.

Jodi, the best friend, PA, proofreader, and best human I've ever known. Thank you for all you do for me, especially with this book.

Thank you to my husband and son, who spend many hours watching my back as I type away in my living room wall office. All I do is for you.

To my readers group, the Rose Garden and my street team the Roses, thank you for your constant love and support.

Thanks to my fellow Speakeasy authors who helped me incorporate some of their characters into Matteo and Melanie's story, and thank you Delancey Stewart, Claire Hastings, and my dear friend Marley Valentine for helping me use your characters and places from The Busy Bean and Vino and Veritas series.

Special thanks to Jenn, Jane, and Natasha at Heart Eyes Press for tolerating my random dumb questions at least a few times per week all these months. I'm so happy to be a part of all of this.